TRIAL BY FIRE

CHAPTER ONE

PRESTYN

It has been a shitty day.

Dropping my keys in the bowl next to the front door, I sigh at my own bad luck.

I really thought I'd found a good guy this time. I should have known better.

It's no secret that online dating is its own special circle of hell. No one likes doing it, but in a world where electronics take the place of the real world every day, there's not much choice if you don't want to be single forever. I thought meeting Gary confirmed that it was the way to go, but I was oh so wrong.

I wander through my small apartment, wishing I had the ingredients for a martini but knowing I can either settle for wine or just to go to bed. I'd love to drown my sorrows in a breezeberry Alani Nu, but I'm already going to have a hard time sleeping tonight. Adding an energy drink would cement that problem.

Settling on the couch while weighing my options, I'm annoyed by how quiet it is in my apartment. Normally it doesn't bother me that I'm alone, but tonight I'm lonely. Sure, I've got friends and a demanding job, but that's not the kind of relationship I desire.

I'm not even sure what kind of relationship I want, but it's something different than this.

I shake my head. What I *need* is a full body massage and a new boss, but clearly I'm not getting either of those tonight. Hell, I can't even get a normal, decent guy to show up for a date.

I'm not heartbroken or anything, just disappointed. It didn't matter to me that he was just an average white collar guy with average looks. He seemed nice. And he had no idea who I am.

I hid the fact that my family is one of the wealthiest in the Tampa Bay area, courtesy of the Caine Resorts and Conference Centers that my great-grandfather founded all those years ago. I'm not ashamed of being the youngest member of the Caine family or that I'm photographed regularly during our high profile events. It just makes it hard to determine who likes you for *you* and who likes you for your family's clout. So I just don't volunteer that information unless it's necessary.

It's why I use a nickname online and make sure my profile picture is one of me with a hat on, in the middle of a hike I took last year. Makes it harder to do a reverse search on me.

It's also why I jumped on Gary's invitation to have dinner tonight. He gave no indication he had any idea I'm not your average everyday girl. He didn't push too hard or move too quickly. And he was nice. So I took a chance and agreed to a date, even buying a new dress for the occasion.

And then he didn't show.

I waited for over an hour, the server getting more and more impatient the longer I nursed my martini, until I finally gave up. I'm sure the twenty-dollar tip I left on the table doesn't make up for what he would have made off two meals and drinks, but it's the largest bill I had on me.

As disappointed as I am, I can't get rid of the feeling that it seems so out of character for Gary not to have at least told me something had come up. Or at least, out of character for what I know about him, which isn't much. Maybe I should message him.

Yeah. Just to make sure he's okay. If he stood me up, I'll know pretty quick, but I'd feel terrible if he was in an accident on the way to dinner and I didn't at least check on him.

I fish my phone out of the large handbag I had dropped next to the couch, searching and finding his contact information.

Sorry to have missed you at dinner. Hope everything is okay. Let me know if you'd like to reschedule for a later date.

There. Done. Not too desperate, gives him an out, and shows I care all at the same time. Covering all my bases.

Not wanting to sit around waiting for a reply, I head to my small bathroom to get ready for bed. It's still early enough I can catch up on the new novel I downloaded yesterday. I'm not a huge reader, but I've made it my new year's resolution to change that. Gotta stop rotting my brain with reality TV and all that mess. I've never read a time-traveling book before, but I'm willing to give it a try. Soon enough, I'm settled in my bed, enjoying the exciting adventure that comes with vampires and werewolves.

Our heroine has just begun tracing the portal with her finger when my phone rings, making me jump.

Picking it up, I see it's Gary calling. My heart beats even faster than it already was from the sudden jolt of adrenaline. He's never called before. We've only recently upgraded to texting after chatting through the website for several weeks. This is exciting. And a little nerve wracking.

I stare at his name on my phone for a little too long before shaking myself from my stupor and swiping to answer.

"Hello?"

"Hi, is this Pres?"

It's a woman's voice. And she used the name I go by on the dating app. That's not what I was expecting. Maybe it's someone from the hospital? Or his sister?

"This is she."

The woman on the other end sighs deeply. "I was afraid of that."

"I'm... what?" Confused. That's what I am.

"I was hoping you were some old man who likes to catfish people for kicks."

Now I'm really confused. "I'm sorry... who is this?"

"My name is Delaney. I'm Gary's wife."

Wife?!

I can barely breathe as I process what she's saying. Gary is married? The sweet man who oohs and ahhs over pictures of my niece and nephew is married to someone else?

"I'm sorry... did you..." I rub my forehead which is suddenly starting to hurt. "Hang on, I'm trying to process this."

"I know. And I'm sorry to drop this bomb on you."

Now I'm even more baffled. "You're sorry? I'm the woman who your husband was planning on cheating with and *you're* sorry?"

Delaney sighs like she's exhausted. "This isn't the first time this has happened."

I hear what I assume is Gary's muffled voice in the background. I can barely make out words that sound like, "That's no one else's business," when Delaney cuts him off with, "If you don't want people to know you're a serial cheater, stop being a serial cheater."

I blink rapidly, not quite sure what to do. I feel like I'm intruding on someone's private conversation, and yet, this is the man I was falling for. Or at least I thought I was. Actually, that's getting way ahead of myself, but it wasn't out of the realm of possibility for the future if tonight had gone okay.

Now that I know I've been snowed, though, I'm not sure I care about invading his privacy.

The indignation hits me like a punch to the gut.

I've been *duped*! By a *married* man!

Granted, I wasn't totally honest with him either. I never told him I'm technically a hotel heiress. But protecting myself from opportunists is a little different than *being married*.

"Delaney," I interrupt their arguing. "I need to assure you I had no idea he was married. Er... *is* married. I would have stopped talking to him immediately if I'd known." I don't owe her an explanation, I'm not the one in the wrong here, but I feel like it's the right thing to do.

"That's what I love about you, Pres."

Wait... what?

"You have so much integrity."

"Um... thanks?" This conversation has just gotten weird.

"I'm making things weird," she says, as if she's read my thoughts. "Let me back up. I found Gary's online account today by accident and started doing some reading. Of all the women Gary was talking to—"

All the women? That cheater was cheating on me, too!

"—your messages were so kind and genuine. And you're so smart and beautiful. I just think you're a really great person."

"Thank you?"

I have run the gamut of emotions today, from excitement and irritation to disappointment and anger. But right now, I'm at a loss as to what I should be feeling as the catfish's wife sings my praises.

"When I saw that he had made plans with you for tonight, and when he stood you up, I felt like you needed to know what happened. And I want you to know it's not anything to do with you. I'm sure you are lovely and if I wasn't married and a heterosexual woman, I'd be half in love with you from these conversations alone. Please know you did nothing wrong and you are not responsible for any of this. But you do deserve to know the truth."

I'm stunned. This is possibly the nicest thing that has ever happened to me with online dating. It would figure that a woman is involved. "I wish I knew how to respond to that."

Delaney laughs. A deep chuckle that makes me think she'd be someone fun to hang out with, if circumstances were different, that is. "I know. I'm sure this feels really odd to have this conversation with me, but I am a firm believer in holding the person who is responsible accountable, not sharing blame with innocent bystanders, so rest assured I have no ill will toward you. I just thought you should know so you can move on and find someone who is truly worthy of you. Unlike my asshole soon to be ex-husband."

More muffled voices in the back to which Delaney replies, "Yes, I alluded to the D word. How many times did you think you could get away with this before I finally kicked you to the curb?"

"Um, Delaney?"

"Yes?"

"Are you going to be okay?" I really mean that. From the sound of it, this isn't the first time she's caught her husband cheating and I can't imagine how heartbreaking that must be. She was so kind to reach out to me, I feel it's only fair to reach out to her as well.

She sighs deeply again, sounding emotionally exhausted, and why wouldn't she? "To be honest, it really sucks to know that he has screwed me over so many times, lied to me so many times, it doesn't even hurt anymore. But at least I'm ready to go now, right?"

"Right." I actually don't know if that's right. I just don't know what else to say.

"Anyway, I just wanted to let you know what was going on. I didn't want you to worry about someone who wasn't worth worrying about."

My lips quirk up on the side a bit. "That really was nice of you. Thank you. And again, I'm so sorry."

"Think nothing more of it. Frankly, I think you're a doll. Please don't let this taint your idea of relationships. There is someone out there who is waiting for you. I just know it."

Warmth fills me. Probably from the deep blush I feel on my cheeks. I'm not used to this kind of compliment from a stranger who isn't trying to get something out of me.

"Thank you. And please keep my number. You know, in case you need me to testify during the divorce or whatever."

A laugh that can only be described as maniacal comes from the other end of the line. "That is a fabulous idea, Pres. Thank you. Now if you'll excuse me, I have to throw my husband's shit in a car and light it on fire."

"Hold on... don't—"

I don't have time to discourage her from committing a felony before the line goes dead.

Putting my phone down, I find myself staring at the wall, thinking about the man who screwed me over. But maybe even more so, thinking about the woman who has enough strength of character to call a stranger and give her a heads up.

I wish I had strength like that. Right now, I feel more deflated than anything.

CHAPTER TWO

NICK

"Push deep into warrior two. Now hook your right arm behind you and raise your left arm up, looking to the sky."

I follow my yoga teacher's instructions and twist my body until I feel my spine relax into the stretch. I've been really tight lately, so I'm glad to be here in the studio.

"Can you push a little further?" Jackie asks and gently adjusts my body so my hips are square to the front.

I take a deep breath in through my nose and push it out slowly, relaxing my muscles even further, centering my body and my thoughts.

A grunt next to me uncenters me real fast.

"How the fuck do you do this?" my teammate Anthony, also known as Tiger whisper-shouts. "This is fucking brutal, man."

"Shh!" someone whisper-yells next to him.

"Sorry," he responds quietly before turning back to me. "No seriously. I'm about to rip my dick in two."

"Then you're pushing too hard." I come back through warrior two as instructed, then swivel my body into a runner's stretch, *chaturanga,* and end up in downward dog, making an extra effort to stretch my calves.

Out of the corner of my eye I see Tiger skip all the necessary steps to end up in what looks like a bear crawl more than a downward dog.

"Ohhhh. I get it now."

I glance over to figure out what he's talking about, only to see him paying less attention to his form and more attention to all the leggings-clad butts in the air.

"You're gonna get me kicked out of here, you ass," I remark and lift my right leg as high as I can get it. "I'm not here for women. I'm the fucking goalie. My job is to keep myself limber at all times."

I neglect to tell him the part about trying to get a strong handle on controlling my breathing through the crazy anxiety plaguing me. That's grounds to be razzed regularly and I don't like the amount of chirping I have to endure in the locker room as it is.

"Then why am I here?"

Bending my knee, I adjust my hips to open up my core more. "I thought you were here to loosen some of those joints that have been tightening up on you and maybe get a little stress relief. Clearly, I was wrong to think you wanted any actual help."

"Are you calling me a crybaby?"

"Pretty much."

"How are we doing over here?" Jackie approaches with a too-tight smile and a too-chipper voice. If she's trying to mask her irritation with our conversation, she's doing a shitty job of it.

"Just trying to concentrate," I reply, squaring my hips and pulling my knee to my chest before placing my foot on the floor and moving back into warrior two.

"I'm doing my best to—oh shit! What are you doing? Why are you leaning on me?" Tiger practically squeals.

"Sometimes it takes a second person to make sure we're pushing our bodies to the limits." Jackie is resting her body weight on top of Tiger, forcing his hips back and his calves to stretch more.

Surely she's not torturing him on purpose. Then again, he's been a big baby the whole time we've been here so she could be trying to discourage him from coming back. Hell, I'm ready to discourage him, too.

Except for the occasional "son of a bitch" I hear whispered next to me, I do my best to go back to ignoring my teammate as I center myself.

As I move through the motions I've been working on for the last few months, I let my thoughts drift to the ice. The swivel of my hips when I drop one knee to the ground. The stretch of my obliques when I reach to stop a goal. The placement of my ankles when I'm upright, waiting for the next puck to come sailing at me.

I run through scenario after scenario making extra effort to really feel my muscles as I push my body to its stretching limits. Yoga is a relatively new thing for me, but something our team trainer, Dom, and I discussed as a good option for me. Not that I don't already stay fit and flexible. But I want to be better than just flexible. I want to be strong in the joints long term. Yoga is something I can keep doing long after retirement.

That's the physical benefit I keep reminding myself of. The mental benefits are what actually got me in the door. For some reason, management thinks I don't pull my weight enough when it comes to interviews and media presence. I don't disagree with them because I hate that part of my job. I don't like prying eyes in my life and cameras in my face. The thought of it makes me sweat. I just want to play hockey.

Management disagrees. I've been told I'll be doing interviews from now on, stage fright be damned. That's the other reason Dom suggested yoga. Maybe it'll help me control my anxiety when a microphone is shoved in my face and personal questions are lobbed at me like tennis balls.

Still, I've been learning to enjoy the benefits I wasn't expecting from practicing yoga. I can focus more which helps my game, my stress levels have gone down, and since I'm not exactly a people person, I enjoy that it's a silent exercise program.

"Ohmygod, I think my balls just fell off."

Well, mostly silent.

"Do you want to just go?" I ask, giving him an out. "It's okay if you need to take a break. Yoga is a different kind of exercise."

That's all the encouragement Tiger needs. "Actually, I need to make a call."

He takes off and the shift in focus in the whole room is almost palpable now that we don't have an unwanted distraction. We're free to center our minds and our thoughts and push our bodies as far as they'll go without trying to ignore the bitching.

Forty minutes goes by quicker than I expect, but soon enough we're on our backs, concentrating on our breathing and relaxing all our muscles. I think I hear a soft snore from the other size of the room which wouldn't surprise me. Someone always falls asleep during Savasana. I get it. It's the most relaxing part of my life, too.

Jackie's gentle voice breaks through the repose. "When you feel ready, open your eyes. Turn on your side in fetal position and slowly push up to a sit."

She waits until almost everyone is upright, still quiet as to not disturb those who are not as ready to go yet.

"Put your hands together in prayer form and bring them to your heart." We follow her gentle instructions. "I look forward to seeing you all here again next time. *Namaste*."

She bows to us and we bow back, saying "*Namaste*" right back at her.

Before standing I reach my arms over my shoulders. I really do feel so much better every time I come here. Not necessarily interview ready, but I doubt even yoga could completely help with that.

Jackie makes her way around the room, answering questions

and giving recommendations. I wipe off my mat and roll it up while I wait, feeling like I need to make an apology on Tiger's behalf. Finally, she gets to me.

"How are you feeling now that you've been coming for a while?" Jackie smiles brightly at me. She's got a quiet, gentle demeanor when we put in the work, but is able to turn on the charm outside of that bubble. It's one of the things I like about her as my instructor. But only as my instructor. She's a little too talkative once class is over.

"I feel good. It's nice being able to come a couple times a week. But listen, I'm really sorry about bringing my buddy today. He's not usually disruptive like that." That's actually a lie. He's disruptive a lot of the time and I should have known better, but she doesn't need to know that part.

Jackie's smile pinches tightly. "It's okay. The more the merrier. But he's not coming back, is he?"

I laugh. "Don't worry. I'm uninviting him."

"Oh good." Her eyes widen. "I mean... oh gosh I didn't mean to say that. I just meant..."

"It's okay, Jackie. I know exactly what you meant and I make no judgment at all."

She covers her eyes for a moment. "I'm so embarrassed. I shouldn't have said that. Can I make it up to you over a cup of coffee? Or better yet, a chai tea?"

Is she...hitting on me?

I feel my eyebrows raise but quickly school my expression as I figure out a way to gently decline her offer. "Really, there's no apology necessary. And I have to get us to practice anyway."

We don't have practice. We had a short skate this morning since we have a game tonight, but she doesn't need to know that either. How many lies can I tell this woman in a two-minute conversation?

"That's okay. Maybe next time." She pats my arm, and I swear

I feel a squeeze as well, but it happens so fast before she leaves to approach the next student, that I'm not sure it happened at all.

I'm still pondering this turn of events when I meet Tiger in the lobby.

"Dude, do you get felt up everywhere you go?"

Maybe I wasn't so far off base.

"You saw that?" I ask.

He gestures with his head, barely taking his eyes off his phone. "The entire wall is made of glass. Of course I saw the hot yoga instructor checking out your guns. I was actually hoping she was going to bend over and demonstrate another pose, but instead I got to see yet another woman wanting to take you home. Lucky me."

I sigh and head for the door. "Women don't always hit on me."

He scoffs. "Okay. We'll go with that."

"It's true."

"No it's not. You have more fan signs being held up during games by hot women. You have more tweets from hot women propositioning you. And may I remind you, you were voted Tampa's most eligible bachelor a couple months ago?"

I shift uncomfortably at the reminder. I don't enjoy being the center of attention like that. I just want to play hockey and enjoy a good book afterwards. I don't need the scrutiny and accolades that come from being an athlete. I'm not a hero like our first responders. I'm just a dude who likes hitting a puck around.

"I'm not eligible," I argue and press the trunk button for my Range Rover so I can stow away my yoga mat. It's a bigger car than I originally wanted, but I have a lot of gear and a lot of really large friends. "That would mean I'm looking for a woman and we both know I'm not."

"Not yet anyway. Just wait. Some sweet honey is going to sweep you off your damn feet and there will be no going back."

I grimace and close the trunk before walking around to the

driver's side door to climb in. "Did you just use the term *sweet honey?*"

He follows my lead and get in the passenger side. "What's wrong with that?"

"So many things, man."

"Regardless, I've seen this script before. The minute a guy starts saying he's not looking for a relationship, BAM! That's when it hits him out of nowhere. Mark my words. You're going to be married by next year."

I give him a side-eye as I buckle up. "You've lost your mind."

"Well see, Nick. We'll see."

I hope he's wrong. I don't have time for a woman in my life. I'm too busy, and dating takes too much effort. Speaking of, I still have to find a date for the gala in a couple weeks. I would go alone but my sister has already made it very clear that's not happening.

As if she's listening to my thoughts, which is possible since we have that twin-to-twin telepathy thing going, the phone rings.

"What's up, sis?" I ask as soon as I connect the call via the Bluetooth in the car.

Tiger's eyebrow raises. "Sis?" he mouths. Not sure where he's been. It's not a secret I have a twin sister.

"How is my favorite brother doing this fine day?"

"Uh... I'm fine. But why do you sound like you're overcompensating for something?"

"Because you're not going to like this conversation."

I groan as I pull into traffic. There's only one topic I despise discussing with her and it's my love life.

"Don't act like that," she chides. "You know this gala is important and you know you need a date for it."

"Gala?" Tiger asks and now I'm really wondering about his attention span.

"Hang on, Delaney. Tiger is sitting next to me and he's claiming he doesn't know anything about this."

"I don't."

"Dude. Coach has mentioned it like seven times. The annual Glaze gala to raise money for the community?"

"Doesn't ring a bell," he claims, staring out the window.

"You're full of shit. It's practically a requirement for all of us to be there."

"Sorry, I'm a rookie. I wasn't invited," he says, shrugging one shoulder.

I just shake my head. I can't help it if he wants to get on Coach's bad side.

"Your funeral. Anyway," I turn my attention back to my sister. I might as well get this over with. "What do you want to know, Delaney?"

"First," she says in a clipped tone. "It's rude of you to not introduce me to your teammates. Hi, Tiger. I'm Delaney, Nick's twin sister. Nice to meet you."

"You, too." Turning to me, he says, "She sounds hot."

I slug him in the shoulder while my sister laughs.

"Ow. Was that necessary?"

"Yes. She's married, you dick."

Tiger shrugs and turns back to the window.

"Flattery will get you everywhere, so thank you for that, Tiger," Delaney says with a little too much pep in her voice.

"Don't encourage him," I grumble.

"Can't help it. I love the compliment. Anyway..."

Crap. I was hoping she'd have forgotten what we were talking about.

"Do you have a date yet?"

I sigh deeply because no, I don't. Which can mean only one thing.

"I heard that sigh. It's a good thing I met a woman you're going to love."

If I wasn't trying to navigate my way through traffic, I'd drop my chin to my chest. "I highly doubt that."

"You could ask your yoga instructor," Tiger chimes in. "She

was really into your...muscles...today."

"Dude. You aren't even going. You don't get to help her find me a date."

"Who says I'm trying to find you a date? I was helping you get laid."

Delaney laughs again and I find myself happy these two haven't met in person yet. No telling what kind of torture they'd put me through if they were working together.

Trying to keep this conversation on track, I switch back to my sister again. "Where did you meet her this time, Delaney? Coffee shop? Shopping? Some online group?"

"It's a long story, but it's not the point anyway."

Well, that's sketchy. Why wouldn't my sister want to tell me how she met this woman? I don't get a chance to ask her because she's on a roll.

"Before I invite her, I want to make sure you're still unattached. She's an absolute gem and she's gorgeous. Really a bombshell."

"In my world, bombshell is synonymous with psychotic, so this isn't a ringing endorsement."

Tiger snorts a laugh but nods in agreement. Patrick's wife is example number one of that. She's drop dead gorgeous and completely unhinged most of the time.

"Well," Delaney continues as if my opinion doesn't matter. "She's also smart and well educated. She's kind and empathetic. I just adore her and I think you will, too."

"Okay, okay." I hold up my hand to stop her, even though she can't see me. "It's only for the gala, right? You're not trying to set me up on a real date or anything?"

"Well, I'd love to." Of course she would. She's been meddling in my love life for years. "But the more pressing issue is the gala. I've put a lot of work into it with the committee. This is important to me."

And there it is. The way she gets me every time. I can never say no to my sister when it's important to her.

"Fine," I grumble. "But make sure she knows this is a one night only thing. I'll meet her there and we're leaving separately. There will be no follow up date."

"Yay!" Delaney says a little too enthusiastically. "I will make sure she knows all that. Scout's honor."

"You have never been a Scout."

"Regardless. I promise this will be fun. You're going to love her."

"Mm-hmm," I hum noncommittally.

"Okay that's all I needed. I'll let you and Tiger get back to whatever it is that you're doing that I probably don't want to know about."

"No you don't," Tiger yells. "Not unless you want your brother to drag you to yoga."

"Yoga? That's new. I'll have to ask you about it later. I've got to run. Love you."

"Love you, too."

She hangs up before I can say anything else, leaving me to stew in my own despair. I was hoping to get out of going to this damn event, but now I'm roped in even more.

"I told you so," Tiger says. "When you're least expecting it, the right woman is going to land in your lap. I think your sister just dropped her."

I roll my eyes and try to ignore the pit of anxiety brewing in my gut despite the last hour of yoga. Tiger may think the woman of my dreams is around the corner but she's not showing up courtesy of my sister. That much I already know.

CHAPTER THREE

PRESTYN

The minute I'd heard her voice again three weeks ago, my stomach dropped.

"Hi Pres?" she clarifies as I answer the phone. "This is Delaney. We spoke briefly a few days ago about my soon to be ex-husband, Gary."

How could I forget? It shook me to my core.

"Oh hi. Is something wrong?"

"Not at all." Delaney laughs lightly. "Actually, I'd say things are going better than they have in a long time. But I have a favor to ask of you..."

I can't believe I agreed to this, but in that moment, I felt like I owed Delaney Edwards. Or... soon to be Williams, again. Like it was my fault her marriage had fallen apart. Logically I know it isn't, but that didn't stop guilt from creeping in.

And now I'm here. Standing in the lobby of my family's hotel, waiting to meet the woman whose life I ripped apart so I can go on a date with her brother.

Sort of.

Delaney invited me to tonight's gala event for the Florida Glaze hockey team. It also happens to be an event our hotel hosts annually. When she asked if I would accompany her brother since he was having a hard time securing a date due to his "shyness", I thought, "What the hell?" I'm already attending as a member of the Caine family, not as an employee of the hotel. There really wasn't a reason to say no, and my guilt was enough to make me say yes.

Now here I stand, in the lobby where I'll meet Delaney.

Wringing my hands together, I can't stop the nervous thoughts running through my brain.

What if she's not as kind as she seems on the phone? What if she's setting me up with the world's douchiest brother? What if she's figured out who I am, who my family is, and is bringing the paparazzi with her all while planning to punch me in the face?

"Get ahold of yourself, Prestyn," I mutter to myself. I smooth my hands down my dress, mostly so I'll stop fidgeting with my nails. "You're being ridiculous."

A low whistle behind me has me turning around.

"You look fabulous." Bayleigh walks around me getting the whole three-sixty degree view. "You clean up nicely don't you?"

"You don't look so bad yourself."

She really doesn't. Bayleigh may be wearing a work uniform, but she looks crisp and put together. It's unfortunate she has to work tonight, though. I'd much rather see her in a gown so we could hang out together during the event.

Bayleigh is an Executive Sales Manager in the Catering Sales department. Usually our paths wouldn't cross, what with me working in Retail Operations, but ever since my idiot boss begged to oversee both departments while we're interviewing new Catering Directors, we talk almost daily. She's a lot of fun to work with and is truly the only bright spot of helping to oversee her department, which is not my favorite. Hence, why I work in *retail*, not catering.

"I admit our work uniforms are pretty sharp, but you look like true Caine royalty," she gushes.

If I was the kind of person who blushed, my cheeks would be pink right now. "Thanks." I pat my hair to make sure it's still smooth, the butterflies in my stomach still fluttering. Bayleigh doesn't miss it.

"Why do you look nervous? You never look nervous."

"I'm meeting someone."

My friend's eyes widen with delight and she clasps her hands together. "A date?"

"No. Well, yes."

"Is it one of the hockey players?" She grabs my arm excitedly. "Please say he's a hockey player. Those guys are hot."

I've been so nervous about meeting Delaney, I never stopped to remember that there are probably going to be a bunch of Glaze players here tonight. Oh boy. I hope Delaney doesn't have a hockey playing brother. I prefer to stay out of the limelight. I don't need to get stuck with some pretty boy who documents his whole life with mirror poses and duck-lips for hourly social media posts.

"It's not like that," I say quickly, hoping that I'm right. "I'm meeting my date's sister here first."

"His sister?" Bayleigh looks understandably confused.

"Yeah, it's complicated."

"You're meeting your date and the family at the same time? That's a little fast, don't ya think?"

"It's not like that. It's—"

"Bayleigh!"

Aaron, the idiot boss and the man responsible for overseeing Bayleigh as well stalks over to us, a scowl on his face.

"We're not paying you to stand around and chat with the *guests*." He eyes me up and down, clearly unhappy with my role for the evening.

I've known Aaron Ford for most of my life and he doesn't intimidate me. He's never liked me. He and my older brother Hoyt were best friends growing up so he's been around since I was a kid, and one thing has always been painfully obvious to me —Aaron wants to be a Caine more than anything. He's always tried to suck up to my dad and was bound and determined to be the third Caine sibling when I accidentally came along. He's hated me ever since.

Me, being fifteen years younger than Hoyt and twelve younger than Gavin who is general manager of this particular location, could still peg Aaron as disingenuous at a really young age. He's just... smarmy. There's not another word to describe him.

Well, except lazy. I honestly believe that's why he was put in the lead roll of the smallest department of our Tampa resort where Gavin is in charge. There's not a whole lot he can screw up, not for lack of trying. Just last week, we lost a major retailer because Aaron upped the rent and didn't bother to tell them until a couple weeks before their current lease was up. It's been a nightmare trying to fill the empty space in a timely fashion.

"You need to be in the ballroom." Venom drips from Aaron's order for Bayleigh to get back to work. "Ready to serve our guests."

"Yes sir," she says, but doesn't move. What's he going to do, fire her for speaking to the owner's daughter? Doubtful.

That doesn't stop his power trip, though. "Right now," he tacks on, just to be a dick.

She half rolls her eyes, trying to make it look like she's merely turning to address me, but I catch it. "I'll see you later, Prestyn. Have fun tonight."

"Thanks. See you in there."

I turn back to my post, waiting for the mystery woman to arrive. Aaron, however, is still hanging around.

"Is there something you need?" I finally ask, feeling uncomfortable with him standing here, giving me the evil-eye.

"I would appreciate if you wouldn't monopolize my employees' time during the event tonight. They have a job to do and don't need you as a distraction."

Cocking one eyebrow, I turn my head slowly. "Careful now, Aaron. I'm Prestyn Caine tonight, founder, owner and CEO's beloved daughter. Not your employee. Wouldn't want any of the men in my family to overhear you say things like that to me, would you?"

Not that it would matter, but he doesn't know that. All he knows is I've got the right last name and he doesn't.

Working for this hotel has always been my dream. From the time I was a little kid and would run the halls while my dad worked, I dreamed of being in charge. The magic of it has never been lost on me. The smiles on people's faces and the way the employees all seem to enjoy their jobs, it's an environment I've always wanted to help create.

As the youngest Caine sibling, it should be a no-brainer. No one has ever been a lowly assistant. My brothers both graduated from college and were immediately put in director positions. But me? That's not the way it's been. I was a freshman in college and therefore too young to take over when this position came open. That's when Aaron weaseled his way into the job.

Now that I've gotten my Master's degree in business management and have several years of "assisting" under my belt, you'd think someone, my brother, my father, *someone* would start grooming me for a better position. Director at the least.

But no. My great-grandfather built this hotel on the backs of the *men* in our family. I can practically hear my grandpa spouting off some misogynistic bullshit about "no female Caine having ever worked here, not even in housekeeping!" I've been determined to break through the glass ceiling by proving I deserve more, but so far no one has taken me very seriously. It's a battle I fight quietly every day, carefully easing my way in so eventually they'll know they need me.

That day is coming. I can feel it. Aaron has no problem letting me run the show while he takes all the glory. It makes me want to kick him in the balls, but I try to remember I'm doing the job I love, and eventually, if I play it right, I'll get the credit I'm owed.

Speaking of the family...

"What are you two discussing?" Gavin strolls up looking dapper in his tux. He kisses me on the cheek and I can't help but smile up at him. With his dirty blond hair, hazel eyes, and a body made for formalwear, he's quite the looker. He may find himself a hook-up dressed like that. "Looks like things are serious between you guys."

"Aaron was just complimenting me on my dress," I say sweetly.

Aaron's face practically turns purple from anger. But what can he do? "And reminding her that just because she works with our staff doesn't mean they have time to fraternize tonight."

"Relax, Aaron," Gavin says as he tucks me under his arm. "Caine family members have been attending these events since birth. Prestyn is all Caine and knows how to conduct herself."

Aaron smooths down his wrinkled tie. I'm not sure why he's even here tonight. He doesn't have to be. But I guess he can't pass up an opportunity to hobnob with some of Tampa's elite under the guise of working. The fact that he's got Florida Glaze memorabilia all over his office is probably another reason.

It's on the tip of my tongue to ask, just to put him in a tight spot, when a woman approaches.

"Pres?"

I recognize that voice.

"Delaney?"

She smiles and both men seem to swallow their tongues. She's that beautiful. Her long blond hair falls in waves halfway down her back. Her smile reveals perfect white teeth. Her lashes are long and thick and frame big blue eyes. And don't get me started on that dress. The red satin gown with off the shoulder straps hugs every curve on her body.

Just looking at her, I can't figure out for the life of me why Gary would cheat on her. Hell, I have no lesbian tendencies in me at all and even I would never cheat on her.

"It's so nice to meet you." She reaches in for a hug, surprising me, but I like it. She smells like vanilla and brown sugar, probably from her lotion.

Lotion I suddenly realize I forgot to put on myself. Not ideal, but it should be okay. At least the humidity is good for something around here.

The men quickly excuse themselves leaving us alone.

"I'm so glad to finally meet you," I squeak out, still nervous about meeting the woman whose husband picked me as his partner in cheating. "And again, I'm so, so sorry—"

She cuts me off, the stern look on her face leaving no room for argument. "Stop with that. You are not the one at fault. It was all him."

"I know. I just feel bad about the whole situation."

"I don't." She grabs my hand and clasps it tightly in both of hers. "I knew long ago that it was time to leave. I just needed a kick in the pants to finally go. I wish I could say it was painful, but it's not. I'm finally free."

I hate that she feels that way. Not because she's okay with getting divorced, but it sounds like she never had the kind of relationship she should have had. The kind that I want. The kind that I may be giving up on. If someone who seems to be as dynamic as Delaney can't find her perfect match, there's no hope for someone like me.

"Anyway, enough of the Debbie Downer talk." She swivels, still holding my hand, and guides me toward the ballroom. "We have a party to attend, and I need to make sure the silent auction is organized the way we want it."

"Wait... you're part of the committee?"

"For the last three years!" That megawatt smile is back. Clearly she's proud of her work. She should be. This event is known to raise a ton of money for local charities. "Obviously the community engagement and fundraising departments for the Glaze are in charge of everything. But they love when the families get involved. As Nick's twin, I felt it was the best way I could support his career, ya know?"

"Hold on, Nick is part of the Glaze?"

My mind is swirling with this new information. All she told me is Nick needed a date for this event. She neglected to tell me that he's less of a guest and more of a participant. And that he's her twin.

Delaney's eyes light up as she talks about her brother. "He's the starting goalie. We got so lucky that he got a contract here. Players are at the mercy of where the organization sends them, so it's rare that their contract brings them right back home."

"It's really nice that you're so involved in his career like that."

She shrugs. "Family is everything, so I admit, I hope my involvement is one more reason they want him to stay. It's a way to do my part to build him up, while doing something I'm good at." She laughs. "Lord knows I can't help him with drills."

The more we chat, the more I like her. And the more I realize I dodged a bullet with Gary. Or maybe I dodged a bullet with men in general. Based on Gary's clear narcissism, Aaron's douchebag behavior, and my brothers' inability to see past the *good ole boy* club, I'm no longer sure there are men of quality anywhere.

All thoughts of disingenuous men leave my mind as soon as we arrive at the party. The ballroom is arranged exactly as it was before I left it a few hours ago to get ready, but with the dimmed lighting, it looks amazing.

The huge chandeliers on either side of the room provide a soft, ambient glow, the wall lighting is a little brighter so people can see as they dance to the live band. Tables covered in spotless white cloths with silver accents are set up around the room, complete with reservation numbers all the attendees will get when they sign in at the door. Silent auction tables have been set up on one side of the room and touts everything from a one-year gym membership to season passes for the Glaze, to an all expenses trip to Tahoe, including the use of a private jet. That was donated by my dad who cares less about hockey and more about raising money for the community. He may be an entrepreneur, but he's also quite a philanthropist.

Two different bars are located on the back wall, one on each side of the room, and are fully stocked with any kind of beer or liquor one could want. And what we don't have out here, is probably in the back, ready to be pulled out at a moment's notice.

It's impressive and ostentatious and will hopefully bring in big money from Tampa's elite.

Delaney finally drops my hand. "I need to go check on a few things and make sure everyone who needs to know I'm here, does. As soon as my brother gets here, I'll introduce you, okay?"

"Okay." My response comes out confident, but I'm not sure this is a good idea anymore. What exactly are Nick and I supposed to do tonight? Hang out around the bar? Dance? This agreement is starting to seem like a bad idea.

Delaney whisks away and leaves me standing alone. I hate this feeling. I know I'm a guest tonight, but no one is here to schmooze yet and I don't like standing around doing nothing. The line between being the owner's daughter and being an employee is very thin, a line I don't seem to be straddling well in this moment. I should probably check in with the staff. I'm not technically on the clock, but if they need something, I'd much rather them come to me than Aaron anyway.

"Is he here yet?" Bayleigh asks as she walks up next to me, putting some last minute silverware on the table before the doors officially open.

"Nope."

"Well, that's disappointing. I'll be keeping my eyes on you tonight."

She points at her eyes and back at mine before she walks away, leaving me standing around, feeling useless again.

CHAPTER FOUR

NICK

There are a dozen things I'd rather be doing than riding in a limo with a bunch of rowdy teammates, dressed in a monkey suit so we can attend a pretentious event with our boss. Number one on that list is eating shards of glass.

Unfortunately, doing so would probably mean a hospital stay and being medically benched for the rest of the season, so I guess I'm stuck with these clowns.

It's not that I don't like my teammates. I really do. Poker night is awesome. And I enjoy when Tucker Hayes has a pool party at his new place. I just don't like having to force conversation with people I don't know and answer the inevitable zillion questions about my job. It's exhausting to me, especially when we just got back from a road trip.

When I'm hanging out with the guys, I can be myself. At events like this, I'm never totally sure what to say. But the front office is starting to lose patience with my lack of public appearances so I don't have much choice. If I stick to talking about hockey, I should make it through.

"Listen guys," Tucker calls out from the opposite side of the limo. "There are some rules when it comes to the silent auction."

His hand is placed possessively on his live-in girlfriend-slash-baby-mama, Lacy's, knee. "The most important one is to not outbid me on the trip to Tahoe."

"Because you can't afford to pay for your own trip after buying that big ass house?" Becker Bell chides causing the others to laugh and razz Tucker a bit.

"No, it's because I provide all the supplies and food for poker night every time, you dickhead," he razzes back.

Becker holds up his hands. "Don't look at me. Maks is the one who eats all your food every time."

"What?" Maks looks up, his eyes hooded after being interrupted from nuzzling the neck of whoever his woman of the night is. I've never seen this one before. Then again, Maks's longest relationship spanned a mere three days. And only because it was a weekend in Vegas and they never left the bed long enough to part ways.

"You owe me eight G's for food and beverages," Tucker says.

Maks licks his lips before turning back to his date. "Send the bill to my accountant." Then his mouth is back on her neck.

This is turning out to be a real classy night so far.

The limo rounds the corner to the hotel and Patrick's knee starts bouncing double-time.

"You okay?" I ask our captain.

"Yep."

"You sure? 'Cause you're vibrating the whole car."

He glances down at his knee and cusses when he realizes how fidgety he is. "Sorry. I haven't attended one of these as a single man since my rookie year. Just not sure what to expect."

The car goes silent as we all remember that Patrick was served with divorce papers during our road trip. It came as a total shock to him. Not so much to the rest of us. We've been listening to them bicker and argue for the last year. It was only a matter of time. That doesn't make it any less painful for him, though.

"What? You think a bunch of puck bunnies are going to jump

out from the bushes and accost you now that you're back on the market?"

That gets me a small laugh. "Hey, I am a prime catch, man. Fifty bucks says there's already a line of ladies waiting to meet me."

And he's back to a little bit of normal. That's what I was hoping for.

"My bad. I'll be sure to stay out of the way so they don't get distracted by my charms," I joke, eliciting yet another chuckle from him.

"Don't you have a date?" Tucker asks as he finishes the last of the champagne the limo company generously provided to the tune of two hundred fifty additional dollars.

Lacy gasps, like me dating is such a huge surprise. "With who?"

I should be offended by her shock. I don't date often but I'm not celibate or anything. Not that my answer is going to squelch her excitement.

"I'm not sure," I admit with a shrug. "My sister is setting me up with someone."

"Oh, a blind date!" Lacy leans forward, her eyes dancing with delight. "How did she meet this woman? What's her name? Is your sister a good matchmaker?" She is a little more invested in this conversation than I feel totally comfortable with.

"Uh...I have no idea. She basically threatened me so I'm going in totally blind."

A series of "ooh..." and "you're so fucked" murmurs circulate around the car.

Amazing. The thought of this date already makes my throat dry without these fuckers confirming my worst fears. I really hope this woman isn't a huge hockey fan. I never know if the women are genuine or not and I don't want to get stuck in a situation I don't want to be in because my sister didn't vet someone properly.

The last thing I need is to be blasted all over social media by some fame hungry fan.

I don't want a girlfriend, I'm not even close to looking for one. But if I had to be in a relationship, I'd want something like what Tucker and Lacy have. They have a certain chemistry I've always desired. It's not just sexual, although I see the way he looks like he wants to eat her up sometimes. No, it's so much more. Granted, they were apart for four years with Lacy going through hell so they're making up for lost time, but they love where they're at now.

Fortunately, the limo comes to a stop in front of the hotel so there's not enough time to continue our discussion or for me to go down a dangerous rabbit hole of thoughts. Instead, everyone finishes their drinks and checks their cuff links and ties while the driver pulls over. As soon as the door opens, we emerge one by one and are greeted by the hotel staff.

I button the jacket of my three-piece suit as flash bulbs light up the red carpet. Media vans are lined up across the street, ready to report on the "Who's Who of Tampa" and what they're all wearing this evening.

Fortunately my teammates are much more comfortable answering questions, so I'm able to stroll right past the reporters, flashing a smile for the cameras and waving as I hurry by. Thank God most of my teammates are spotlight whores.

The grandiosity of the event continues as we make our way into the hotel. Banners with the names and logos of all the businesses who sponsored tables are draped on the walls, making them look more like decorations than the advertisements we all know they are. Waiters mill about, handing people champagne as they wait to check in at the registration table. Small talk and laughter fills the area.

Everyone catches up to me at registration, and the easy-going but elegant vibe continues into the ballroom. It's classy with a sexy spin on it, from the dimmed lights to the band's song choices. I'm not sure how much my sister was involved with the planning and prep, but they did a great job.

"I'm gonna hit the bar," Tiger announces practically the second we step through the door. And yes, he ended up being threatened by Coach if he didn't show up tonight, which had me chuckling. "Anyone want to join me?"

"I'm in," Becker replies, and the two of them take off. Maks follows slowly behind, his arms wrapped tightly around his date who is wrapped just as tightly in her dress.

"We're heading to the silent auction first," Tucker says.

Lacy pulls back from his embrace to look up at him. "You were serious about Tahoe?"

"Uh...yeah I was. There are kids and roommates and guests crawling all over our house. We need some alone time."

Lacy looks at him like he's two screws short. "So rent one of the rooms here and save us the travel time."

"Lacy." He turns to her and holds both her hands between them. "I don't think you know how men work."

She snorts out a laugh. "Oh really."

"Yes, babe. I need to fuck you on the kitchen counter, in front of a giant window, over the back of the living room couch, and maybe in a hot tub. I can't do any of those things in a hotel room."

I clear my throat, suddenly feeling very uncomfortable overhearing this conversation.

"If I agree to let you bid on it, will you shut the fuck up right now?" Lacy's voice is sweet, but her words have bite to them.

He plays along and cups her cheek reverently. I assume he knows how ridiculous this whole scene looks and is doing it for fun, because truly... this is weird.

"Of course I will, baby."

"Fine." Lacy turns on her heel and grabs his hand to drag him away. But not before turning to me. "Sorry about his lack of filter. You know how he is."

"Yup." That's all I need to say. I've always wondered if part of the reason he's friends with Maks is because he enjoys seeing how far he can push people's buttons, too.

Suddenly, I'm standing alone. I'm not sure where Patrick went, probably to check his phone and see if the soon to be ex-wifey has changed her mind. I know I'm horrible to wish for his pain, but as much as they were driving me crazy, at least they were a distraction from the upcoming potential blind date doom.

"There you are!"

I'd know that voice anywhere. The one person in my life who I feel totally and completely comfortable with, no matter what the situation. I guess sharing a womb with someone for nine months will do that to a person.

"Hey, Sis." I greet Delaney with a kiss to the cheek, careful not to smudge her make up. "Did you help with the decorating? It looks great in here."

She beams with pride. "I may have decided on the center-pieces for the tables. You like them?"

Each table has a tall, clear vase filled with flowers in soft shades of blues and whites. The vase itself has small white lights inside, making the whole thing glow.

"I do. They give off a very wintery vibe."

"That's what I was going for. Anyway..."

Oh boy. Here we go.

"Are you ready to meet your date for the evening?"

"Remind me again why I need a date?"

Delaney adjusts my tie and smooths down my lapels, like she's getting ready to present me to someone important. "Because there are photographers here. You don't like going to events, you don't like giving interviews, and you need some good PR. Why not hang out with an absolutely lovely woman and get a little exposure."

I groan. "Seriously, Lane? This is your attempt at getting me some PR?"

The gleam in her eye says there's more to it than just that. "I love you, Nicky. But you need to get out more." She threads her arm through mine and pulls me forward. "Come on. Let's find your date."

I huff but resign myself to my fate. "Fine. How do you know her anyway?"

My sister stiffens next to me. Now I know something else is going on.

"Lane?"

My warning tone must sound serious because she hesitates to answer me. That's not a good sign.

"It's a long story," she finally says. "I'll tell you all about it later, I promise, but she's right over there."

I give her one last glare, thoroughly irritated by this situation already. Until I turn around and see the woman approaching.

Holy. Shit.

"Is that her?"

"That's Pres." I can practically feel my sister's delight. Likely because I can't take my eyes off the brunette bombshell coming towards us.

She looks just as nervous as I feel, but she doesn't have any reason to be. She clearly is supposed to be here.

Delaney reaches my date and gives her a quick hug before threading their arms together. "Pres, this is my brother Nick. Nick, my new friend, Pres."

It takes me half a second to register my sister's words. "*New* friend?"

Pres squirms in her mermaid style green dress. Delaney, on the other hand, doesn't seem to notice her discomfort.

"Like I said, Nicky, it's a long story," Delaney says with way too much pep in her voice. Something is up with that and I'll find out what. Later. Right now, I'm interested to find out why my sister thinks this beautiful woman is a good match for me and she is... wow.

"Now that introductions have been made," Delaney says. "I'll leave you guys to it and go check on the centerpiece that seems to have stopped glowing."

After directing a wink at me, she glides away, a huge grin on her face.

I, on the other hand, am leaning toward the dumbfounded side. I'm not sure what to say to the breathtaking woman standing next to me. It seems that she's not sure either.

We stand there in awkward silence for a few minutes before we both speak at once.

"Would you—"

"Do you want to—"

We both laugh softly. Being the gentleman that I am, I gesture for her to go ahead.

"I was just going to ask if you'd like to grab a drink so we can cut through some of this awkwardness."

"You've read my mind."

I let her walk ahead of me and follow closely behind. We're stopped a few times by VIPs who want to speak to Pres, which ignites my curiosity about her. How do Tampa's rich and famous know her? Does she run with the elite crowd in town? And how the hell did my sister meet her?

There's surprisingly no line at the bar so we get right to the front to order drinks—martini for her. Scotch for me. Both on the rocks.

"So you're a goalie, right?"

I almost stiffen at her bringing up hockey right off the bat, but something about her tone indicates she has no idea what I actually do on the ice.

"Yep. That's my day job."

"Quite an unusual day job." The bartender places our drinks on the counter and Pres thanks him, then picks hers up.

"Working in an office never seemed appealing to me. And I love being on the ice, so it worked out well for me."

"I can see that."

She takes a sip of her drink and glances around the room. I'm not sure if she's looking for someone in particular or is trying to buy herself time to come up with another conversation starter. Yet another indicator that she's nowhere close to being a puck bunny.

"Now you know how *I* ended up here. How did you score an invite?" I ask as I guide her away from the bar and to a high top table tucked away against a wall. My hand is on the small of her back, where it fits perfectly. A little too perfectly. Her physical beauty stuns me. If she's just as beautiful on the inside, I may be fucked. Despite my sister's insistence on me dating, I'm not in the market for a girlfriend.

Pres clears her throat before answering me. Is she... nervous?

"I...um. I work here."

"Ah," I respond. "So you got the invite before I did." It's a lame attempt at a joke, but it makes her smile briefly.

"I had it on my calendar almost a year ago, when we started planning it."

"Are you part of the planning committee or something?"

"Not really. I work in retail operations, but we're in between catering directors so right now we oversee this department."

This woman is surprising me all over the place. Not only is she beautiful and demure, she's sharp and goal-oriented. She knows nothing about hockey, and doesn't seem to care, and she's friends with my sister.

"Well, I'm glad you got the night off, Pres."

"Me, too." She looks up at me through thick lashes and I'm about knocked over from how perfect she is.

I'm going to be really pissed if Tiger is right, and the perfect woman just dropped into my lap.

Nick is turning out to be a really great date. We got a couple drinks. We perused the silent auction and laughed about Tucker Hayes starting the bidding for the Tahoe trip at a hundred bucks. And then Nick put in his own bid of ten grand, just to piss Tucker off.

We danced. And lord, how that man can move. At one point, during a slower number, I was close enough to smell his cologne and I almost forgot where we were and who we were with. I just wanted to wrap my legs around him and dry hump him on the dance floor. That probably would have ruined the mood, though. In spite of the reservations we both initially had, we've had a really great time. And the chemistry between us is palpable.

All my reservations about going on a blind date with a professional athlete have faded away. I know there's probably a bad boy side to him, but tonight Nick has been a perfect gentleman. The minute I said my feet were starting to hurt, he guided us to our table so we could sit for a while. And he hasn't pulled his phone out to take a picture once.

"So how did you end up getting the night off for this shindig?" he asks as he lifts his drink to his perfect lips.

His question makes me pause momentarily. I'm not positive I want to tell him who I really am. In the past, that's become... problematic. I'm not getting the vibe from him that he would care that I'm a "hotel heiress", though. Maybe it's because he's his own kind of celebrity. He doesn't need my money. He has his own.

Now that I think about it, I wonder if Gary really did know who I was the entire time we were talking, and that was his whole game from the beginning. Makes sense. The only thing I have that Delaney doesn't is a gigantic trust fund that I'll come into when I turn thirty.

Still, I feel comfortable with Nick. Maybe a little too comfortable. I might as well see his reaction to my status as "Caine royalty."

I stir my martini with the stirrer toothpick that still has one olive left on it and clear my throat. "My full name is Prestyn Caine."

"Okay."

He says it so nonchalantly, I'm not sure he understood what I'm getting at.

"Caine." He continues to look at me blankly. I clarify, "As in Caine Resorts and Conference Centers."

Nick's eyebrows furrow. "Like this Caine Resort?"

I nod and that's when the lightbulb seems to go off.

"You don't just work here, do you?"

I shake my head and smile, glad I don't have to explain much further. "No. My great-grandfather started this hotel and my grandfather grew it to... well..." I look around the massive room, letting myself really take in the grandiosity I normally don't notice. I gesture to our surroundings. "This. My dad is really into philanthropy, though, so he likes when we attend these events as guests. You know, mingle with the wealthy patrons, make connections and encourage donations. That kind of thing."

Nick smirks. "Is that why you agreed to go on a date with me? So you could encourage my donation?"

I know he's joking, but I still feel the need to explain myself a little. "No. Delaney never even said your name so I had no idea who you were. I didn't know what to expect so it's been a nice surprise that you're so... normal. And nice. You never know when someone is setting you up, right?"

He makes a noise in the back of his throat like he knows exactly what I'm talking about.

"But I've had a really nice time with you."

Nick cocks his head and looks at me, really looks at me. I can practically feel his warm gaze on my body. It's not unwelcome. It's also been a really long time since I've had sex. Maybe Nick could help me change all that. He's hot and he's super nice. I bet he's a really generous lover. We could have a really great fling.

"Me, too," he says as he smooths down his tie. "I'll be honest, I was nervous when my sister called and said she'd found me a date."

I giggle. "Couldn't find one on your own?"

"Wasn't really looking. If I'm being honest, I was trying to find a way out of it, but Delaney has this way about her, ya know?" He lifts a brow and huffs humorously. "Of course you know. You got pressured into this, too."

"It didn't turn out all bad though, did it?"

"Not even a little. It's nice being with someone who doesn't seem to care about the difference between a drop pass and a flip pass."

That elicits a laugh from me, partially because I have no idea what either of those terms mean. "That's very true. Sounds like in a way, we're kindred spirits." I hold up my glass to clink his. "Here's to me not needing your money, and you not needing mine."

"Hear, hear."

We drink and take a few minutes to watch the room around us. Everyone seems to be having a good time. Gavin is schmoozing with some of the big wigs in the room. Delaney is laughing with who I assume is a hockey wife based on the age and size of the man next to her. The dance floor seems to have been taken over by the entire Glaze hockey team. And Maksim, probably the one person on the team I know because his antics are legendary in Tampa... Maksim is slow dancing to a fast song, his hand solidly squeezing the ass of his date. At least I hope that's his date. From everything I've heard about Maksim Ivanov, that could be someone else's date he's pawing possessively.

I'm glad to see so many people having a good time. So why do I still feel such discontent?

"Do you ever feel... lonely?"

The words are out of my mouth before I can stop them and I'm not really sure why I even said them. I chance a look at Nick, hoping he isn't about to bolt at my emotional turmoil. But he's not. He's looking at me intently, like he's seeing a new side of me.

He licks his lips before answering. "All the time."

That's not the answer I was expecting. "Really? You seem so settled."

"I'm different than the guys on my team."

"How so?"

"I'm not into all the flash that comes with being a professional hockey player. I don't like interviews. I don't like going out and partying. It exhausts me to have to talk to so many people all the time. I'm never really sure what I'm supposed to say. Don't get me wrong, I love my fans. They can be amazing. But they only know me as the goalie who keeps the other team from scoring. They don't know *me*. So it can seem very surface level. Not real, ya know?"

I do know. So many people in my life know me as the only daughter of Richard Caine, and that's all they know. They don't know how much I love working with our retailers. They don't know how much fulfillment I get from helping our business part-ners stay afloat and make a good life for themselves and their families. They don't know my favorite part of my dad isn't his pocketbook, but his love of giving back.

Suddenly I want to know more about Nick. Not the side everyone gets to see, but the parts he keeps close to himself. Who he really is.

I lean in, getting closer for such an intimate question. "Tell me something real."

"What?"

"Tell me something real about yourself. Something the fans have never taken the time to know."

Nick thinks for a few seconds and I'm starting to learn he likes to think through his words before responding. Unlike me who has to bite her tongue before words I can't take back just roll right off them.

Finally, he comes up with an answer.

"I read poetry for fun."

Like they have a mind of their own, my eyebrows shoot up.

"I know. Shocking."

"No not shocking. Just not what I expected from... from..."

"A testosterone-filled professional athlete?"

I open my mouth to correct him, but realize he's right.

"Well, yeah. I guess. That's really shallow of me to stereotype but I've never met any man interested in poetry, let alone one who looks like you."

He smirks, like I've said too much. And I probably have. He asks, "And what do I look like?"

The air around us begins to shift and I have to bite my bottom lip to keep from saying something I shouldn't. Something like, "Take your pants off so I can straddle you right now," because, holy moly is he sexy. His tousled blond hair and chiseled jaw line, topping off what I'm sure is a very cut body underneath that finely tailored suit.

It takes everything in me to come up with an appropriate answer for where we are. "A jock. You look like a jock."

Nick snickers, like he can see right through me. "That's not what you were thinking."

"How do you know what I was thinking?"

"Because you blush when you're thinking dirty thoughts."

My jaw drops open at this information. "I do?"

"Yep. You've been doing it all night."

"And how do you know I've been blushing when I've been thinking dirty thoughts? Maybe I was just overheated."

Nick leans in further and the air around us continues to move in a sultry way. It's like our pheromones are off the charts and there's nowhere for them to go except around the both of us, blanketing us from the outside world.

"Because you have them at the same times I do."

My breath hitches and my stomach clenches. When I agreed to this date, I didn't expect to have so much fun. And I certainly didn't expect this level of attraction.

"That's a bold statement, Mr. Hockeyman."

"Mr. Hockeyman, huh? Not even my first name anymore?"

"Just keeping you humble."

Nick leans back and pulls his drink to his lips, stopping his arm halfway up. "You're right. Now is not the time, nor the place for this level of conversation."

"No. But later might be."

He chokes on his scotch and I can't help but laugh.

"Serves you right for trying to embarrass me about my blush."

He nods in acquiescence. "Touché. So back to the original conversation. What's one thing your fans wouldn't know?"

"Fans? I don't have fans. I'm not Paris Hilton."

"No, but I'm sure there are people on the outside of your world looking in that have different ideas about you than you have about yourself."

I don't tell him there are people *inside* my world who do the same thing. Namely my brothers and my father. Even though the truth is that except for a select few who have never had any real expectations of me, no one's really expected anything of me. And no one at all knows this particular dream. Until now.

"I want to go to Virunga National Park."

"Where's that?"

"In the Congo."

Nick looks shocked. "That's quite a dangerous place to visit."

"That's why I want to visit."

"I'm not following."

"The park rangers not only help protect the people, but they work hard to protect the wildlife that lives in the region. Did you ever see the video of that pilot who had a chimpanzee on his lap while he was flying?"

"I vaguely remember seeing something like that on Instagram. I'm not really on social media that much."

Just another point in Nick's favor tonight.

"Virunga is where that pilot works. He and a couple other guys do flyovers all over the park to help stop poachers from killing the apes and gorillas. Elephants. They do such amazing work, and I'd like to see it first hand. See how I can help and what kinds of resources they need to stay afloat and make it safer for the rangers."

"Wow. That's... wow."

"It's weird, I know."

"No. Not at all. I think it's really cool that you're empathetic to the plight of one of the most dangerous parts of the world. Not many people can think past the number of likes on their social media accounts."

His approval warms me for some reason and I'm not sure if I like how it makes me feel, or hate that I'm so starved for validation I'll take it from a virtual stranger.

Then again, Nick isn't really a stranger anymore. He cares about his friends, but he also cares about those around him. He's an introvert who loves poetry and the way it makes him feel. He's an athlete who loves a sport and recognizes how lucky he is to play it for money. He's so very multi-layered and like no one I've ever met. And holy hell, the complete package is just so sexy.

"Well thank you. I—"

Don't get a chance to finish my sentence when the band leader begins his announcement.

"Ladies and gentlemen, if you would kindly begin taking your seats. The silent auction is officially closed and the winners are about to be announced."

People begin making their way toward the tables, the excitement to find out who won palpable.

"I'm going to grab another drink before we're stuck at here for a while," Nick says. "Would you like me to grab you another dirty martini?"

I nod. "Please. Extra dirty and—"

"All the olives they can spare, right?"

Now he remembers my drink order, too. Can this man be any more perfect?

"You got it."

As Nick walks away, I can't keep my gaze from following him. I know I have some serious attraction toward him, but it's more than that. I feel safe. Like I could tell him all my secrets and he'd keep them. I'd never have to worry about them being sold to a tabloid or used against me later. That's part of why I'm careful to guard my words with Aaron. He may be a family friend, but that doesn't mean he wouldn't turn on me in a heartbeat.

"If you don't take that hunk of sexy home and fuck his brains out, I just might."

If I didn't know that voice so well, I'd be concerned by who has been paying such close attention to me.

I lean into Bayleigh, who is bending over the table to 'pick up dirty glasses,' which is a sneaky way of making sure Aaron doesn't see her fraternizing with a 'guest'. "He's amazing, right?"

"I'll have to take your word for it since I'm not part of your conversations. But honestly, Pres, I haven't seen you light up like this in... probably ever. And he's so into you."

"You think?"

"I do. I'm serious." She collects the last of the glasses and places them on her tray. "Take advantage of it. When are you ever going to meet another guy like this who has as much money as you do?"

Well, probably not that much. Trust funds have a tendency to grow exponentially when you aren't moving any money out of them. But I see her point.

Before I can thank her, she glides away, off to clear another table, leaving me to sort through my hormones.

CHAPTER SIX

NICK

The steaks for dinner were perfectly made. The band played great music. The bartenders didn't skimp on the alcohol. But the best part of the night was the silent auction. In particular, when the results of the trip to Tahoe were announced.

Tucker was so determined to win it, he staked out the table all night and immediately outbid anyone who offered more money. What he apparently missed was Maksim coming up right behind him at the very end and outbidding him by just one dollar.

The look on Tucker's face when the winner was announced and he was halfway to his feet, only to find out he lost, was priceless. Considering how little Maks pays attention to everyone around him, he can be really astute sometimes. And this time it worked to all of our benefits. I haven't heard so much laughter from my teammates since the night Tiger beat everyone out at the poker table, in spite of them moving him away from his lucky chair.

Far and away though, an even better part of the night has been getting to know Prestyn. She is electric. That's the only way I can describe her. She knows how to talk to just about everyone, as seen by the way she worked the room tonight. She's fucking gorgeous, from her dark hair that was pulled back to show off her neck and collarbones, to the strapless green number that hugged her body. But that's nothing compared to the dreams she has and how much she wants to make the world a better place. I admit, the whole package is sexy as hell.

"Did you have a fun evening?"

The night is winding down and most of my teammates are already gone. I felt like I needed to stay behind in case Delaney needs my help, but getting to spend more time with Prestyn hasn't been a hardship either.

"I did. More fun than I expected," I admit.

Prestyn runs her finger around the rim of her glass as her teeth gnaw on her bottom lip. I'm getting the impression she's feeling nervous about something. Her lip finally pops out, the color immediately pinkening as I watch her mouth a little too intently.

"Can I ask you a really personal question?"

I wasn't expecting that, but something about her has me wanting to tell her all my secrets. Like I can trust her with just about anything. "Sure."

"When was the last time you had sex?"

It's a good thing I'm not eating or drinking or I would have choked on her unexpected question.

She continues before I can answer, and I admit I'm dying to know what she's going to say.

"I know that question sounds like its coming from out of the blue, but here's the thing..."

Oh man, what's the thing? I *need* to know what the thing is now.

"It's been a really, really long time for me."

She blinks a few times looking up at me from underneath her long, dark lashes. Is this really happening? Is she propositioning me? Or is this just wishful thinking?

Well no, I know it's wishful thinking. But is this for real?

"Most of the time, I don't know if I can trust the person who is flirting with me," she continues, and I'm unable to look away. "Do they really like me, or are they trying to get close to my family? Do they really find me attractive, or are they only attracted to my money? Can I trust that what happens between us will stay between us, or am I going to end up having personal details about myself made public for a profit?"

Yikes. I've had all those thoughts about dating myself, but her family is like billionaires. I can't imagine the kind of extra pressure that puts on her.

"You don't give me that feeling at all." Prestyn taps the rim of her glass gently. "You make me feel... safe."

I may have come on this date under duress, but the fact that I've made her feel so comfortable makes *me* feel like I've done my job. Which is odd because I shouldn't feel so protective of her, should I?

"I think because we met in this setting..." She gestures with her hand toward the opulence of the chandeliers that have now been turned up while the room is being torn down. "I think maybe its made it easy to see what's real. Like... because the back-drop to tonight was so very obviously not reality. I mean, who spends every day in glamorous dresses and dripping in jewels? No one, right?"

I nod, only because I'm not sure how else to respond. My heart is pounding and I've lost my breath waiting to hear the rest.

"I also think since Delaney is the one who officially set us up, it's not like either of us were pursuing each other, you know?"

I do know and I think I see what she's getting at. It's easier to believe someone when they've already been vetted by the person you most trust in the world. That's Delaney for me. She's my twin. She would never put me in a bad position. Hell, she volunteers with my organization just to show her support for me. I don't know of anyone else who's sister is that involved with their hockey career.

"Plus, your organization needs our help. It wouldn't be smart of you to burn that bridge." Prestyn cocks an amused eyebrow at me. Then she licks her lips and shakes her head. "I know I'm rambling, but I'm trying to get to the point, I promise. I just feel so... lonely sometimes. For human contact. Real, genuine human contact." She huffs out a small laugh and glances at the table. "I'm sorry. I'm rambling."

I place my hand over hers, wishing I could tangle our fingers together, but that feels too intimate. "I don't mind. I like hearing your thoughts. Please continue."

She takes a deep breath and her face begins to blush. If that means what I think it does...

"I just want one night of unbridled passion. Just to scratch the itch. I want the feel of a man's body over mine, the touch and the... the I don't know how to say it without sounding like a porn star..."

"The feel of skin-on-skin contact?" Her eyes whip up to mine. "Fingers running through your hair and the grip of a hand on your hip?"

I'm not sure where all those words came from, but I better slow down. As my body responds to the images I've conjured, my pants are tightening, and that's not a look I like to sport when my sister is in the same room, no matter how big the room is.

Prestyn swallows hard. "Yes," she whispers. "That's exactly it."

I lean forward, not wanting even the possibility of anyone overhearing this conversation, but unable to stop myself from moving this close. "Tell me what you want, Prestyn."

She licks her lips again and my eyes immediately latch onto the movement.

"I want to know if you'd like to be my fuck buddy tonight," she blurts.

My thoughts come to a screeching halt. I was beginning to expect a proposition, but her words are so out of left field, I start laughing, and suddenly I can't stop.

"It's not funny," Prestyn says with a flirty smirk and smack to my arm. "I didn't know how else to say it."

"You could have gone with anything, Prestyn," I tease. "Just a simple, 'would you like to come home with me tonight,' would have been more than sufficient."

"I know, but I don't want you to misunderstand me. I like you, Nick. I really do. But I'm not asking you to date me or anything. Not that I wouldn't. You're a great guy. Amazing actually. Oh god, I'm rambling again."

"Keep going. You're really boosting my ego."

"I think I might stop here. Forget it. I take it back. I was kidding. It was nice to meet you."

I know she's joking when she starts to stand, but that doesn't stop me from playing along. "No, no! Don't leave. I'll stop, I promise. You want to have a night of hot sex. That's what I'm hearing."

She sits back down and nods, only there's no blush this time. "Assuming we're compatible, I'm not saying it has to be an everyday thing. But wouldn't it be nice to have someone you can trust enough to sleep with, enjoy some time with, and not have to worry they're with you for the wrong reasons?"

This is the strangest conversation I've had in a long time, but she's also not wrong. I get lonely a lot, too. I, myself would love that same skin-on-skin contact I'm joshing her about. And frankly, I really want a night with her. Or three.

"How do you want to do this? Do we need a schedule? Rules? A secret rendezvous location?"

She tips her head toward me. "You realize we're inside the hotel my family owns. I already have a key to a private rendezvous location."

"You don't think people will find it weird when I'm here all the time?"

She laughs lightly. "There are over two thousand employees at this hotel and we service over a million visitors per year. Unless you lose your key regularly and ask the front desk for a new one every time, no one will even know you're here. And if I do decide to grace you with a key, if you lose it, ask me to get you a new one. It's less suspicious if the person who is supposed to be there needs it."

"I find it incredibly convenient that you have a room reserved just for you."

"It's my family's suite, one that no one usually uses. Well, that's not true. Hoyt likes to stash his mother-in-law there when she visits so he doesn't have to deal with her, but that's maybe once a year. I used it tonight to get ready and thought Gavin might need it but he left early so it's empty tonight. Sometimes I'll crash there if work keeps me super late. Which means I always know who is coming and going."

"Seems like you've got this all figured out already."

Prestyn shrugs, her bare shoulder lifting. A shoulder I may be sucking on very soon.

"I just believe in grabbing onto opportunities when they come along. I wasn't expecting you, but here you are. I think this could be... mutually beneficial to us."

I stall, not because I'm not considering her offer. I've had fuck buddies in the past. But I've always just fallen into the situation. It hasn't been quite so preplanned. Then again, I've never been with someone of quite the same pop culture status as Prestyn either.

"I leave on a road trip in a couple days so I can't promise you more than tonight."

"And I have a major meeting in a couple days so I can't see you after tonight anyway."

I study her expression, looking for any indication that she's having doubts, but there're none. Her eye contact is unwavering. Her head is held high. She's a woman who knows what she wants.

"If you'll give me five minutes, I need to say goodbye to my sister, and then you can show me where your suite is.

Prestyn smirks, a glint in her eye. "I hope to show you more than that."

I groan and lean my head back. "Save the sexy talk until after I speak to my sister, will you?" I push up from the table, making sure I don't need to adjust my pants. "Don't go anywhere."

"Don't worry. I'm only *coming* with you tonight."

My step falters and she laughs behind me. "That was unnecessary."

"But too much fun to pass up."

I shake my head, a smile on my face as I weave through the tables to find Delaney. I can't believe I just agreed to this. Not that I'm sad about it. I'll be taking full advantage of the situation for as long as Prestyn will have me. My visions of how tonight's blind date would go were very different from the reality in my immediate future.

Finding my sister picking up silent auction materials, I put my hand on her shoulder. "Need any help?"

Delaney doesn't turn around. She probably knew I was coming from fifty feet away. That twin thing again.

"I'm almost done, actually. The hotel is doing most of the tear down so that's covered. I'm just gathering the last minute items that weren't picked up and paid for yet. There's always a few who have too much to drink and forget before they leave. Gotta make those calls on Monday to get the rest of those bills paid!"

"You did really great tonight, Sis."

Delaney turns and wraps her arms around me. "Thanks, Nick. It makes me happy to be able to support you like this."

"Doesn't hurt that it's raising money to help charity, huh?"

"Not even a little."

I drop a kiss to the top of her head and begin to pull away, ready to say goodnight.

"Oh!" Delaney exclaims before I can make my escape. "What do you think of Prestyn? Isn't she sweet?"

Sweet is not at all the word I was thinking when she propositioned me a few minutes ago. But I hold my tongue. My sister doesn't need to know anything about that. We may share almost everything, but our sex lives have always been a hard limit. So I go with "She's nice. Thanks for setting me up with her."

"Are you going to see her again?"

I almost laugh as I think about how much I'm about to see of her. "It was a blind date, set up by my sister. I'm not sure I see this becoming a long-term thing."

Delaney's shoulders slump. "Oh man. I like her. I was hoping you'd hit it off."

"If you like her, you date her." I kiss her on the cheek. "I'm sure Gary would go for kinky shit like that."

She tries to swat me on my chest, but I'm too fast and agile for her.

"See you later, Lane."

Delaney waves me off and gets back to it, her mind on a million other things than what I'm up to tonight. And thank goodness for that. Because I only have a one-track mind in my pants right now, and he's guiding my way right back to my date.

CHAPTER SEVEN

PRESTYN

I know Nick said to wait for him at the table, but I've been schmoozing all night while drinking more liquids than I should have and I have to pee. I don't want to kill the mood by making a run for the toilet when we get upstairs—the walls aren't thin here, but they're not soundproof either—so I figured now was the best time to relieve myself.

Besides, it gave me a chance to do a quick pit check, smooth my hair, and add just a touch of color to my lips. All things I've been taught to do during swanky events all my life.

All things that come in handy before getting your dress ripped off so you can be thoroughly fucked, as well.

Coming out of the restroom, I round the corner to where my date is probably waiting, and almost run right into the table Aaron is rolling to the storage closet.

"Oh!" I exclaim and hold out my hands so I don't barrel into it the table.

"Prestyn." Aaron's voice is practically a sneer. "Not a bad turn out tonight."

I appease him with one quick nod of my head. "And there is

chatter that we exceeded our fundraising goal, so I'd call it a success."

"Why haven't you changed out of your dress yet?"

Furrowing my brow, I try to figure out what game he's playing at. With him, there's *always* a game.

"So you can help the crew tear down," he continues. "That's part of the job when you work in catering."

I fight the eye roll threatening to break free and turn on my sickeningly sweet voice instead, unable to stop myself from pulling 'rank'. "First, I don't work in catering. I work in retail sales. And I'm a Caine, Aaron. That would look terrible on the hotel, and the department, if the richest men in Tampa saw a Caine moving furniture into storage tonight, don't you think?"

His nostrils flare and he almost drops the table he's holding upright. I'm definitely paying for that one on Monday.

"In that case, the party is over. You need to vacate so us *working folks* can finish the job we're paid to do."

Sounds like I hit a giant, insecure nerve. I always knew he wanted to weasel his way into my family, but I didn't realize how much it irks him that he's still not included on nights like these. I move that little nugget to a secure part of my brain to use at a later date.

"I'm on my way out now. Just looking for my..." I look up and see Nick sauntering toward me, looking sexy as hell in his very dark grey suit. "...date."

I can't take my eyes off him. He carries himself with such confidence, which comes as no shock. Not only is he a fantastic goalie, or so I've been told, from the chatter around the table tonight, he's also been offered numerous modeling contracts, all of which he's turned down.

I just realized I'm about to have sex with a world-class athlete and potential runway darling. He better be as good in the sack as my fantasies think he is.

Aaron's voice begins to break through my thoughts, though

I'm not really listening.

"...those cost breakdowns on my desk first thing Monday morning. Are you listening to me? Prestyn?"

"Hmm? What?"

I finally glance at him to find him fuming at my very obvious lack of concern about his opinion.

"I'm glad you had fun playing the hotel princess tonight, but you still have a job to do. What could be more important than listening to your boss's very explicit instructions on reports... due..."

Aaron's voice trails off as he finally sees who is coming. His eyes blink several times and a weird red color starts to creep up from under the collar of his shirt.

"Are you ready to go?"

From the weird noise that comes out of Aaron's mouth, I think the sound of Nick's voice made my "very important boss" fangirl a bit. That's my cue to turn this conversation around.

"Nick, I don't believe you've met my boss, Aaron. Aaron, this is Nick Williams, goalie for the Florida Glaze."

Aaron fumbles with the table and finally puts his hand out to shake. "Yes... yes, sir... yep... so nice to meet you, Mr. Williams."

He pumps Nick's hand way too hard and for way too long. I have the fleeting thought that it's probably how he is in bed, too. Ew.

Wondering if there's a way to bleach the thought from my brain, I refocus my attention on the scene in front of me.

"Always glad to meet a fan," Nick says kindly. He's smiling, but somehow it's not reaching his eyes.

"Any time you need anything, anything at all," Aaron gushes, still holding on until Nick finally pulls his hand free of his grasp, "Just give us a call and I'll get Prestyn right on it. I'm her boss so she has to do what I say."

Nick looks at me for just a split second, probably wondering how I'm going to react.

I give him a tight smile, my eyes just a little too wide as I grit out, "Yes. Aaron's my boss."

"Oooookay. Well thanks for the offer Aaron. I'll be sure to let you know. I'm heading out now." He turns to me and I know he's trying not to blow our cover. "Are you on your way out, too? Can we continue discussing that donor idea I wanted to run by you?"

"Sure. I know a private exit so you don't have to worry about walking the red carpet again."

We quickly say goodbye to Aaron who yells, "If you need help with that donor thing, call me." Nick doesn't even respond.

As soon as we're out the door and out of earshot, Nick begins laughing. "Ohmygod, is he always like that?"

"What? The biggest Florida Glaze fan in the world?"

I'm joking. I know exactly what Nick is talking about.

"No. *I'm her boss. She has to do what I say,*" he says in a nasally voice, imitating what has to be one of the most uncomfortable work-related conversations I've ever been part of.

"He's like that all the time," I answer truthfully as I lead us to a bank of elevators most people don't know are here. "Actually, that's not true. He's usually worse."

"Worse than demeaning his employee, who is also the owner's daughter?"

"You'd be surprised how much men can get away with when you work in a misogynistic environment like this one."

"Misogynistic?"

"It's a long, not so pretty story. But as a hotel 'princess',"—I flash air quotes since I don't really feel like royalty—"I'm determined to have a hand in changing that. But not tonight. I don't want to talk about that right now. It's depressing and squashing my libido."

Nick laughs again as we arrive at the elevators. As soon as I press the arrow pointing up, the door opens and we step into the enclosed space where I press another button to the seventeenth floor.

"We certainly wouldn't want to *squash* your libido."

"Are you making fun of me?" I look up at him through the very long false lashes I wear for important events.

He pinches his thumb and forefinger together until they're almost touching. "Just a little bit."

"It's a good thing. First step of sneaking around this hotel— knowing there are cameras in every elevator in the building. Picture and sound. Likely, a security guard is watching us and listening in right now."

Nick's eyes shift around the small area, trying to spot the cameras.

"You'll never find them." He looks down at me with a smirk. "We need the security for a myriad of boring reasons, but we keep them well hidden. We never want the guests to feel like we're spying on them."

"But they're spying on *you*."

"That's different. I'm alone with a man they haven't seen me with before. They're either waiting to see if you are going to harm me, or waiting to see if I'm going to start sucking your face, neither of which are going to happen. We have a great team, but those pictures would still sell for a lot of money."

I catch Nick's grimace in the reflection in front of me.

"You can't even trust your own staff?"

I look up at him, cocking one eyebrow. "Do you trust every single staff member at your job?"

He presses his lips together and nods once. "Gotcha. Are there any more tricks I need to know about this place?"

"Just one." The elevator dings and the door opens to our floor. I step off and call behind me. "Don't get lost."

I hear him chuckle as he follows me down the long hall to the family suite. I open the app on my phone and unlock the door, pushing it open to step inside. I've been here a million times since I was a kid, so nothing about it is unusual. Nick's mouth, on the other hand, is gaping wide open as he looks around.

Tossing my clutch onto the foyer table, I watch as he takes it all in, waiting to see what draws him in the most. I expect it'll be the multimedia system or maybe even the view of the ocean from the floor to ceiling windows. Instead, he stops right in front of the built-in bookshelves, his eyes raking over the titles.

"Are you a big reader?"

He runs his fingers over some of the spines and I feel a shiver up my own, just from watching how gentle his touch is.

"I don't know if you'd call me a reader. Like I said before, poetry is more my style."

I lift one eyebrow, surprised by this declaration. I'm obviously not the first person to be shocked by the information.

He turns to me with a wide, beautiful grin on his face. "Not what you were expecting me to say?"

"Not what I ever expect anyone to say. I don't know many poetry lovers."

He pulls a book off the shelf and opens it, flipping through the pages. "I'm usually the only one. It's too bad. People are missing out on some beautiful lyrics."

"Lyrics?"

He slides the book back into place and pulls out another, fingering its pages with reverence. The movement makes my thighs squirm with anticipation. Will he treat my body with the same gentleness?

"Poetry always sounds like music in my head." He snaps the book shut, but doesn't put it back. "I'm sure I'm not the only one. Everyone knows song lyrics are just musical poetry. But for some reason, my brain automatically sets it to music."

"Sounds like you missed your calling to become a musician."

He laughs and I feel the rumble deep down into my core.

"I didn't say the music was any good, only that it was there."

I watch as he slides the book back into place, at an achingly slow pace. I've never had such an erotic reaction to books. But something about Nick's hands on them, touching the pages, devouring the words with his eyes, turns the entire experience into something completely different than just reading.

I'm not sure how much more I can take before I rip my dress off and dry hump his leg.

"Would you like to see the rest of the place?"

Nick turns to me, his eyes twinkling. He knows I'm trying to move our night along. How is he so patient?

"I'd love to."

We take our time, meandering through the different areas of the suite. I show him the full kitchen that has probably never been used, and the large balcony where you can hear and smell the ocean. He's impressed by the shiny black grand piano in the sitting room, even though none of us can play. I even take him into the very impressive master bathroom. The white marble counter is still scattered with my makeup and hair supplies from when I got ready for the gala earlier. The room comes complete with a bedroom sized walk-in closet, an oversized marble tub that can easily fit two, and a shower that has not just a rain head, but eight different sprays in the wall.

"It's opulent, but it's my favorite part of the entire suite," I admit as I explain how each individual spray can be adjusted for temperature or pressure. That elicits both of his eyebrows raising in surprise. "I don't want to be presumptuous, but feel free to come on over and try it after an extra hard practice."

He smirks at me. I can't read what it means, but I hope it's excitement over trying my favorite toy. "I'll have to do that."

"Anyway," I say quickly, moving through the doors and into the master bedroom. "That's the whole thing. I'm sure there are details I forgot, but you've got a good idea of how over the top it is now."

"I wouldn't say it's over the top."

I purse my lips. "Mm-hmm."

"I'd say it's a nice home away from home when you just need a break but can't go far."

"You overestimate the intentions behind why this suite was built in the first place."

"I don't really care about the intentions. I care about what we're going to use it for."

I gasp as he come up behind me, his lips gently resting at the juncture of my neck and shoulder. The way his hands grab my hips reminds me of the tender way he handled those poetry books. My breathing picks up as I wait for him to squeeze or kiss or move or *something*. But he doesn't. He stands there patiently, still, building the anticipation and I wonder what he's going to do. What he's going to do to me.

Finally, after what feels like an eternity, he speaks.

"If we do this..." The puff of air from his breath grazes my shoulder making me weak in the knees. "We have to be on the same page."

"Yes, yes. Same page." I'm practically panting and I can't stop my hand from raising and sliding into his hair.

He lets out a small groan from the contact. "This is not a love match. This is two high-profile people finding pleasure in each other. And it stays between us."

"Yes," I whisper, my chest heaving like I can't catch a breath.

And then his lips begin to move. He nibbles on my shoulder, my neck, and when his teeth graze behind my ear, my legs practically give out.

Before I can get my bearings straight, I feel Nick's hands at my rib cage, his deft fingers pulling the zipper down on my dress. The silky material slides straight down my body and lands in a pile at my feet. I hear Nick gasp when he realizes I'm in nothing but a thong and my heels.

The sound gives me a feeling of empowerment. Carefully, I pull away, stepping out from the material on the floor and turn to face him. Channeling my inner sex goddess, I reach up, grabbing the pins in my hair and pull.

CHAPTER EIGHT

NICK

I have two thoughts as her dark hair cascades down her shoulders.

One, my mouth is completely dry and I may have stopped breathing.

Two, she's the most beautiful thing I've ever seen.

I knew Prestyn was stunning. There's no denying her beauty, but right now, standing in front of me, in nothing but a scrap of red lace, a pair of sky high heels, and a hint of vulnerability on her face, I've never seen anything more stunning.

Her flat stomach and breasts that will fill my mouth just right aren't even the best part about her. It's the softness in her eyes. The plumpness of her mouth. Her teeth betraying her nerves as she bites her bottom lip.

I slowly peel my jacket off, tossing it to the side, my eyes never leaving hers. Stepping forward, my hands grace her legs and the words to one of my favorite poems begin to pour out of me.

"I thirst for thy kisses; let me lay my lips on thine which are as fresh and ruddy as the pomegranate."

She gasps, eyes widening in surprise as I slowly move my hand up, circling her belly button with my finger.

"Ah! I die within thine arms."

My hand flattens as I sweep it over her stomach. "Let me press thy lovely breasts, firm as the golden apples in the garden of Cama..." I continue to move, my hand going where the poetry takes me. "...and sweet to smell as the jasmine-flower."

With my hand now holding her head in place, I lean down and nip at her bottom lip. She sucks in a short breath before melting into me. She tastes like pomegranate, which, of course, brings more words into my mind as my tongue invades her mouth.

Press me tighter in thine arms and let an amourous embrace unite us like the tree and bark.

She finally pulls away, her eyes hazy with lust. "Did you come up with those words on the fly?"

A smile breaks out on my face, knowing she's about to be shocked. "No. It's called "A Love Letter From India"."

She blinks rapidly as she processes my words. "So you didn't write it?"

I shrug. "No one knows who wrote it. It's a great poetic mystery."

"Wow," she breathes and I take her lips with mine again, poetry be damned.

Prestyn's fingers begin working the buttons on my dress shirt as I pull the knot free of my tie, tossing it across the room, words suddenly escaping me.

What started slow and sensual, is now speeding up at a rapid rate. By the time she is pushing my shirt over my shoulders, I already have my shoes off and my belt unbuckled. I'm hardly able to wait when Prestyn pushes me away.

Stepping back, I allow my eyes to take her in again. This time her lips are puffy and it's a good thing I practice yoga or I'm not sure I'd be able to control my breathing at this point.

"What's wrong?" I ask.

"You're wearing too many clothes."

I can't disagree there. Channeling my inner Zen, I slowly slide the zipper of my pants down, push them over my hips and let them fall in a heap. My socks are next, and despite my attempt at drawing out this moment, we're suddenly wearing the same outfit —underwear and a smile.

Prestyn licks her lips as she gets an eyeful of the bulge I'm sporting in my boxer briefs. Threading my thumbs into the elastic, I push them to the floor, reveling in the small intake of breath I hear when I'm finally revealed.

Taking myself in my hand, I stroke slowly, watching as Prestyn's chest heaves, her breasts rising and falling in time with her breath. A drop of pre-cum weeps out of my tip and Prestyn whimpers as she tries to hold herself back. I know she's enjoying the anticipation as much as I am.

"Nicholas." My full name on her lips is like music to my ears. Words begin to form in my brain again, but nothing I can put in sentences yet.

"Hm?"

"Please tell me you have a condom."

My hand comes to a screeching halt.

"Fuuuuuck," I groan realizing I just cockblocked myself. "Nope. I'm guessing you don't either, do you?"

"It was a blind date arranged by someone I don't know well. I didn't have high hopes we'd get to this point."

I run my hand through my hair and blow out a breath, disappointed in this turn of events.

"But…"

My eyes snap back to hers. Maybe our evening isn't ending like I thought. "But what?"

"There are other things we can do."

I raise my eyebrows, intrigued.

"What do you have in mind."

Her eyes glance down at my cock again, before she looks back up through her lashes, tilting her head to the side exposing more of the creamy skin on her neck. "Keep stroking yourself."

I comply, enjoying how her eyes darken and her lips part, how she wets her mouth with her tongue as she watches.

"What do you want me to do?" Her voice is raspy with need which makes me squeeze just a little bit tighter.

"Play with your tits."

Her hands immediately slide up her stomach, grabbing a handful of beautiful breast in each one. She circles her fingers around each nipple, causing them to stand at attention. I watch as she plucks at them one at a time, her thighs squeezing together, searching for relief. My body aches for release, but I can't leave her hanging like this.

Stepping forward, my gaze darts all over her body. I'm having a hard time figuring out what I want to watch the most. She's so beautiful and sexy. I have the fleeting thought that I could watch her like this forever.

"Let me help you," I whisper.

Taking her hand in mine, I move it from her breast to my cock, squeezing her small hand around me and helping her stroke the way I like it. Taking my hand off hers so she can take over, I slide my fingers beneath the waistband of her panties, slowly gliding down until my finger finds her clit. Never taking my eyes off hers, I begin circling gently, matching the movement of her hand.

Her breathing is shallow, her eyes hooded, and I slide deeper until I find her entrance. She whimpers and widens her stance as I slide one finger deep inside her, then add another one, pushing until I find the bundle of nerves I'm looking for.

Prestyn gasps and her hips begin moving, riding my hand as she chases her orgasm. Her hand stops stroking, but I can't find it in me to care, too intrigued by her eyes rolling to the back of her head, her eyelids tightening, and her head falling back as she gives herself over to the sensations.

Mere seconds later, I feel her tighten around my fingers and she cries out, my fingers suddenly more wet than they were, but I don't stop. I just slow my movements as she comes down from her high, and when her eyes open, a look of pure contentment crosses her face.

"You're so beautiful." I know I've said it already but I can't stop saying it because it's true. Suddenly I want to see that look on her face again, and again, and again, as many times as I can before I die.

Dramatic, yes, but not untrue.

When Prestyn regains her balance, I slide my fingers out of her and into my mouth where I suck her juices off me.

Pomegranate.

That's the only word that comes to mind.

Prestyn kisses me on the lips before shoving me backward. "Lay down on the bed."

"Prestyn, you don't have to do that. I'm not asking for recip-rocation."

She laughs deeply. "Who says it's reciprocation? I'm just not done with you yet."

Giving the lady what she wants, I fluff up the pillows, adjusting them against the headboard so I can lean against it. If she's about to do what I think she is, I want to watch her mouth move.

She slides her panties off, not having any more use for them, and crawls up between my legs, kissing the inner parts of my thighs as she goes. Her dark eyes continue to hold my gaze and I know she's watching for my reactions. She smiles against my skin with every intake of my breath, every gasp when she finds a tick-lish spot, every grunt when her hair grazes my cock.

But when she finally slides me into her mouth, I lose the ability to keep my eyes open, the sensations overwhelming.

I reach for her head, but think better of it, knowing my strength.

Prestyn doesn't miss my movement. "It's okay," she says quickly. "I have a tough head and I like having my hair pulled."

My cock twitches at her words and immediately thread my fingers in her silky strands.

She continues to suck, pulling me deep into her throat, and I can't take how only one of us is getting pleasure from this. It's not in my nature to be a taker. I can't not make her feel good, too.

Sliding my body down so I'm flat on my back, I tap her shoulder.

"Hmm..." she responds, never taking her mouth off me.

"Prestyn." It takes everything to get her name out of my throat, but I need this. Need her. "Prestyn, give me your pussy."

"We don't have a condom."

"I know. Swivel, baby." I tap her shoulder several times. "Bring your pussy here. Sit on my face."

Prestyn pauses, her eyes blinking in surprise before she moves. She tries to keep sucking me deep, but can't as she turns her body and straddles my face.

Fuck. Me. That is a beautiful sight. Her pink pussy is glistening just above me and my tongue practically moves on its own, swiping her from front to back, enjoying her flavor. She squeaks at the sensation but nothing can stop me from devouring her.

Pomegranate.

She takes my cock deep again, the angle hitting differently now that she's on top like this, and my hips begin gyrating of their own accord.

I grab onto her hips, holding her in place, not caring if I ever breathe again, perfectly content to stay here until I die. This would be a great way to go.

The faster I move, the harder she sucks. The slower I move, the slower her mouth strokes. We get into a coordinating rhythm and I feel the familiar tingle of my spine. Knowing I'm close, I latch my lips onto her clit and suck. Hard.

Her legs twitch and her body tenses, juices coating my face as she comes, never taking her suction off me. So I let my body go, the orgasm racing up my spine and slamming into me so hard, I couldn't stop sucking on her clit if I wanted to.

As I come back to my body, my mouth falls limp and her legs go slack. Prestyn rests her cheek on my thigh, breathing heavily.

"Holy shit." She's barely able to get the words out, completely spent. "That was intense."

"Yep." My eyes are closed as I live in this moment, feeling the soft skin of her ass under my fingers, smelling her just underneath my nose.

"I'm kind of glad we didn't have a condom."

A chuckle rolls out of me. She's not wrong. That was the best blow job of my life.

I tap her hip. "Come here."

Her head lifts and she looks back at me. The picture of her looking over her shoulder, her leg over my shoulder and just a glimpse of her very satisfied pussy between her ass cheeks has me wanting to flip her over and take her seven ways to Sunday.

"What?"

"I know this is just sex, but I'm still a man who likes to cuddle after an orgasm."

Her eyes brighten and a huge smile breaks out across her face. "Good," she says as she moves. I'm a little sad her pussy isn't in my face anymore. "I'm a woman who gets cold after an orgasm, so I need your heat."

She snuggles up against my side and I grab the end of the oversized comforter, tossing it over us. One of my legs is sticking out, but I don't mind. I'm overheated anyway.

We lay there for just a few minutes before I feel her breathing get heavy and I know she's fallen asleep. I wonder if I should wake her up to take her make up off, but before I can make up my mind, I'm out, too.

———

I roll over on the bed, but something doesn't feel right. My pillow, it's not the pillow I like to sleep with.

Because I'm not in my bed.

I'm at the Caine hotel, in a suite, sleeping after sixty-nining the most amazing woman I've ever met.

Raising my head to get my bearings straight, I listen for any sound, anything that would indicate I'm not alone.

There's nothing.

I wipe my hand down my face, clearing the sleep from my eyes and glance over at the night table. I don't have practice until this afternoon, so I'm not late for anything, thankfully. My phone is right where I left it, but there's a piece of paper underneath.

Grabbing it, I see it's a note from Prestyn, so I settle against the headboard and read.

Nick-

Thank you for an amazing night. Not just here, but at the gala as well.

I hope you are still game for our little arrangement. I think it's safe to say the itch will be back and I'd love for it to be you who does the scratching.

I was serious when I said this is just a fuck buddy situation, so please don't be concerned about my feelings. If you never want to see me again, that's okay, too.

But if you do, I've added my number in your contacts, and I installed the hotel security app to your phone so you can come and go in the suite as you please.

I slide my phone open and sure enough, the Caine Resorts and Conference Center logo is right on the home screen. Tapping it open, I can see the room number and how to disengage the front door lock. Fancy.

Text me before you want to meet again, though. Since this is a family suite, I'll just have to double check no one plans to be here when we want to meet up.

Also, put a password on your phone, for god's sake! It should not have been that easy to get in and mess around with your stuff!

No rush leaving today and feel free to rummage through the kitchen if you need. Can't guarantee there will be anything there, but you're welcome to whatever you find.

Thanks again for last night.

-P

I slide my hand behind my head and breathe deep, letting the memories of last night assault me.

Prestyn is fucking amazing. She's not like anyone I've ever met before. She's hard working, doesn't like the limelight, and if I'm guessing correctly from the way her boss treated her, completely underappreciated around here.

She's the kind of woman I could fall for.

But this is just sex and we're both determined to keep it that way. Which means remaining friends, or at least friendly. I can handle that.

Pushing up off the bed, I quickly use the facilities and get dressed in my wrinkled clothes. Suddenly, I'm feeling dehydrated so I head to the kitchen, hoping there may be a bottle of water I can snag on my way out.

Opening the fridge door, I find it almost completely empty except for one lone container.

It's a carton of pomegranate juice.

CHAPTER NINE
PRESTYN

I swing my conference chair from side-to-side as I gnaw on my pen—two things I never do.

Today, though, I'm having a hard time concentrating on our staff meeting. Aaron is droning on and on about shit he doesn't know anything about, tossing out words like "corporate synergy" and "core competency", trying to impress everyone. No one is falling for it.

Instead, we're all just biding our time until he's done.

Unfortunately, it gives me way too much time to think back on the weekend and the amazing oral I had with Nick.

Or Nicholas, as I think I like to call him. I haven't decided which one fits him better.

God, he is one fine specimen of a man. I knew he was hot, but once he was naked, he was practically scorching.

His abs are just straight rock that flex beautifully when he moves. His thick thighs that were so much more flexible than I knew until I was crouched between them. His muscular back that arched right as he was about to come. His huge...

"Prestyn!" Aaron nearly yells, pulling me out of my memories.

"Hmm?"

"Are you done daydreaming?"

I really want to tell him I was replaying the memories of my night with his favorite goalie, and *ha-ha, he likes me better than you*. That would probably shut him up. But I'm on a mission in this office, a mission to prove I'm just as capable as my brothers, and giving Aaron any information that he can twist on me is not a smart idea.

"Sorry. I was going over the final numbers from the gala in my head."

Aaron narrows his eyes, probably looking for any dishonesty in my answer, but not sharp enough to actually find it.

Finally giving up, he moves on. "You have those numbers already? It was less than forty-eight hours ago."

I lean forward, pulling open my folder. "Yes. Delaney Edwards, is one of the committee members for the gala and emailed them over to me this morning at my request."

That's not a lie. I'm always curious how our charity work goes, so I asked. It's the only reason I have the information since it's not our department. I just texted Delaney to see how we did. I expected a roundabout number with a heart emoji or something from her, but I'm learning Delaney is very meticulous. She sent me her complete spreadsheet instead. A spreadsheet I'm pretty jazzed about having at this moment.

I pull it out and fly by the seat of my pants as I roll out the numbers. "Of course a significant amount went to all the event fees, but my father requested we give a twenty percent discount off the top, so that helped with the proceeds."

"Why would he do that?" Aaron questions. I'm not surprised. He doesn't have a philanthropic bone in his body. Plus he's never had to oversee an event before since *it's not our department,* so he has no idea how charity events like this one are done.

Once again, I wonder how the hell my father came to the conclusion that Aaron could do this job. Although I'm starting to suspect the reason he was placed under Gavin instead of at Hoyt's location was to ensure things didn't totally fall apart. Or maybe that's just my assumption that the higher ups see the same ineptness I do.

"He usually donates a bit for major fundraisers," I explain, more for the other people in the room who may not already know this information than for the one who should. "It's a nice tax write off for the hotel, and means more money actually gets into the charities' hands."

From the way Aaron sneers, I know he hates that I have this information and he doesn't. It's like he's trying to forget I've been attending these events since I was a teenager and he's been to one. The one on Saturday where he moved tables into storage.

I ignore him and continue doling out information, knowing my colleagues will at least be excited for the results.

"When all was said and done, and thanks to a sizeable donation from Frank Zapata... you guys know him. He owns the chain of new grocery stores that have been popping up in Central Florida."

A few people nod around the table.

"We raised a grand total of two-hundred-nighty-eight thousand and one dollar."

Aaron puffs out a haughty laugh. "One of those uber rich people couldn't cough up another two grand to bring it to an even three-hundred grand?"

I ignore the fact that *I am* one of those uber rich people he's trying to insult and set him straight. "It's because of the silent auction. Since people are trying to outbid each other, the numbers end up a little strange. And it looks like Maksim Ivanov outbid his teammate by..." I make a show of shuffling through my papers, even though I was sitting at the same table when the drama happened, but I can't miss the chance to throw out yet another Glaze player's name. "... one dollar."

There are chuckles of amusement around the table, and I sit

back, pleased with my ability to look capable and one-up Aaron at the same time. But does he let it go? No, no he doesn't.

"I'd like a copy of that spreadsheet before the end of the day."

"Sure." He sits back, looking satisfied, but I'm not done. "I'll double check with Delaney that this version isn't confidential and can be distributed."

Aaron opens his mouth, but Gavin interrupts. That goes to show where my focus has been all morning. I didn't even see my brother come in.

"The event turned out very nice. Unfortunately, I had to leave early, but from what I heard, the guests were all very happy to be there and any issues we ran into were minimal, not noticeable by the attendees. That just goes to show the quality we provide here at our resort. So I want to thank all of you for your hard work."

There's a low murmur of thanks around the room for Gavin's appreciation. He's really a hands-on boss, especially considering he could be hiding in his office most of the time and it be justified. But that's not Gavin. He prefers knowing his employees and getting a feel for any problems that arise, just like I do.

"And I want to give an extra special thanks to Aaron for keeping both departments running at the same time." Annoyance rises within me. Once again, I'm doing all the work with Aaron taking all the credit. My heart sinks as Gavin continues. "I know there's been a lot of work happening lately for some of you, but we've had some interviews for the Catering Director position and I'm confident we're only a few days away from securing our final candidates."

This is the first I've heard that the candidate search is finally almost over. I'm a little pissed to be finding out this way. I know there's no official reason for Gavin to keep me in the loop, but I'm still a Caine, dammit.

"Well I appreciate you recognizing all my hard work," Aaron says without missing a beat.

I glance up to see Bayleigh making a gagging face. I twist my lips, trying to keep the smirk I'm fighting off in check.

"If there's nothing else, let's get back to work."

The room comes alive with people shuffling papers and making small talk as Aaron shouts out things like, "Make sure to have those reports on my desk by noon, Anderson."

Bayleigh immediately approaches me, threading her arm through mine as I down the last of my watermelon wave Alani Nu and toss it into the trash can, and dragging me out the door.

"I thought we'd never get out of there." She blows out a breath, like she's winded from the effort it took to keep her emotions in check.

"If Gavin hadn't cut in, I'm not sure we ever would have."

"Speaking of Gavin..."

Here it comes. Bayleigh is the one person who seems to have noticed how much my brother overlooks. At least, she's the only one who's said anything about it to me.

"Why haven't you told him the truth about Aaron yet?"

I play dumb. "What truth?"

She huffs in irritation. "That he spends all day on TikTok while making you run all the reports for two departments, and coordinate all the work assignments, all while keeping up with your actual responsibilities?"

"Oh that."

"Yes, that."

"You know why."

"Because you're trying to prove your worth, blah, blah, blah. Prestyn, Aaron is a schmuck. He's slimy and gross and is getting paid to play Candy Crush."

I glance up at her in question. "Is that game still around?"

"I saw it on Aaron's computer once, which is more proof he doesn't keep up with the world around him. So why do you let him get away with it?"

I don't know how to answer that. Maybe it has to do with the fact that I've always been the one playing catch up with the boys. My brothers both got into Ivy League schools with scholarships while I barely qualified to get into Tampa State. Immediately after graduating with their MBAs,they both had business connections out the ying-yang while I focused on getting things done with hard work and building relationships with our clients. They're both so much older than me and I've always been the little sister, scrambling to be taken seriously. When you add in the fact that I don't have a penis, well, it's just not a battle I can fight loudly. I need to be more methodical than that. Less emotional than say... Aaron.

"I'm playing the long game."

Bayleigh scoffs. "Exactly how long of a game? Because it feels like Monopoly night and its been time for some of us to go a long time ago."

"Ha ha. I promise I'm working on it. But I don't want to talk about this anymore. Let's talk about whether or not you're one of the candidates for the Catering Director position."

Bayleigh's eyes widen and she shifts gears quickly, avoiding my new topic. "You're right. We shouldn't talk too much shop. It's depressing."

I snort a laugh. "You didn't think so when we were talking about me."

"And we're still talking about you." Bayleigh begins bouncing with excitement. "Tell me about that hottie from Saturday night."

I roll my eyes but don't even bother biting back a smile. "You already know about him."

"Nuh-uh," she argues. "Don't even pretend like your date didn't go on longer than the gala. I saw you slipping out the door with him, his huge hand resting on the small of your back as he guided you out of the room." Her tone takes on a swoony quality.

"You know you sound like a romance writer when you say stuff like that, right?"

"Someday, when you read that exact line in book, you'll know it was me who wrote it."

"Uh... won't I know by your name on the cover?"

"Who uses their real name anymore? There are too many crazies out there. I'm using a pen name. But stop trying to distract me from the real issue."

Dammit. I tried. It didn't work.

"Tell me you took that giant of a man home with you Saturday night."

I turn my head away from her, avoiding Bayleigh's knowing gaze.

"Ohmygod, Prestyn Caine! You slept with him, didn't you?"

I shush her squeal, hoping no one heard her alude to sex in the same sentence where she said my name.

"Keep it down. You know how it is around here."

"Sorry, sorry," Bayleigh whisper-yells. "I'm just excited."

"I haven't even said anything!"

"You don't have to. I can see it in your body language. You did, right? You've been walking like you rode a horse all day. Please tell me you did. Ride him, I mean. I need to live vicariously through you!"

Her words have all the dirty details drying up on my tongue. I love having a work friend like Bayleigh. Someone I can have lunch with every day and share gossip with, and that sometimes I see after hours for drinks. But I know better than to tell anyone my secrets. Like it or not, as normal as I feel when I'm on the job, I'm not normal. I never will be. I'm a Caine and information like this would make the front page of national gossip news channels.

My lack of response must tip Bayleigh off that something's wrong because she suddenly cocks her head to the side and assesses me.

"Come here." She changes directions, dragging me down a side hall.

"What? Where?"

"Here."

Bayleigh pulls me into a random closet that is just large enough for both of us between wall-to-wall shelves of cleaning supplies.

"Um, why are you hiding us in a closet?"

"Because I need to say something and it needs to be done in private."

"Ookkkaaaaaayyyyy... but you know security is going to make up some wild rumors if we stay here for long."

She ignores me and continues. "I like you, Prestyn."

Not what I was expecting for her to say, but I'm listening.

"You are my friend and I would never betray you."

My heart softens in appreciation because I know what she's doing. But I've heard this before from other "friends." And I've learned that everyone has a price.

"In a more logical sense, since I can see my integrity has no bearing on you..."

I shake my head, half amused she went there and half concerned she knows me so well.

"...I like my job. I have twenty-five vacation days a year, all major holidays off, the best medical benefits money can buy and a higher salary than I expected when I took this job. Plus, I get a deep discount on rooms at any of the Caine hotels anywhere in the world. Do you know why I'm telling you this?"

I shake my head. "Is there an employee survey or something being passed around?"

"One that says to give you our answers directly? That would be weird." I huff a small laugh. I can see Aaron doing that just to spite me. Bayleigh continues, "I'm telling you this because I have always known we'd have this conversation someday and I want you to know where I stand. Now let me ask you... do you know how much the gossip rags would pay to know you and Nick Williams, Florida Glaze goalie and Tampa's Bachelor of the Year, did the nasty?"

I feel my face pale "I... I never said that happened."

"You didn't have to. I saw you daydreaming while Aaron droned on. It was written all over your face."

I gulp, wondering if I'm about to be blackmailed, or if Nick and I are about to be all over the internet.

"Anyway, top dollar for a story like this is worth one year of my salary. One year, Prestyn." She leans in closer. "That's it. None of the other perks come with it. And if I were to sell the story, once I run out of that money, I'd be out of a career too, because I'll have been blackballed from ever working in a hotel like this again. So give me one good reason, not in a moral sense which I know isn't something you believe easily, but one good logical reason why I would bother spilling the beans on this?"

"To humiliate me?" It's happened before.

"My best work friend and the only person I can make gagging faces to behind our boss's back? That would be really dumb of me."

Bayleigh puts her hands on my shoulders. "Listen, you don't have to tell me anything about what happened that night. But just know for the future, I have no interest in tanking the first career I actually like for fifteen minutes of fame. And not even that! I'd have to be an anonymous source, so there's no point at all, even if I wanted to."

My lips quirk to the side. She's got some very good, kind of humorous points.

"And I don't. You're my friend."

I gulp down a knot of emotion in my throat and nod.

"Just know," she says quietly. "I'm here for you. *You*. My friend Pres. Not 'Prestyn Caine'." She uses air quotes on my name to emphasize the persona I always have to be in public. "I just hope he was good in the sack because holy shit that man was hot, and you deserve a few good orgasms to relax sometimes."

Her rapid shift in subjects makes me laugh.

I grab my only real friend, and the first person I've trusted even a little bit in a long time, and hug her. "Thanks Bayleigh. I appreciate you more than you know."

Pulling away, I give her an ornery look. "And for the record, he's so much hotter naked."

With that, I walk out the door, laughing, while Bayleigh yells, "I knew it!" behind me.

CHAPTER TEN

NICK

I'm a sweaty, stinky mess and I just want to get home so I can stand in my shower for a solid hour or so, letting the water work out the kinks in my muscles.

Beginning the tedious process of unpadding myself, I ignore the sounds of Patrick's dramatic conversation with his divorce attorney. I have no idea why he doesn't wait until he's alone to discuss private matters, but it's starting to affect more than just our locker room chatter. It's affecting his ability to lead this team. Any time a captain is more interested in getting to the locker room to check his phone than to discuss key issues that came up in practice, it doesn't bode well for the organization as a whole. We need him to lead us, not make us carry his moody ass through all our games.

"What does she mean it wasn't what she signed up for?" Patrick yells. "Her dad owns the organization. She should have known more than any other hockey wife."

Yep. That's my cue to hightail it out here. I have no interest in listening to this shit again. There's a reason I stopped rooming with Patrick and started bunking up with Tucker when we're on the road. I got tired of hearing him argue with his wife all night, and now I'm tired of hearing him argue with his attorney.

I chuckle under my breath. I should take my own advice since I'm clearly in my own mood.

I toss all my body gear to the side, barely missing Maksim's legs. He stops in front of me on his way to the shower, completely naked like always. The man is a true exhibitionist and doesn't care if it makes any of us uncomfortable. I just make it a point to keep my eyes off his ding-a-ling.

"What's up, Ivanov?" I lean over and begin undoing all the laces on my leg pads. I have more equipment attached to me than anyone else in here and it takes me way longer to get out of it. Not that I'm complaining. When a puck is flying at your face at a hundred plus miles an hour, you want all the protection you can get. But it's the reason I'm stuck listening to Patrick's life implode and avoiding Maks' dick swinging into my face.

"We're going out. You coming?"

"Depends on what you mean by going out." With Maks, it could mean a simple dinner. Or it could mean an impromptu road trip to some random strip club where there is an illegal high stakes poker game happening in the basement. There's not a lot of in between with him.

"Dinner and a club. I need to get laid."

I grimace. Thankfully I'm looking at my pads so he doesn't see my reaction. That would only mean more peer pressure.

"Nah." The last sweaty pad slides off my leg and I toss it to the side. "My body doesn't like the shift from afternoon practice to morning skate before a game, so I'm going to get some rest tonight."

"You can rest when you're dead."

I chuckle under my breath. No one can ever say Maks isn't persistent.

"I'll get there sooner if I don't treat my body like the temple it is. You should take a page out of my book."

He grunts, clearly unhappy with my answer. But he struts his naked ass away from me and into the shower. I guess I'm off the hook.

Tucker drops down next to me, towel around his waist and smelling like soap. Ever since his family moved in with him, he's been one of the first clean up so he can get home to them.

"You're the third person to tell Maks no."

I finish stripping off my sweaty clothes and pull on some loose work out shorts and my favorite grey hoodie.

"I was wondering why he gave up so easily on me."

"It's because we're right." Tucker slides on some deodorant followed by a fresh shirt. "Morning practice is going to suck if we stay out until it's time to be here."

I shove my feet in my crocs, which aren't fashionable but I appreciate the function. "He's done it before. I'm sure he'll be fine."

"That's because he can go home as soon as practice is over and catch up on sleep before the game. Some of us don't have that option anymore."

I do, but I know Tucker's not talking about me. After finding out he has a three year old daughter, he's been determined to never miss another moment in her life. So he moved Lacy and their daughter into a giant home in a gated community. It came complete with a pool house for Lacy's best friend and her son, so Tucker's bachelor ways are officially over. There are too many kids and activities happening in that place to expect to get any rest during the day. No wonder he needed that Tahoe trip so badly.

As a side benefit for me, Tucker's conversations with the kids on road trips are a hell of a lot easier to tolerate than Patrick and his wife yelling at each other.

We hear a bang from the other side of the room and from the way Patrick is sitting on the bench, his fingers twisted in his hair while he rests his elbows on his knees, I'm guessing the noise was his cell phone being thrown into his locker.

I shoot Tucker a look. He just shakes his head. We're all waiting for this divorce to hurry up and be final. The sooner those two stop all communication, through their lawyers or directly, the better.

"On that note, I'm out." I shove my keys and phone in my pocket and clap Tucker on the shoulder.

"Later dude."

I nod at several other guys on my way to the parking lot, but mostly I'm thinking about that shower I'm going to take and the sushi I have waiting for me.

I know it seems strange that I shower at home, but there's only so much peopling I can take. I'm in introvert by nature so after a while I need to be alone to recharge. And Patrick's intensity combined with Maks' nudity after a long practice is one of those times.

Sliding the screen of my phone open, I stop walking for a split second as I take in what I'm seeing. I have four missed calls from my sister.

Four.

Hightailing it to my truck, I quickly crank the engine and wait for my Bluetooth to connect. As soon as it does, I'm pressing the call button. It only takes seconds for her to answer.

"Hey, Brother."

"What's wrong?"

I always know when something's going on with my sister, even if I can't put a finger on what it is. I've been getting that vibe since the night of the gala. Just hearing the tone of her voice now, I already know this is about her dickhead husband Gary.

She sniffles and sighs deeply. "I thought you'd want to know I filed for divorce the other day."

Internally, I cheer. Delaney has always been way out of Gary's league. He's not attractive in the traditional sense, and he comes across as disingenuous to everyone except my sister. It's like he's constantly working an angle. I've never known what she saw in him, but I played nice only because she loves him. Or did love him. I'm not sure yet.

Regardless of how elated I am, she's in pain. That's what I need to focus on.

"What happened this time?"

Her voice immediately gets some fire to it. Good. I prefer hearing her angry than sad. "I wish you wouldn't say it like that. 'What happened this time?'" she mocks. "It's not like we've had more problems than any other married couple. It happens to everyone."

"Except in your case, he's always the one to screw up and it's like a cyclical pattern."

"It is not."

"I'm not going to argue about it, Delaney. You know I can feel it when things are going on so you can't pull that shit on me. I know even when you don't tell me. I've held my tongue long enough, but if you're getting divorced, I'm finally going to tell the truth."

"I don't need you to tell the truth right now, Nick. I need you to tell me you love me and listen right now." I can hear the tears in her voice again and it makes me want to punch my future *ex* brother-in-law in the face. "Don't try to fix this. Just listen."

I take a deep breath, relying on my new yoga techniques to steady myself before she tells me the latest drama. This guy has run up credit cards, bought a car without talking to her about their budget first, given her presents that are obviously for him to use. He's a piece of work. I can only imagine what was finally the tipping point.

"Okay. I'm listening."

"He's been cheating on me."

Just like that, my yoga lessons fly out the window. "That mother—"

"You said you'd listen," she interrupts.

I have to physically bite my tongue while I wait for my rage to subside so I don't keep going. It takes a few seconds to feel calmer, or at least less impulsive. "Fine," I say through gritted teeth. "I'm listening."

She sniffles again and I envision her wiping under her eyes, like she always does when she's upset.

"A few weeks ago—"

"A few weeks ago?" I interrupt. "And you're just filing a few days ago?"

"It takes time to wrap your brain around ending your marriage, Nick. Are you going to listen or do I need to hang up now?"

I get hit with a pang of guilt. She's right. This isn't about me. "Sorry. Sorry. I'm done."

"A few weeks ago, I was using his work laptop to find a website I had been on, I don't even know what it was. Anyway, I went to the history because I couldn't remember the name of the store I was looking up and it was right there. This... this dating website."

"Son of a bitch," I mumble under my breath. My sister is a gem. Absolute gold. There is no one kinder or smarter or more interesting than her. She's the kind of woman men fight to be with. She doesn't deserve any of this.

"Of course that had me curious so I clicked on it and he hadn't even logged out. It took me straight to the last messages he sent."

"Did you read them?"

"Of course I did."

I blow out a breath, trying really hard to keep my truck going toward my house and not veer off to Gary's work so I can confront him. "Lane, why did you do that to yourself?"

"I don't know," she cries. "Morbid curiosity, maybe? Or maybe I was hoping to find evidence that he was reaching out to people to do research for his job or something."

"He's an engineer."

"I didn't say I was being rational, Nick. I wasn't exactly thinking straight."

"I know, I know. You're right. I'm just really mad right now and wishing I could protect you from all this."

She sniffles again but stays remarkably calm under the circumstances. "I wish you could, too. But you can't. Right now the best you can do is just be there for me."

"And give you a place to stay."

"Oh hell no." Delaney lets out a maniacal laugh and I know her vicious side is about to come out. "He's the one who screwed up. He can go."

I let out an evil chuckle of my own. "We can toss his shit in his car, douse the whole thing with gasoline, and I'll hand you the match to toss on it. You say the word, and I'll stop to get matches on my way over."

"You're a good brother, but no. I was *this close* to doing that a few weeks ago, but then I remembered I don't feel like fighting an arson charge. I need to stay on the up and up so I can rip his ass to shreds in court if it comes to it."

"I disagree. We'd get you off with a misdemeanor due to mental distress and drag your divorce out long enough to bankrupt him. Drag it out and make him suffer."

"I'm going to lock onto that fantasy and pull it up whenever I need a little ego boost."

"It's not a fantasy if we can make it into a reality."

She lets out a light laugh, which makes me feel like she's going to be okay. It's going to take a while to heal, but she'll be alright eventually. "While I appreciate it, I'm not using your money for something like that. The best thing I can do is cut my losses. He's going to be shocked enough when he realizes I'm serious. It's over."

I hate to admit it, but she's right. She should have divorced him years ago, but he's always convinced her to stay, that he's learned his lesson and will do anything to keep their marriage together. He's usually on his best behavior for about six months before his demeanor starts to revert back to the assholish façade he normally sports. It's going to be interesting seeing how he reacts to her holding the line this time.

"The good news is, we get Prestyn out of the deal, right? Isn't she great? Have you talked to her lately?"

I furrow my brows in confusion. "What does Prestyn have to do with this?"

"That's where I met her," my sister says nonchalantly. "She's the girl Gary was messaging with on the dating sight."

My fingers tighten around my steering wheel. If I didn't have so much control, I'd probably have run off the road already.

"Hold on. Prestyn is who Gary was cheating with?"

Delaney scoffs. "No. Prestyn is who Gary completely snowed. She had no idea he was married and was appalled when I called her."

The words she saying don't make any sense. My sister found out her husband was cheating, and called the other woman? And then she set me up with her to be a public date?

"What the fuck, Delaney. You set me up with a home-wrecker?"

After everything we went through as kids. After the rug being ripped right out from under us, why would my sister do this to me?

That night of the gala comes crashing into me. The amazing conversation and laughter we shared. The connection with another person who likes to stay out of the public eye. The fucking amazing oral sex that left me wanting more.

Pomegranates.

I'm so pissed. Not just at my sister, but at myself for falling for the charms of a woman who clearly isn't what I thought she was. And for her ruining the memory of my favorite poem.

"Why the fuck would you do that to me?" I practically roar.

"Do what?" Delaney's voice drips with anger right back at me.

"Prestyn is amazing. She's gorgeous and smart and kind. She's the kind of woman I would have picked for you if I'd found her first. Well, I guess I did kind of pick her. I'm kind of glad Gary found her for us."

"Delaney. Stop."

She finally stops her rant long enough to let me process what she's saying.

"I need to get this straight in my brain. Gary was cheating on you."

"Yes."

"With the woman you set me up with."

The woman I had a one-night stand with. The woman I was hoping to see again. The woman I was duped by.

"That's not how it happened," Delaney seethes.

"I can't care how it happened," I pop off. "I care about the fact that you set me up with some... some whore Gary found on the internet and didn't even think for a second that it was a shitty thing to do to me. What if the press catches wind if this?"

"Catches wind of what? That your sister set you up on a blind date with Prestyn Caine? She's a fucking hotel princess, *Nicholas*, which I didn't even know until the gala. She has more to lose than you do, so get over yourself and your huge athlete ego, would you?"

I tighten my fingers on the steering wheel and clench my jaw. My sister and I don't fight often, but when we do, it can get nasty. I'm trying hard to remember that Delaney is grieving her marriage right now and I need to give her some grace for her stupid fucking decisions.

"You're going to be friends with her, aren't you?" I finally ask.

"I am," she says with no room for argument. "I think she's delightful. And I think you should see her again, too."

My head shakes rapidly even though I can't see her. "No way, Lane. I have boundaries. Unlike you and mom."

"You shithead," she yells but I ignore her. "You can think she's a great person and all, but don't suck me into this bullshit. I'm not crossing that line."

I don't tell her I already crossed that line with Prestyn a few too many times. I keep that information to myself. Not just because it's private, but because I feel stupid. Like I was scammed. If I'd had this information to begin with I would have made very different choices.

"And don't you dare start inviting her to birthday parties and shit to try and push us together." I tack that on for good measure.

"Scout's honor," Delaney says sarcastically.

"You've never. Been. A scout," I say through clenched teeth.

"It doesn't matter. I was crossing my other fingers behind my back anyway."

I open my mouth to continue to argue with my sister but she cuts me off. "I gotta go. Gary is home and he was served today so we need to hash this out."

Coming back to the real issue at hand, my anger begins to ebb. "Call me when you're done, will you?"

"Maybe. Depends on how this goes. I don't want to argue with you, too. It's already going to be a long night."

Now I feel bad. I shouldn't have jumped all over her when she should be saving her emotional energy for the conversation she's about to have. "I'm sorry, Delaney. I shouldn't have yelled. It just triggered some stuff in me. You're not the one at fault here. Just do me a favor and dig deep for that Williams anger so Gary doesn't trick you into forgiving him again, please?"

She chuckles softly and I don't miss the fact that there's almost no humor in it. "Trust me. I'm not mom. The minute he opens his mouth to defend his actions, is the minute any remaining tears will dry up."

I have no doubt. My sister may be one of the kindest people I know, and she may give too many chances, but when she is done, she is *done*. I've seen the aftermath of it before and it's not pretty. I can't wait for Gary to feel it.

"Love you, Lane."

"Love you, too. And thanks for warming me up to throw down."

Just like that, the call disconnects.

I still need to shower when I get home, but suddenly my sushi and the new poetry book I was looking forward to reading no longer have much appeal. I may need to see what Pay-per-view fight was on the other night and order it. Seems like a good dose of screaming at my TV while watching two men beat the shit out of each other is a better option considering my mood.

CHAPTER ELEVEN
PRESTYN

Hosting conventions isn't rare at this hotel. There are always fandoms meeting their favorite creators, influencers taking selfies with followers, authors signing books for readers. Almost weekly there are squeals from the ballrooms as some kind of fan gets excited to meet their favorite something-or-other.

What we don't usually have, though, is back-to-back events with the same people.

I guess technically it's not back-to-back. But less than two weeks ago I was sitting at a table with several members of the Florida Glaze hockey team, laughing over a trip to Tahoe that everyone seemed to be fighting over.

Today, I'm looking over the roster for the annual local athlete meet-and-greet seeing which of the hockey favorites are going to be signing memorabilia for fans.

Everyone I would expect is on the list: Tucker Hayes, Patrick Smith, Maksim Ivanov.

The one name I don't see on the list is the one I was hoping for: Nick Williams.

I haven't heard from him since our night together and I'm a little disappointed. I thought we'd hit it off pretty well.

Nick was funny and charming. Our conversations never faltered. I like that he's a bit low key and has no desire to be in the limelight any more than he has too. Plus, his affinity for poetry was surprisingly sexy.

And speaking of sexy, I thought our night together was really hot. I'd been hoping to have another go at it, this time with a little planning ahead and a condom.

Instead, I haven't heard from him at all.

Oh well. I could spend time dwelling on it, but I knew what I was getting into. I said one night with no strings and that's what I got. Well, that and a very intense orgasm while riding his face. Even if I never see him again, I still have a great night to remember.

Setting my thoughts aside, I race through the ballroom that's been outfitted for today's event. The panels that usually separate two rooms were opened to make one huge space. There are several booths set up with tables and banners, where guests will find their favorite local athletes. It's not just the hockey team here today. We have a professional baseball team, football team, and basketball team participating as well. The event is massive, hence the massive room.

Satisfied that everything is prepped to our liking, I head toward the door.

"Prestyn!"

I stop with my hands on the lever and grimace. I was so close to avoiding Aaron until we began and it was too late for him to stop me.

Putting my game face on, I swivel around. "What's up, Aaron?"

"What's up? We're thirty minutes away from the doors opening and no one has checked the green room yet."

Green room? "You mean Ballroom Eight?"

He sighs like I'm the problem and not the fact that he's

renaming the conference rooms. "Celebrities don't like being tossed in a spare ballroom. They prefer green rooms."

"But we don't have one of those."

"Today we do. Ballroom Eight is currently labeled the green room. There is a sign and everything. Honestly Prestyn, you should know these things. When was the last time you checked your email?"

Roughly five minutes ago, and I can say for certain there was no email explaining how a green piece of paper covering the room plaque will trick anyone.

Aaron doesn't wait for my answer, just continues wasting my time. "Anyway, I need you to check the *green room* and make sure catering has everything they need. I'm hearing complaints that there isn't enough silverware. We're not paying full price for shoddy service."

I bite my tongue from reminding Aaron that we *are* the service so we provide utensils. Details aren't Aaron's strong suit.

I'm not sure what his strong suit is anymore, but details are definitely not it.

"I'm headed that way, anyway, so I'll make sure it's all done."

"Good," Aaron says, but I'm already pushing my way out the door. "Let... uh...Isaac..."

"Ian."

"...Ian know I expect better from now on."

I don't respond, anxious to get away from my so-called-boss. Today is going to be non-stop. The further away I can get from being Aaron's keeper, the better.

I'm racing down the hall when quick footsteps catch up to me.

"Here." Bayleigh hands me one of our walkie talkies and some ear buds so I can plug into the running conversation with the staff that's charged with hanging close to our local celebrities. "Have you been to the green room yet?"

"I'm heading that way. What the hell is it with Aaron changing the name on us?"

"I didn't stop to ask," Bayleigh admits and she pushes one ear bud into her ear. "I was too busy checking out the hot men."

I chuckle and clip the walkie-talkie to my waistband. "Of course you were. Are all the handlers prepped and ready to go?"

"Yep. And I hope it's okay with you, but I told Justine to stay close to Maksim Ivanov."

"You read my mind."

"No. I just paid attention at the gala. That man is a loose cannon. Too bad he's so hot. His looks are wasted on someone even I wouldn't touch with a ten-foot pole. And I haven't been laid in months."

"Well I have—"

"Show off," she grumbles.

"—so if you need me to take over with him, let me know. I doubt he could charm me if he tried."

"Oh he won't."

The singsong quality in her tone has me side-eyeing her.

"What does that mean?"

She presses her lips together and bits back a smirk. "Have you checked the roster?"

"Just a few minutes ago. Why?"

"Was it the most recently updated roster?"

I feel like I'm missing something. Pulling out my phone I notice an email that came in just a few minutes ago. Opening it, I scroll through it quickly.

Please note the following changes to today's meet-and-greet.

Patrick Smith from the Florida Glaze will no longer be in attendance.

Nicholas Williams from the Florida Glaze will be taking his place.

I don't realize my eyebrows have raised until Bayleigh bumps me and lets out a quiet squeal.

"Told you Maksim was going to leave you alone. I bet that hot goalie already warned him to stay away from you."

"I highly doubt that. I haven't heard from Nick since..." I glance around, remembering we're in public with a lot of ears in line, waiting for the doors to open. "Anyway, we hardly know each other."

"So what?" Bayleigh continues. "The gala was only like ten days ago. And the Glaze went on a six-day road trip last week. He's been busy."

I *hmm* noncommittally as we round the corner to Ballroom Eight. The line to get into the event is down the hall and wrapped around the corner. The excitement is radiating off the ticket holders in waves. Whenever the door to the ballroom opens, voices start piping up.

"That's the green room! Is that where everyone is?"

"I wonder what they're serving for lunch in there."

"Did I see Maksim Ivanov doing a handstand on the table through the crack in the door?"

That last comment makes me glance up at Bayleigh who is looking back at me like she's reading my mind.

"Smart idea... making sure every single fan knows exactly where the celebrities are hiding, huh?"

Yep. That's exactly what I was thinking.

We make our way through the door, greeting our security guard on the way in, and Bayleigh heads straight to Maksim who is not doing a handstand, thank God. Satisfied she's keeping him reined in, I go check on the food.

"Hey Ian," I greet. "Did you get the silverware that was needed?"

He scoffs as he stirs a large aluminum platter of corn. "Let me guess, Aaron is making a big deal about something that's not?"

My inner bitch wants to laugh and tell him he's bang on, but my professionalism takes over instead. Ian doesn't seem to notice, or care, too used to Aaron's antics.

"Before the words were even out of my mouth, someone restocked it. Everything is going well," Ian says with a smile. "I've gotten a lot of compliments on the food."

"Can't go wrong with a little bit of everything, right?"

"You mean a *lot* of everything. These guys keep my teams winning! The least I can do is make sure they get enough calories today."

"You're a good man, Ian."

"Thanks, Prestyn. You aren't too bad yourself."

He gets busy serving more food and I turn on my walkie-talkie.

"Okay guys, it's almost go-time. Everyone have their assignments?"

Several voices respond, confirming everything is in place and we're all ready to go. Being a celebrity "handler" isn't a hard job. It's mostly making sure our guests are where they're supposed to be when they're supposed to be there, and get to take bathroom and water breaks. Mostly.

"Justine, you good with Maksim?"

If I'm not mistaken, I hear some chuckles from around the room.

"Yeah, I'm—" Her voice cuts out temporarily. "Dammit, he already took off on me."

"I've got eyes on him heading toward the back, hot on catering's heel," someone interjects

I swivel my head and sure enough, our problem child is trying to sweet talk one of our servers. Justine is right behind him though. I almost laugh when she stops him and he tries giving her puppy dog eyes. Even if she did bat for his team, I doubt they'd work on her. Justine grew up with brothers like I did. No amount of flirting works on her if she doesn't want it to.

Satisfied that everything is ready to roll, I glance around the room and my eyes finally land on the one person I was hoping to see today.

Nick.

He looks as sexy as ever in a navy blue t-shirt and jeans. It's not a formal three-piece suit like last time, but the cut of his shirt does nothing to hide the flex of his biceps every time he turns the page of his book.

I bet he's reading poetry. Maybe something he could recite to me the next time we're naked together. Or maybe I'm getting ahead of myself.

Still, it doesn't hurt to go say hello, right?

My feet move quickly until I'm standing right in front of him.

"Well, hey there stranger."

Nick looks up at me, slightly startled at the interruption. He was probably so engrossed in the book, he didn't realize anyone had approached.

His face suddenly hardens. "Hello."

I pull the chair next to him out and sit. "I hear you went on a road trip last week. How'd it go?"

He narrows his eyes at me. "We won four of the games."

"Oh that's great."

He's silent, which isn't completely strange considering what I know about him, but I'm getting a strange vibe. Does he think I've been following him online or something? Turned into a puck bunny or whatever hockey groupies are called?

"I honestly didn't know you left. My friend, Bayleigh, just told me since she saw that you were here." My eyes widen. "Not that she was looking for you either. Just, she was working the night of the gala and knew you were my date."

For some reason, I can't seem to stop babbling. I know I should. I should just close my mouth and walk away, but my brain isn't following instructions very well.

"So that's why I know you were out of town. Not because I have alerts on my phone or anything." *Oh God.* "Because I don't! I just… I guess I was hoping to hear from you but it makes sense as to why I didn't."

Why? Why is this floor not opening up and swallowing me whole instead of leaving me here to make a fool out of myself?

"Are you done?" Nick finally asks. His tone is sharper than I think my rant is worth, but maybe he doesn't believe me and is afraid I'm now a super fan.

I admit I'm a super fan of his tongue, but not his hockey career.

"Sorry. Yeah. I'm done. I didn't realize you were going to be here until about three minutes ago so I'm feeling a little frazzled."

Nick quietly snaps his book closed and lays it on the table. "I was going to call you."

My heart rate speeds up. I was hoping he would say that. Not because I was hoping to see him, necessarily, but because I have more itches to scratch.

Oh who am I kidding. I would love to see him again, even without that itch.

"You were?"

"Was. But that was before I talked to my sister."

"Delaney? What about her?"

Nick leans back, looking cool and collected. And harsh. I wonder if this is his mean hockey face.

"Delaney filed for divorce from her husband. I hear you know him. Gary?"

My heart sinks and my blood runs cold. Now I understand the cool reception I'm getting from him.

"Delaney finally told you how we met."

He nods slowly. "She did. And then we had words about why she would set me up with the woman that destroyed her marriage."

I rear back like I've been slapped. "Destroyed her marriage? I didn't even know they were married until Delaney called me."

Nick blows an irritated puff of breath from between pursed lips. "Do you know how many times I've heard that before?"

"I don't know. How many times has Gary cheated on Delaney? Because from what I understand, this isn't the first time."

"What?"

The malice in his voice doesn't frighten me. I get it. Nick is angry his sister would be treated that way. But I didn't do it. And I'm tired of being held responsible for things that aren't my fault or responsibility.

"That's Delaney's story to tell, so feel free to ask her. Then you can ask her why she thought "the other woman" was worthy of going on a date with her twin brother. You know what she'll tell you?"

"Do I want to know?"

"She'll tell you I didn't know. Gary lied to me, tricked me, and then stood me up. I've never even met the guy. The only reason I even know I got snowed is because Delaney had the decency to call me and tell me it wasn't my fault. That an asshole had wormed his way into *my* life." My voice hitches with emotion. "She was decent and kind and I've carried the guilt around for weeks, even knowing I'm not the one who cheated on her and had I known he was married, I never, ever would have spoken with him on a dating website."

Nick's face softens minutely, but I ignore it, too pissed off to care.

"Do you know how humiliating it is to think a guy actually likes you, only to have him treat you like you are completely inconsequential? Like your feelings don't matter at all?" I stand up, ready to leave this conversation and Nick behind. "Of course you don't. But you sure do know what it's like to treat women like Gary does, don't you?"

He grimaces and I know I've hit my mark.

Leaning in, I make sure my voice is low enough that he's the only one who can hear me. "I know we agreed to no strings so no feelings would get involved. But that doesn't mean you can blatantly shit over my feelings for fun."

I press the button on my walkie-talkie. "Quick change of plans guys. Nick Williams is going to go with Group B. Bayleigh, add him to your list. Miguel Velasquez is going to be with me instead."

I hold Nick's gaze and shake my head in disgust before turning and walking away.

I am a dick.

A big fat hairy dick.

A disease riddled, flaccid, useless disgusting dick.

I am Maksim Ivanov's dick.

Taking a drink of my water as I lean against the wall away from prying eyes, I glance over at said teammate who signs a fan's boobs with a black Sharpie. As soon as he caps it, he leans down and bites her nipple gently through the fabric of her shirt. The fan squeals with delight. I grimace.

Maybe I'm not as bad as Maks' dick. But I'm still a terrible person.

All day, while I've tried to concentrate on the people in front of me, signing my name on pucks and sticks and headshots, smiling for pictures, I've been mulling over the conversation Prestyn and I had. How I was cold and judgmental toward her, and how she finally snapped back.

Comparing me to Gary was a low blow. But was she wrong?

I have a bad feeling there is more to this story than I'm privy to. It may be time to find out.

Grabbing my phone, I check the time. I've still got a few

minutes until I have to be back in my chair. It's just enough time to get the information I want.

I dial, but it only takes one ring for her to answer.

"Hey there, little brother. How's it going?"

"You're older than me by two minutes, Delaney. And I've got a hundred pounds on you. Maybe you can stop referring to me as the little one."

She laughs and I'm glad to hear her sounding better than she did the other day. I'm sure she's still sad about the demise of her marriage, but it's good to know she's not devastated or hiding under the covers and ignoring the outside world because of it.

"I will never stop reminding you that I'm older."

"Not even when we turn forty?"

I'm met with silence. That's what I thought.

"We'll see," she finally says. "I've got time to figure that out. What's going on, anyway? I thought you were at some meet-and-greet today."

"How did you know about that?"

"I have alerts on my phone so I can keep tabs on you. It's really convenient to have a famous brother sometimes. Makes it easier to keep up with your life when the paps do it for me."

"First of all, there are no *paps*. Second, you could just text and ask where I'm at."

"What's the fun in that? I like my way better. But I'm guessing that's not why you called, is it? This has something to do with the event you're at."

I don't know how she instinctively knows these things. Well yes, she's my twin. But her ability to know not just when something is going on with me, but specific details she shouldn't know, is almost freaky.

"I'll cut to the chase since I'm running out of time. Prestyn is here."

"I assumed. And why is that a problem?"

"She tried talking to me."

Delaney groans and I can practically hear her dropping her head back in dismay. "You shut her down didn't you?" she accuses accurately. "How bad was it?"

I cringe, not wanting to tell her Prestyn's parting shot, knowing Delaney would probably agree if she knew the whole truth.

"Let's just say, I may have burned a bridge."

"Why? Why would you light that match? Prestyn is nice, Nicky."

"Because I still don't know what happened between her and Gary, *Delaney*." I take a deep breath and pull my anger back in check. I didn't call to fight with my sister again. I'm trying to figure out what I'm missing. "Look, the only thing you told me is Gary was dating her which is how you met."

"Correct. Because you went all alpha male on me and started yelling about how I set you up with a home-wrecker."

"Fine. You're right. I admit that."

"I'm sorry, what? You cut out."

I should have video called so she could see my eyes narrowing at her. Hopefully she can hear the seething in my tone. "I said, I should have been more calm when you told me what happened."

"I accept your apology. Continue."

I sigh in frustration but get back on track. I'm running out of time. "Prestyn says she didn't even know Gary was married until you told her. That she'd never met him. I don't know what to believe."

"You believe her, you idiot, because she's telling you the truth."

That's what I was afraid of.

"They never actually got to the cheating part," my sister continues. "Gary stood her up for their first date, which was a totally shitty thing to do. Can you imagine the anticipation of a first date and the guy you've been talking to just doesn't bother to show? That can be really humiliating."

So can having the guy you had a one-night stand with turn around and basically call you a whore. *Oh man.* Maybe I am Maksim's dick.

"I read through all their messages, Nicky. Every single one. Prestyn had absolutely no idea he was married. None. When I called to let her know the truth, because some of us women really do try to stick together, she couldn't stop apologizing. She was devastated. She even offered to testify for me in my divorce hearing if need be." Delaney laughs lightly, and I'm starting to realize there's a lot about her marriage I didn't know. "Don't hold this against her. You met her. You spent the entire gala laughing with her and enjoying her company. She's genuine. I think you know that. I think you're projecting what happened with Dad on her and this is not the same. She is just as much a victim in this as I am."

A deep, massive feeling of regret over the way I've acted comes over me. I'm not that person. I don't get irrationally angry unless it's about someone I love. My sister is at the top of that list. That's the only excuse I have for my behavior.

"You said something stupid today, didn't you?" she asks. "That's why you're calling."

I laugh humorlessly. She knows me too well. "Yeah."

"Think you can make it right?"

I lean my head back against the wall. "I hope so."

"She'll forgive you. Just tell her the truth about all this. *All* of it. She'll understand when she gets the whole context."

"Yeah. Speaking of, have you talked to Dad lately?"

"Nope. He doesn't need to know about my divorce until its over and I have no more feelings about it. He's come a long way, but that doesn't mean I trust him yet."

I nod in agreement, even though she can't see me. It was traumatic enough when our own parents' marriage fell apart. There's no reason to bring that narcissistic ass into the middle of all this. He'll just make it worse.

"Nick?"

I glance over my shoulder to see Bayleigh standing off to the side.

"You've got about two minutes."

"Thanks," I say and turn back to my conversation. "Listen, I gotta go. Are you going to be okay?"

Delaney laughs, and not lightly. She truly sounds amused. "I'm better than okay. I'm sleeping better than I have in years alone in that big ole bed. Kicking Gary out is probably the best thing I've ever done in my life. I think the better question right now is, will *you* be okay?"

"Yeah. I just..." I blow out another breath. "I just need to figure out how to make this right."

"Well don't take too long. You'll never meet another woman like Prestyn Caine again in your life. Don't miss out on her because of some old wounds that stupid Gary broke open."

"I won't. Thanks, Lane."

"Love you, little brother."

"Will you quit with the little brother shit?"

"Never!"

She's still laughing as she hangs up.

Shoving my phone in my pocket, I turn back to Bayleigh.

"Everything good?" she asks. "You need water or juice or anything?"

"You wouldn't happen to know Prestyn's favorite kind of flower, would you?"

Bayleigh gets a knowing look on her face. "I don't. I'll try to find out. But between you and me, she's more of an energy drink kind of girl."

"Really?" That's surprising to me.

"Really. A bouquet of Alani Nu would go a long way in winning her heart."

"Huh. Good to know. Thanks."

"Any time. Except now," she adds. "We need to get you back to your table."

Rocking my head back and forth to shake out the tension in my neck, I take a second to pump myself back up.

Once I feel centered and have a fake smile plastered on my face, I take my place in the hot seat for a few more hours of torture disguised as PR.

———

After talking to my sister, I started sneaking glances at Prestyn when I could. What I've discovered is that she's kind to everyone. It isn't just other patrons at a gala or coworkers. Even the maintenance staff she seems to know by name, and they all have a smile for her.

But it wasn't just that. Anyone can fake kindness. Prestyn seems to have a calm about her that draws people in. She can chat easily with the fans, the excited kids who got stuck waiting in line with their parents who are fans, the people who get frustrated from waiting in line for too long. She always has a smile on her face and has a way about her that seems to de-escalate any situation.

It all makes me feel worse. It should. I deserve to feel remorseful. I just hope my regret comes across when I talk to her.

Finally, after what seems like hours, the doors are closed and the event is officially over.

Standing up from my table, I stretch my arms over my head and then out wide, trying to work out the kinks in my back. It's a good thing I have yoga tomorrow. I'm going to need the extra stretch.

Bayleigh approaches, mumbling something into the wire of her earbuds, before directing a smile toward me.

"How are you? You feel good about today?"

I don't want to laugh, but that's kind of a loaded question.

"Everyone seemed happy and it's finally over, so I guess that's a yes."

"Good," she says brightly. "I'm sure you are starving. Ian made some of his green chili enchiladas and all the sides to go with it so you can have dinner before you go."

I salivate thinking about it. "That sounds amazing."

"Oh trust me, it is." Bayleigh begins gathering left over pens and markers, quickly organizing them into different baggies. "There is nothing Ian can't make but this is probably my favorite meal. I'd eat it every day if I could. Can I take you through the back to Ballroom... er... the green room?"

I snicker at her near mistake. No one was fooled by that green piece of paper hanging outside the room we got to rest in. Having met their dickhead of a boss, I'm sure it was his idea in the first place, so I don't feel too bad laughing about it.

"Sure. Lead the way."

Bayleigh leads several of us through the back. Not that she needs to. I can smell the enchiladas from here. If they taste like they smell, this Ian guy may need to make more.

Sure enough, the line to get some food is already a dozen deep by the time we step into the room. I'm disappointed, but not surprised. It's been a long day for all of us. It doesn't matter how many little packages of trail mix we scarfed down. Food is a must.

I take my place in line but before I take my first step forward, my gaze finds Prestyn.

As she's been doing the whole day, she's smiling and making conversation with a staff member. There is not one ounce of discomfort on either of their faces. It's so obvious she makes it a point to know everyone who works here. That she takes pride in the people who run this operation.

Regret rushes over me again. As hungry as I am, I can't wait to apologize to her. My stomach is twisted in knots anyway over this whole situation.

Leaving the line, I beeline my way to her. The person who has been in charge of Maks all day looks up as I approach, her eyebrows shooting up.

I clear my throat. "Sorry to interrupt."

"It's okay," the other woman says. "I'll talk to you later, Prestyn."

Prestyn gives her a tight smile as the woman walks away, but refuses to make eye contact with me. "Did you need something?"

Her arms are crossed and a random spot on the floor appears a little too interesting. I'm really going to have to grovel.

Shoving my hands in my pockets, I try to calm the nerves I'm feeling. "I was hoping we could talk for a minute."

"Not really sure there's anything left to say. No hard feelings and all that."

"Except I was wrong and I need to apologize and make it up to you."

She finally looks up, gnawing on her bottom lip as she assesses me. "Fine."

Glancing around the room, she sniffs and looks back at me, arms still crossed. "But not here."

I breathe a sigh of relief. "Understood," I agree quickly. "I don't want an audience for what I need to say anyway."

Prestyn grabs the wire of her ear buds and clicks a button on the walkie talkie at her hip. "Hey Bayleigh." She pauses for a moment, presumably for a response. "I need to escort Nick Williams to a different part of the hotel for a meeting. Can you take over for me?" Another few seconds as Bayleigh replies, and then Prestyn's attention is back on me. "Follow me."

Without so much as a glance over her shoulder to make sure I'm following, Prestyn takes off toward the back wall and the door to the employee area. She's moving so quickly, I have to jog to catch up.

I don't mind though. With how much I have to say, I need to get my thoughts in order before we're alone anyway.

CHAPTER THIRTEEN

PRESTYN

Taking Nick back to the suite where we had our one super-hot night together may not have been the best idea. But I couldn't figure out where else to go so we could be alone to hash this out and I knew it was unoccupied, so here we are.

I almost told Nick he could shove his apology up his ass, but something in his demeanor made me change my mind. Maybe it was the way his cheeks pinkened just slightly when he approached. In my world, I don't see a lot of men feeling regret, and even fewer are remorseful enough to cause them to blush.

Or maybe I'm just a sucker for a hot guy in a tight-fitting t-shirt.

Because I'm weak. Weak for watching him all day as he tried his best to interact with his fans. No one else seemed to notice how uncomfortable he was, but I did. He just doesn't like being the center of attention and fuck me, if that's not super attractive when I'm surrounded by ladder climbing narcissists daily.

I hate myself for still finding him attractive, but I guess being enamored by someone and accepting their apology are two different things.

The door closes behind us and I untangle myself from the

walkie talkie, tossing it on the table in the entry hall before heading deeper into the living room.

The soft pat of Nick's Nikes' tells me he's following at a respectful distance. Good. He doesn't know if I'm one of those women who gets bat shit crazy and starts throwing things. I'm not, but it's still a smart idea for him to give me space.

Turning around, I resume my defensive position—arms crossed, lips pursed, dry eyes. "So? What do you need?"

He shifts uncomfortably, those damn high cheekbones pinkening again. "Obviously, I need to apologize."

"For what?"

We both know the answer to that, but I want to hear him say it out loud.

"I alluded to you being a home-wrecker."

"You didn't allude to anything. You said, and I quote, that I'm the 'woman who destroyed her marriage', unquote."

Nick closes his eyes and nods, as if this conversation is hard for him. Good. It should be.

"I did say that. And I'm so sorry. I know it's not your fault."

"How do you know that?"

"I talked to my sister."

Pressing my lips together, I nod once. "Right. Well, it's great that you believe your sister when she tells you the truth but you don't believe me. Thanks for the apology. You can see yourself out."

"Hold on." Nick starts to move forward but stops when I glare his direction. "I know I'm in the wrong here, but that's not fair. Of course I trust my sister over you. I've known you for one night. We haven't even gotten to the point of real trust yet."

I look away, knowing he's right. That doesn't diminish the sting though.

This time, when he takes a step forward, I don't move.

"Look, Prestyn, I screwed up, okay? When my sister told me

what Gary had done, it... it triggered old stuff for me that wasn't even about you."

"So you took it out on me." I roll my eyes. "That's so much better."

He takes another step forward. "No, it's not. I didn't even hear my sister out. I just got angry and yelled over her about what a jackass Gary is. Apparently I do that a lot. There's a lot of stuff I guess I didn't know about their marriage." He mumbles that last part, probably more to himself than to me.

I don't respond, refusing to look at him for fear he'll see the hurt in my eyes. Because it does hurt. All of it does. Being lied to by Gary, feeling guilty over hurting Delaney, being wounded by Nick. It all hurts in some way, and I'm not even the one who did anything wrong.

"Listen, Pres." He takes another step. "The first I'd even heard about how it all happened was when you told me today. Not that I should be surprised. I guess Delaney hasn't been completely honest with me over the years because of... my lack of ability to react appropriately."

I huff a humorless laugh at how ridiculous it is that somehow I keep being the catalyst for their family drama. As if I don't have enough of my own.

"Prestyn."

I don't respond, eyes still glued to the floor.

"Prestyn, would you please say something?"

"What old wounds did this trigger?"

"What?"

I finally look up, challenging him with my gaze. "What old wounds did this trigger for you? Why did you get so angry so quickly, without even hearing my side of it?"

He looks taken aback and actually steps away from me. "That... I don't like talking about that."

"Well I don't like talking about this humiliating online dating debacle, but I can't seem to get any distance from it since you guys keep showing up at my job. You don't trust me because you don't know me well enough. Well, I don't trust your apology because I don't know *you* well enough. Either give me a reason to believe you're sincere or get out."

Nick pinches the bridge of his nose before sitting on the edge of the couch cushion. "Look, it's not just my story. It belongs to my family, too."

"Get out, then."

Nick holds his hands up in surrender. "Okay, okay. I'll tell you. It just... it's not pretty and it's a deep wound so if you wouldn't mind keeping it to yourself, I'd appreciate it."

I reel back. "What? You think I'm going to sell your story? We've already established I don't need your money."

"No, it's not that," he says quickly. "Delaney has already informed me, in no uncertain terms, that she's going to be friends with you whether I like it or not. Just... Please don't bring it up with her, okay? Especially not while she's going through this divorce."

I pause briefly to consider him. Whatever he's going to tell me is obviously a source of pain for both he and Delaney. The last thing I want to do is hurt his sister, my new friend, again. I'm still struggling with my guilt over being part of it the first time.

"Of course I won't," I finally say.

He nods and gestures for me to sit on the couch across from him. I do, and settle in, still unsure about all this, but willing to hear him out. Maybe it's morbid curiosity, or maybe there's something niggling inside me encouraging me to not give up on him quite yet. Either way, I've agreed to listen.

"Our parents got divorced while we were in college."

Not what I was expecting him to say, but okay.

"It came out of nowhere. Like literally nowhere. One day my dad was calling us regularly to check on things and showing up at my college games sometimes. The next day, he was gone. Like he disappeared."

"Did something happen?"

Nick shakes his head, as if he still can't believe it. "A lot of things happened, apparently. All my mom said was that he was cheating on her. That was bad enough but didn't explain why he ghosted us, too. After weeks of us hounding her for more information, she finally fessed up that the police had shown up at their door early one morning." My eyebrows shoot up before I can stop them. He doesn't miss it. "I know. It was a shock to us, too."

"What did he do?" I ask gently, my anger suddenly forgotten as curiosity takes over.

Nick sighs a deep, sad breath, like he's bracing himself to feel the effects of the fall out again. "He was arrested on charges of polygamy, insurance fraud and conspiracy to commit fraud."

My jaw drops open. "Polygamy?"

Nick nods sadly. "He traveled for work a lot. But he was some kind of agent or whatever at an insurance company so we didn't think anything of it. He called my mom literally every night and when video chatting suddenly became mainstream, he'd talk to all of us. Trust me, I've thought about it over and over and there was never any indication he had two other families."

I didn't think it was possible for me to be any more shocked than I already was, but here I am. My jaw is practically on the floor. "*Families?*"

"Yep. I have some half-siblings that live in California that I've never met. And I guess there are some step-siblings in New Jersey. If you could call them that. My dad married her shortly before he got caught. Actually, that's how he got caught. He tried to add yet another family to his medical benefits and the company started investigating. They weren't happy to find out they'd been paying out benefits when the marriages weren't even legal. There's more to it and how he got away with it for so long, but that's where all the insurance fraud stuff came in. Anyway, that last wife already had two kids, but they never had any together."

"Holy shit, Nick."

"Unbelievable, I know. But true." He glances away, lips twisting as no doubt, memories run through his mind. "It was such a shock because he remembered every birthday from the time we were born, every hockey game, every father-daughter dance. He was there when I committed to my college team. For my entire life he had us all snowed. So when Gary—"

Nick's voice breaks, and his fists clench on his lap. He doesn't have to say anything else, though. I get where the overwhelming emotion comes from.

"When you found out what Gary had been up to, it felt like your dad's betrayal all over again."

He nods. "Which makes it even worse that I took it out on you. I guess maybe in a weird way, I was hoping you did know. That you just didn't care."

Suddenly it all clicks into place. "Because if I knew, then you had someone to blame, instead of feeling like you're just an idiot for falling for it again."

Nick shrugs in response. "It's not rational. Not any more rational than being mad at my dad's other wives. They were victims like we were. But there was nowhere to lash out. He was gone, completely disappeared. There was no outlet except for on the ice and goalies don't get in nearly as many fistfights as everyone else."

I purse my lips, now understanding this man and his over-the-top reactions. I get it and I realize Nick and I aren't so different. I hate Aaron with a passion that probably has less to do with his ineptness and more to do with unresolved issues with my family. Well, that and he's a dick.

Still, it makes my feelings about my boss that much more acute, just like Nick's feelings about "the other woman" were so much more intense as well. While it sucks that his anger was misdirected toward me, I completely understand how it happened.

We sit with our thoughts for a few moments, me mulling over

this overwhelming information, when a question finally occurs to me. "Hey, how come I've never heard about this or read this anywhere?"

His lips quirk up. "Have you been stalking me."

I smile back, the first real smile I've given all day. "I may have looked you up after the night of the gala, just to see what I was getting into."

"I may have looked you up, too." His eyes catch mine and for just a split second, I feel the heat between us ramp up again. Just as suddenly, he gets back on topic. "Probably dumb luck. With a last name like Williams, an online search won't necessarily put us together. And none of us went to any of his trials, so there aren't any pictures anywhere. I think we're old enough now that people ask less about our parents and more about our love lives."

"You're lucky to have such a common last name."

"I imagine Caine isn't as common."

"*Prestyn* Caine is even less common." Shifting to get more comfortable now that we seem to be more or less on the same page, I slip off my shoes and pull my knees to my chest. "I googled myself one time, just to see if there was any other person in the world with my name. I'm it. The one and only."

"You are one of a kind."

I flash him a coy smile. "Are you flirting with me?"

"Maybe a little." Leaning forward, he rests his elbows on his knees. "I'm really sorry, Prestyn. Truly. None of this is your fault. With Gary."

I look away, not wanting him to see the guilt I still carry.

"Prestyn, you know that's not your fault, don't you?"

I shrug, letting out a soft sigh. "Knowing it logically doesn't mean I still don't feel shame over it. No one wants to be the woman that breaks up a marriage."

"I beg to differ. I've seen a lot of women over the years who are more than happy to wreck a home or two."

He's alluded to this before. It's kind of nice having a kindred spirit in dating woes. "I'm sure you have with your job. How do you figure out who likes you for you and who just wants your money and status?"

He doesn't hesitate with his answer. "Easy. You watch the shit your teammates are going through and not make the same stupid decisions."

"That seems problematic."

"How so?"

"Well, if you don't give anyone a chance at all, how do you know if you've finally found the right person? How do you not miss them?"

He shrugs in what looks like indifference, but I can see what appears to be a little bit of defeat as well. Maybe he's less of the bachelor type than even he likes to admit. "You don't. You just don't get involved at all. There's a reason my sister had to set me up on a date for the year's biggest event, ya know."

I cock my head, really looking at him. He's so handsome but it's not just that. He's humble in a way I don't see often. He sought me out to apologize when he was wrong. He didn't brush it aside and just not think about it again, or twist things to make it my fault. He accepted his own bad behavior and tried to do something about it. That's so much more attractive than any eight pack he could have. Even though I know for a fact that he has that, too. It makes me wish things were different. That we could continue on with the no-strings relationship we started.

After a few seconds of silence, he slaps his hands on his knees and rises. "Well, I know you still have a lot of work to do, so I guess I better let you go. Are we okay?"

There's no way I can't accept his apology. "We're more than okay. I promise."

I don't miss the look of relief on his face. "Good. So uh…" he says awkwardly. "I guess I'll see you next time Delaney throws us together."

"I guess so."

Nick heads for the door. I should let him go. Should let him walk right out, but for some reason, I can't. It's almost as if now that I have a better understanding of him and what makes him tick, I want to know more. I *need* to know more. If I let him walk out that door without giving him some indication that I think he's pretty great, I don't think I'll ever forgive myself.

Without thinking, I call out. "Hey, Nick?"

He turns around, brows pinched as if confused by my sudden outburst. "Yeah?"

"You still have the room key app on your phone?"

A knowing smile slowly breaks out on his face. I swear his eyes darken at the implication of my question. "I do."

Licking my lips, I give him the confirmation he so clearly wants. "Use it sometimes. Sooner, rather than later, okay?"

He reaches his hand down to adjust himself in his pants. The unexpected movement makes my entire core clench.

"I will. I have to go on another road trip in a couple days, but expect a call when we get back."

Neither of us says another word. There's no reason. Nick just quickly makes his way out the door, both of us knowing if he stays for one second longer, we may not leave this room for a very long time.

CHAPTER FOURTEEN

NICK

Vegas is one of my favorite places to play. It's not about the night life. None of that interests me. It's about the arena.

The state of the art arena was only built a couple of years ago and the amenities are killer. The ice is some of the smoothest I've ever played on. The lighting makes seeing the puck sharper than some of the older places. And the locker room has on-demand hot water.

Since I don't have a choice but to shower after away games, being able to just turn on the spray and step in is a huge perk.

I'm fully aware that it seems strange to other people that I don't party like everyone else, but that's just not me. I like my downtime. I need peace and quiet to recharge my batteries. And after a ten-day road trip, I'm about tapped out.

Maybe that's why I'm a goalie. It requires teamwork, but really, I'm on my own. I'm not communicating what I'm about to do to anyone. I spend my time observing what everyone else does and adjusting my own response.

Huh. I never thought of that before. That I prefer watching and responding accordingly than being the initial communicator.

That's what I get for reading a book called *The Psychology of Noise*. It makes me rethink my own aversion to it.

Of course my distaste for too much interaction could also be because Patrick is just three feet away and once again yelling at his attorney on the phone.

I glance over at Tucker who shakes his head.

"He's going to lose his spot as captain if he doesn't get his shit under control," Tucker says under his breath.

I shrug out of my upper body pads before answering. "Coach has been giving him some glares lately. It's only a matter of time."

"I'm shocked Coach has let it go this long," Tucker says. "Is he waiting until the divorce is final? I would have thought the glow of nepotism would have worn off as soon as the divorce was filed."

I've been asking myself the same question lately. Don't get me wrong, Patrick is one hell of a first line center. His aggression on the ice is practically unmatched, especially when he and the wifey are fighting. But lately, he's been making dumb errors. His passes have been slightly off and his aggression is more along the lines of rage, which helps no one. Any of the rest of us would have been dropped to the second line by now. But Coach is probably unsure if it would piss off the soon-to-be- ex-wife who would run to her father, the team's owner, so he can't really shake things up until he's given the go-ahead. In the meantime, we have to ride it out until Patrick gets his head out of his ass.

"I have no interest in using nepotism to keep my job if it means bickering with the person I'm supposed to love the most," I finally say.

Tucker gives me a wicked smile. "I don't know. A little arguing means making up is that much more fun." He waggles his eyebrows for effect.

I ignore his suggestive tone. "That right there," I point at Patrick who is pacing now, "There is no reason for any relationship to lead to that. It's just toxic. No, thank you."

The words are no more than out of my mouth when Patrick stops in his tracks. "She what? No... no way. You can tell Tinsley I don't agree to that. No! Don't call me again until she drops that shit!"

Patrick pulls the phone away from his ear to stare at it, a look of horror on his face. He's holding the device so tightly, his knuckles turn white and I swear I hear a crack from the phone. Something is horribly wrong.

Tucker is up and next to him in a second. "Dude, what happened?"

Patrick may be a hothead, but this reaction seems to be a little extreme, even for him.

"She..." Patrick stops, licks his lips and swallows hard. "She wants to have a quicky divorce so she can get remarried."

Inside, I'm cheering that this toxic relationship is finally over. Kind of like I was cheering for my sister. But just like I was with her situation, I keep those thoughts to myself.

"I'm so sorry, man." Tucker claps him on the shoulder in support. "That's rough."

"She's been... she..." Patrick blows out a deep breath. "He lives in our neighborhood. Says he's around more. Not like me, who travels every single week during the season. Oh god, I can't breathe. It's really over."

In one sentence, Patrick confirms how every marriage I've ever seen ends. It makes me grateful that Prestyn and I worked things out. No-strings sex is clearly the right way to go.

Still trying to process this new information, Patrick leans over, resting his hands on his knees just as the door opens and reporters start filing in for post-game interviews.

"Get him out of here," I tell Tucker, who didn't notice our new audience, too concerned about Patrick's ability to breathe.

As soon as he realizes what's happening, he quickly escorts Patrick down the hall to the coach's office. That's the moment Maksim chooses to strip off his remaining clothes and begin strutting around the room. I'm not sure if he's doing it on purpose, but it keeps the cameras off until the other teammates are safely out of view.

Who knew Maks' love of being naked would come in handy?

As Maks passes me, getting his junk way to close to my face while I'm unbuckling my leg pads because of course he does, he leans over to say, "This means we have to take him out tonight. Make him feel better. What happens in Vegas and all that."

I shake my head, hating to admit to myself that he's right.

———

The strobing lights and overamped bass is making this night practically unbearable. Maks' big idea for a night out to get Patrick's mind off his woes has brought us here, to some random strip club.

While Maks is off enjoying a lap dance, I'm stuck here with Patrick who is practically crying into his shot glass.

"I can't believe she left me for him," he says for probably the millionth time tonight. "He's such a dweeb, man. What does she see in him?"

"All his teeth," Tiger pops off, alluding to the front tooth Patrick had knocked out in a particularly vicious game against San Antonio a couple weeks ago.

Instead of getting angry at the quip, Patrick seems to agree with him. "And that giant nest egg. Do you know how much money these tech giants make?"

He looks straight at me, or as close as he can with this much alcohol in his system, waiting for me to answer. I have no idea so I shrug.

"We make a lot of money." Patrick slurs and points at himself, the movement making him wobble in his chair. "Like a lot. But that little shit Darryl probably has a gazillion dollars." He shrugs in his seat. "Do you know how many spa days Tinsley can get for a gazillion dollars? I never stood a chance."

He wouldn't have stood a chance even if this Darryl guy hadn't just sold a start-up tech company for something ridiculous like two-point-three billion. Tinsley has always been on the look out for whoever has the most money. It was so obvious by the way she flirts with all the players at every group function. I've always thought of her as a professional prowler.

It was only a matter of time before Patrick didn't have the largest checking account balance and was left behind.

I have no idea how Patrick ended up in her tangled web, but I'm not jackass enough to ask. Hell, my sister fell for the same kind of shit and if I judge him, I have to judge her, too. Not happening.

"You know what you need?" Becker Bell, our right wing and another poker buddy asks.

"A better divorce attorney," Patrick mutters.

"Well, maybe," Becker admits. "But we can't do anything about that while we're traveling. I was thinking more of a lap dance."

Patrick's eyes perk up. "But no touching."

Good god, he has lost all his brain cells if that's the only thing he can come up with to Becker's suggestion. Traveling tomorrow is going to be seriously rough on him.

Becker laughs. "Correct. No touching. You aren't divorced yet, man."

He holds up a hundred dollar bill and flags down a topless woman who has long, blond hair and impossibly long eyelashes.

Leaning over the table so we can all get a great view of her tits, she bats those eyes at Becker. "What can I do for you boys?"

"My friend here was just dumped by his wife." Becker pouts his lips and I just shake my head. "Can you make him feel better? There's a Benjamin in it for you."

She snatches the money out of his hands and tucks it into her g-string. Sauntering over to Patrick, she straddles his lap and coos. "What a terrible woman. She doesn't deserve you."

Tiger leans around Becker so he can watch the show. Good thing someone is watching. Patrick looks like he's so out of his gourd, he could pass out at any second.

I flag down a waitress with more clothes on and order another whiskey, just for something to do.

I'm bored, I'm irritated and seeing an almost naked ass gyrating across from me is making me horny. What I wouldn't give to be with Prestyn in her suite right now.

Hell, I'd much rather be in the hotel catching up on some reading, but it feels like a dick move to leave when everyone else is trying to help our teammate feel better. Fucking Tucker already got out of being here buy using a call with his kids as an excuse.

I glance over at Maks whose eyes are rolling back as a buxom blonde gets awfully close to licking his neck.

Well, maybe we're not all here to support our captain.

Pulling out my phone, I open up a text thread with the only person I'd actually care to be with right now.

Hey. It's Nick. What are you up to?

It takes a few seconds for Prestyn to respond, not that I'm surprised. I'm sure she's shocked to finally be hearing from me, but she did tell me to contact her when our road trip was over.

Prestyn: I'm watching shitty reality TV and catching up on some reports my boss should be doing. Are you back in town?

Me: Tomorrow. Is the offer still good to get together?

Prestyn: Gawd, yes. Aaron has been on a rampage for the last week. I could use some stress relief.

I furrow my brow, not happy to hear her boss is still giving her hell.

Me: That's shitty. You don't deserve that. You're too good at your job.

The smiley face emoji comes through first.

Prestyn: I appreciate that. Did the road trip go well?

Me: As well as can be expected. We won most, we lost

one. I'm just ready to be away from so many people. Get my own stress relief.

Prestyn: LOL. That's what I'm here for. What time do you get in?

Me: Our flight lands at ten. I'm going to go home to do laundry and get a little peace and quiet before heading to the hotel. Will that work for you?

Prestyn: Be there at six and I'll have dinner waiting. I know you missed out on those green chili enchiladas the other day.

Me: You don't have to feed me dinner. I'm a sure thing no matter what.

Prestyn: Consider it carb-loading. I have a LOT of stress to work out.

I snicker at her response.

"Who are you texting?" Tiger asks. I guess he's finally managed to tear his eyes away from all the naked bodies surrounding us.

"Just a friend," I answer without looking up.

Me: Understood. I'll bring the condoms.

Prestyn: Don't forget this time. I'll see you at 6.

I send the thumbs up emoji and shove my phone in my pocket, a smile growing on my face. Just the anticipation of tomorrow has the stress in my body already starting to melt away.

The ding of the elevator as it reaches my floor has my nerves cranking up a notch.

Maybe it's not nerves as much as anticipation. It would suck if I walked into an empty suite, but I remind myself that this is about sex, nothing more. My feelings won't be hurt.

I hope.

I don't have to worry though, considering the man I've been fantasizing about all day is right where I should have anticipated him to be as soon as I walk in the door—sitting at the dining room table with a mountain of enchiladas on a plate.

The sight is so unexpected and cute, I can't help but snicker, the awkwardness I was feeling fading away. "Do they live up to the hype?"

"More so," he mumbles around his bite of food and then moans his appreciation. The sound makes my stomach clench. I've heard that sound before when he was eating. It was just *me* he was feasting on at the time. "I could live off of these."

Dropping all my stuff on the foyer table, I head straight for the food, the smell making it too hard to pass up and knowing I'll probably need the energy for what will hopefully be a long and intense evening.

"Now you know why they're so popular. I have them at least once a week."

"I really should have gone back down to the green room or whatever it was last time I was here."

Scooping food onto my plate, I take extra assuming I'm probably about to share. Before I sit, I grab the last of the Alani Nu's Nick sent me as an extended apology a couple weeks ago.

Yes, he sent a "bouquet" of my favorite energy drinks to work with a sweet note. Of course I had to forgive him completely at that point. And every time I've grabbed one from the suite's fridge, I've been reminded of how he went above and beyond when he screwed up. The idea of his true remorse made it a no brainer to continue with our arrangement. As long as there's food to start us out, it seems.

"I guarantee there wouldn't have been any left. Not with how much food those guys ate that day."

Nick holds up his fork and points at the tray. "I'm calling dibs on those leftovers."

That gets a laugh from me as I sit in the chair catty-corner to him. "Understood."

I take a quick bite of food more as something to do than because I'm hungry. While I love the enchiladas, I'm feeling a bit out of my comfort zone. I'm not sure how to begin just having sex with a virtual stranger. Do we talk first? Share about our days? Strip our clothes off and go for it right here? I've had sex before, but never in an arrangement sort of way.

I think on it for a few bites before deciding on the answer that seems most comfortable to me... random conversation. "Did you get any rest today?"

"A bit." He takes the napkin off his lap and wipes his mouth.

So he has table manners, too. Yet another thing I like about him.

"To be honest, I was a little anxious about coming here so I had a hard time sleeping."

The fork that was on its way to my mouth stops. I catch his gaze and try to give him a confident smile. "Does that mean you're as nervous as I am?"

Sitting back in his chair, he stretches his legs out under the table. They brush against mine, but I don't move, frozen as I wait for his answer, and enjoying the feel of him so close to me.

Nick scratches his jaw then crosses his arms before answering. "I'm less nervous and more not quite sure how to go from sitting at the dining room table eating dinner to bending you over the bed and eating you out."

I instantly regret the bite I just took as I start choking as soon as I process his words.

He hands me his water bottle, which I take gratefully. Holding up my finger to signal I need a minute, I take a quick swig.

"Sorry," he says sheepishly. "I wasn't going for shock value, I swear."

I'm still coughing a little but am finally able to answer. "It still did the trick. Shocked me, I mean."

"Are you having second thoughts?"

"No," I answer a little too quickly. Setting aside the water bottle, I push my plate away. "I think I'm like you. Not quite sure how to get to the good stuff."

His lips quirk to the side. "Enchiladas aren't the good stuff?"

The air in the room begins to change as we stare at each other. The sexual chemistry suddenly ratchets up a notch. I bite my bottom lip and peek up through my lashes. "Not even close."

Quickly pushing away from the table, Nick comes around behind me and pushes my hair to the side. Just that slight touch has me shivering. When he bends down, his breath brushing across my skin, goose pimples break out all over my body.

"And what is the good stuff?"

His lips find the skin beneath my ear and a very needy moan falls from my lips.

"Is this the good stuff?" he whispers and continues to nibble on my neck. His hand slides down the front of my shirt, into the cup of my bra and his fingers begin twisting my nipple. "Or maybe this?"

Needing something to hold onto, my hand makes its way to Nick's hair so I can grab and pull. "Yes. That's definitely some of it," I finally squeak out.

"Do you want more of that?" His other hand slides down the front of my body until his fingers are rubbing against my core, creating just enough friction to make me want more.

"Yes, please."

Nick growls... literally growls... against my neck. "I love it when you say please."

With a strength I didn't know he had and speed I never anticipated, Nick grabs me and lifts me in his arms, my legs wrapping around him instinctively. Our lips immediately find each other and a sort of frenzy begins.

Tongues invade, teeth nip, lips suck, all while he massages my ass, his fingers so close to my cleft I know my panties must be soaked through. My fingers dig into his scalp, which seems to spur him on and makes him carry me faster into the bedroom. When the door slams behind us, I drop from his arms, desperate to be naked with him.

I'm practically heaving with need as I tear my clothes off, not able to wait one more second for him to be inside me.

"Please tell me you remembered the condoms," I beg as my top ends up somewhere across the room and my pants wind up pooled at my feet.

"They're on the bed already." His own shirt goes flying. When his pants drop, so does my jaw.

"You went commando?"

"No sense in wasting time." He works his feet out of the

pantlegs and reaches for me, stretching around to unclasp my bra and practically ripping it off my body, throwing it behind me so hard I hear it hit the window.

His eyes drop to my breasts and he stalls. "You're so fucking gorgeous."

A warm emotion I know I shouldn't feel runs through me at his sentiment. I'm not sure anyone has used those words with me while in the bedroom. At least, no one that has looked so genuine and truthful when they said it.

That spark inside me scares me just enough to brush his comment aside for me to evaluate later.

"As much as I enjoy your appreciation for my body, would you rather stand here and say sweet nothings or get inside me?"

Nick's nostrils flare and he reaches for me again, shoving his thumbs in my panties and pushing them to the floor. "I can do both. You're fucking gorgeous and I can't wait to fuck you."

I didn't know it was possible to get any more aroused but Nick just brings out that side of me without even trying.

Suddenly, he takes a step back, his eyes darkening even further. He rips the comforter off the bed and looks back at me. "Get on the bed," he demands, leaving no room for argument.

Not that I would. I'm so ready for this, my whole body is vibrating with need. Sliding myself up to the middle of the mattress, I never take my eyes off him. The rasp of the sheets against my body leads to more delicious discomfort. I need him, *need* him, to fuck me.

I situate myself to lean on my elbows and wait for his next command. I don't have to wait long.

"Spread your legs."

Bending my knees to ensure the angle that will give him an eyeful, I let my legs fall open.

"Fuuuuuck," he groans. His eyes go from my pussy to my eyes and back again.

"Why are you waiting?" I finally ask, about ready to do this myself if he doesn't hurry up.

"I'm trying to decide if I want to take you with my tongue or my cock."

"Oh," I breathe, his words completely unexpected. I have no idea how he can make dirty talk sound so sensual, but he does. But talk doesn't satisfy the ache I still feel. "Why can't we do both?"

"Good point."

I squeal in surprise as he's suddenly on me, his tongue making one long, deep swipe up my center before he slides up my body mumbling something about pomegranate. His weight is finally on top of me, his mouth back on mine. His fingers make their way back down my body and plunge inside me, making me gasp.

They don't stay there for long. He gives me just a few thrusts, just enough to make my hips begin gyrating before pulling out again.

"I think we can skip the foreplay, don't you?" he asks.

The condom package crinkles distinctly near my ear. I've been so focused on the heat between us, I didn't even notice it sitting next to me.

"I think we had enough foreplay the night of the gala," I respond, grabbing his cock and squeezing. The hiss that comes out of his mouth encourages me to continue.

Nick pushes back, allowing me to continue stroking him as he rips the package open. He pushes my hand away and sheaths himself quickly, leaning forward to hover over me. He doesn't even use his hands to line himself up, just maneuvers those strong hips to get himself right where he wants to be.

With his eyes locked on mine, he pushes inside and we groan simultaneously.

Within seconds, our frenzy is back.

His hand grabs my leg, pulling it closer to his hip which causes him to hit a spot inside of me I didn't even know was there.

My hand slides under his arm and grabs at his back, leaving a few scratchmarks neither of us seem to care about.

He thrusts at a frantic pace, and I try to keep up, enjoying every bit of pleasure he's wringing from my body.

"I've dreamed about this," he says quietly in my ear. "Being inside you, thrusting deep, claiming all your pleasure."

The only word that comes out of my mouth is "Yes" as he continues pumping in and out, trying to get us as close as two bodies can get.

Suddenly he sits back on his heels, still buried deep inside me and looks down to where our bodies are joined. "Fuck, your pussy is magnificent. I can't take much more."

He licks his thumb and presses right on my clit, rubbing in small circles.

As I look into his eyes... eyes I could fall deeper into if I let myself, I have the fleeting thought that this heat between us, this connection, could be very dangerous for my emotional well-being.

That thought quickly disappears when my body detonates with such a force, I cry out, practically screaming my release as I come and come and *come*. Nick's answering groan of pleasure rebounds through the room.

As we finally come down off our high, chests heaving as we catch our collective breath, Nick begins to move off me.

"No." I grab at his back, holding him close. "I like the feel of your weight on me."

"I don't want to suffocate you." His words are still coming out in sharp breaths.

"You won't. Just... stay."

Nick snuggles in, wrapping his arms under my shoulders to hold me close. We stay like that, content in the afterglow of the best sex we've ever had. Or at least the best I've had. I'm not sure about him, but judging by his willingness to stay right where he is, I think it's a safe assumption.

Several long and satisfying minutes later, he finally pulls out, holding onto the end of the condom. We both hiss as we disconnect and I find myself strangely sad at the loss of contact.

I refuse to think about that.

No strings, Prestyn, I remind myself. *Put any and all emotion away. No. Strings.*

"I'll be right back." He gives me a quick kiss and walks away.

I watch the muscles of Nick's backside shift as he moves into the bathroom to clean up. When he heads through the door, though, I furrow my brow but don't say a word.

Seconds later, he's back and I burst out laughing.

He holds up a plate of enchiladas and takes a bite. "Second best thing I've eaten tonight."

As he climbs back on the bed to share with me, I feel those emotions I'm trying to bury come right back to the surface.

Nick is a dangerous, dangerous man. And I have a bad feeling I'm going to get burned.

CHAPTER SIXTEEN
NICK

It was a shitty practice. It always is the day after we lose a game. And yet, I can't stop smiling as I unhook my pads from my skates. Because while these losers are going home to wallow in their sad misery, I'm heading to the hotel for a mid-day quickie.

Usually Prestyn and I meet after she's done with work but for whatever reason she was available earlier today. Not that I'm complaining. The last couple of weeks have been some of the most relaxing of my life, and all because of a certain heiress who would kick me in the balls if she heard me call her that.

"What are you smiling about?" Becker plops down next to me, yanking his sweaty shirt over his head and tossing it in the laundry bin.

"Nothing." I keep my head down, focusing on a stubborn knot while I try to school my expression.

"I don't believe that. You did just as many drills as the rest of us and Coach's mood is nothing to smile about."

He's right. After we were slaughtered last night by Chicago, Coach was pissed. I take full responsibility in missing three shots, that led to us getting our asses kicked, but it's a hell of a lot easier to block shots when the defensive line is doing their jobs, too.

"Can't a guy just be happy that a bad day is over and we're all moving on?"

I finally get the knot undone and toss my pads to the side so I can begin working on my laces.

"Nope," Becker says with a shake of his head. "That's not it."

I make a fatal mistake and look up at him. Whatever he sees on my face gives him the answer he was hoping for.

"You slick motherfucker."

I furrow my brow in confusion. "Huh?"

"You're getting laid, aren't you?"

"Oh geez," I breathe and return to my task.

Becker doesn't let it go, though. "You are! Who is she? Do I know her? Wait. It's the chick living in Tucker's pool house, isn't it? What's her name?" He snaps his fingers a few times before her name comes to him. "Ellington! No, Ellie. Ellie, right? That's who you're fucking?"

"Oh hell no. I like Ellie. And I really like her kid. But she's a little too aggressive for me."

"Then who is it?"

After sliding my feet out of my skates, I pull off one sock. "Who says there's anyone? You came to this conclusion on your own."

"Nuh-uh. I'm right. Hey, Tiger." Our teammate stops right in front of us, his hand holding the towel wrapped around his waist closed. "Look at him." Becker gestures to me. "What do you see on his face?"

Tiger cocks his head as he looks at me before he smiles. "Oh you're totally getting laid."

I roll my eyes and grab at my second sock.

"I told you," Becker exclaims victoriously. "Now spill. Who is she— Fuck, you asshole." He bats the sweaty sock out of his face that I just flung at him. "Those are your lucky socks. They smell like you rubbed them under your arm after taking a shit in your own armpit."

"Quit making up stories about my love life and I won't have to go to such extreme measures." I step over the bench so I can grab my clothes out of my locker.

"I'm not talking about your love life," he responds with an edge of superiority. "I'm talking about where you dip your stick."

"Your fascination with my dick is causing me some concern," I deadpan, still trying to deflect this conversation. I already spend too much time thinking about Prestyn because she's fucking phenomenal.

Not only do we have the best sex I've ever had, she's smart and funny and kind. Every time we get together we end up in a post-coital conversation about books and music and our goals for the future.

I love that she wants to become the boss on her own merit and not because of her family name. I hate that she lets her boss shit all over her while she proves herself, but her resilience and ability to brush off his remarks, the fact that she knows who she is no matter what anyone else says, is admirable. The woman exudes confidence.

She doesn't need me and she knows it. She just *likes* being with me and chooses to enjoy our time together. It's so fucking attractive I have to stop myself from begging for more time with her.

That's not what we agreed to. We have a no-strings attached sexual relationship, and that's how it's going to be.

Even if I find myself dreaming about her smile when we're not together.

"I'm not any more interested in your junk than I am anyone else's."

I shoot Becker a look. "I don't think that's the deflection you think it was."

"Stop trying to sidetrack me. Who is she? Is she hot?" He waggles his eyebrows, which I try to ignore.

I'm obviously not getting out of this conversation, but I'm not telling him the truth either. There is a reason Prestyn and I are keeping this on the downlow and it only takes one person accidentally overhearing to blow our cover. That's not an option.

"Unlike you fuckers, not everything in my life is about sex."

"Yeeah..." Becker draws out. "I think you're lying."

"I don't care what you—"

"Williams!" Coach yells my name, looking around the room until he finally sees me. Gesturing over his shoulder with his thumb he barks, "My office. Now."

I slip my shirt on and slide my feet into my crocs. "Welp, gotta go."

"This conversation isn't over," Becker yells at me as I walk away.

"The hell it isn't," I mutter as I beat feet to Coach's office. No one wants their name yelled through the locker room by Coach. It's a sure sign you're about to get your ass handed to you. But this time I'm just grateful to get away from Becker and a conversation I refuse to have.

I knock twice on the door jamb before walking into Coach's office. "You wanted to see me?"

He doesn't look up from his papers, just points his pen at the chair in front of his desk. "Sit."

As soon as my ass hits the chair, he leans back in his and I know the lecture is about to begin.

Coach gives me a pointed look, fire in his eyes. "I've had a really shitty morning so far." *Uh oh.* "Do you know why I've had a shitty morning, Williams?"

I think for a second, but the answer seems pretty obvious to me.

"Because we got slaughtered last night on our own ice."

He shakes his head slowly. "That's why I had a shitty night last night. I was feeling better after my wife helped me take the edge off." *Ew.* "And after putting you guys through the ringer with drills this morning. And then I came into my office." He leans forward, clasping his hands together and resting his arms on his desk. "Do you know why my reasonably good mood was ruined when I got in here?"

I have a sinking feeling that I can guess and the answer isn't going to be pretty for me. Still, I try for deflection. "Did Maks walk by naked as a jaybird again?"

"Nice try. But no. This is about you."

Fuck.

I'd successfully dodged the reporters last night and was hoping that was the end of it. From the look on Coach's face, I'm making an educated guess that I was wrong.

I sigh and lean back in my chair. "I've been trying, Coach. I did that meet-and-greet for hours, and that was last minute."

"It was also weeks ago."

"But I went to the gala, like you told me to," I argue.

"I have it on good authority that you spend the entire night talking to your teammates and didn't mingle with anyone else."

He's got me there.

"I let them interview me for that Most Eligible Bachelor thing."

"That was last. Fucking. Year." Coach pushes himself upright, resting his hands on the armrests of his chair. "We got our ass handed to us last night and you were part of the problem."

I wince, because he's right. I'm better than letting three goals get past me, even if the defensive line is off their game, too. And yet, I choked. Let the other team get in my head and let everyone down.

"Instead of manning up for the cameras and owning up to your shit, you slunk away like a little bitch."

I look at the floor, digesting his words because he's not wrong. In my attempt to stay out of the spotlight, I forced the rest of my team to pick up the slack for me. To accept their own responsibility while I shirked mine.

"From this point forward," he continues. "You will do a post-game interview after every game."

I lift my head up, eyes wide.

"Don't give me that look," he says before I can utter a word. "This is part of your damn job and I'm tired of getting calls from the PR department saying you're not holding up your end of the bargain. Need I remind you that interview availability is *part of your contract*. The one *you* signed."

Dammit. I had always hoped that was more of an optional thing. "No sir."

"Good. Because as good as you are on the ice, I need *team* players. That means every single part of the job. I've already got my hands tied with other people causing issues. I don't need it from you, too."

We both know he's talking about Patrick and his relationship woes. No wonder Coach is so adamant about me being in front of the cameras. I'm not his only problem child.

"Sorry, Coach," I utter, my apology much too little, much too late.

"Nope. Don't wanna hear it." He shakes his head. "I'm not having this conversation with you again. Next time I get my ass chewed by the front office, I'm gonna rain down the fire on you so hard you'll be lucky if you can squat in front of that net at the next game. Hear me?"

"Loud and clear."

"Good. As much as you hate it, just be grateful I'm not even considering you for this reality TV bullshit I'm figuring out." He lifts a piece of paper off his desk and looks at it disgustedly before tossing it back down.

"The what?" My interest is suddenly piqued, not because I want to be on television more than I absolutely have to, but because these aren't words I've ever heard him say before.

Coach huffs. Obviously whatever this is is another factor in his overtly bad mood. "Some network exec has got all the team owners on board with a reality show. One person from each professional hockey team to compete for some charity money."

"That's unusual."

"It's fine if they want to do it, but why the fuck did they leave the decision of which player signs on to me? I don't give a shit about any of this."

"I'll do it, Coach."

We both swivel our heads to look in the doorway where Maks stands, surprisingly clothed.

Coach rubs his hand down his face. "The fuck are you talking about, Ivanov?"

Without waiting for an invitation, Maks saunters in like he owns the place. "It's on my bucket list to be on a reality show."

"Of course it is," I say under my breath. Honestly, this isn't as surprising as it should be. No one has ever accused Maks of shying away from a camera. And I'm sure he'd love the extra notoriety he'd get from female fans.

"Not sure you want to do this one. You'll be stuck on some tropical island. That's the only thing I know about it," Coach explains.

"Perfect. I don't even need to pack clothes."

Coach palms his face while I stand quickly.

"I assume you don't need me here to discuss where Maks is likely to sunburn in this scenario, right?" I offer.

Maks lowers himself into the chair I just vacated. "You act like I don't tan my nuts regularly. Giving your butthole regular sunlight improves your libido and helps keep sunburn away."

I look back at Coach, eyes wide, practically begging him to let me out of here for the rest of this conversation. Funny, he's looking at me the same way.

"No really. Can I go?" I point over my shoulder at the door with my thumb. "I'm not paid enough for this."

"Neither am I, and yet, here I am," Coach sulks. "Yes. Get out of here." He waves his hand in dismissal. "But don't forget what I said. I will rain fire on your ass if you skip out on another interview."

"Understood," I call back as I high tail it away from what is sure to be an uncomfortable conversation.

I'm still not looking forward to dealing with reporters, but at least it's not sunlight on my butthole. If nothing else, I'm less likely to get sunburned in doors.

CHAPTER SEVENTEEN

PRESTYN

"Come on, Prestyn," Nick demands, winding up my body even more. "Give it to me, baby."

He pushes my hips down softly so I'm forced to bend my knees just enough to create a new angle. My hands are braced on the bed toes digging into the carpet as Nick takes me from behind, his thrusts quick and forceful. I'm so close, *so close* but I can't seem to get there.

"What do you need, baby," Nick asks and bites the juncture between my shoulder and my neck. His athletic endurance comes in handy at times like this.

I gasp. "You know what I need," I say, because he does. He always knows what my body needs.

Nick slides his hand down my ribcage, reaching around the front and finding my clit where he rubs small circles. I tilt my hips up ever so slightly and that's all it takes.

"Dooooon't stoooooop," I yell, but there's no need.

Nick plays my body like a musical instrument. He knows exactly how to stroke and pluck to make the most delicious music out of my body.

But the sound, the sound that comes from deep in his throat when he finds his own release is the best music to my ears.

As the tension finally dissipates, leaving my muscles unable to hold me up anymore, I flop face first over the edge of the bed.

Nick chuckles and I can feel the reverberations inside me before he grabs the condom and slowly pulls out.

"I take it that was good for you?" he asks as he makes the familiar trek to the bathroom to dispose of the evidence of our love making.

Er, sex. Because that's all this is. Sex.

"My legs are wobbly." The sound of my voice is muffled by the blanket my face landed in.

I lay there, halfway on the bed and butt still in the air as I try to catch my breath. But there is no getting my muscles to work. I'm spent.

Well, for now. If I have my way, we'll take a break, get something to eat, and go for round two. Maybe three if I'm lucky before he leaves.

"Don't you have a road trip coming up?" I ask. My voice sounds groggy, my head barely lifted from the bed.

"We leave in a couple days."

The sound of Nick's voice behind me surprises me. I've been so content in my own little postcoital foggy world, I didn't realize he'd already come back from the bathroom.

I hear him chuckle before he runs his big palm up my spine. I practically purr at the feeling of his touch.

"You're not that wiped out, are you?"

"I told you my legs are wobbly. They're still shaking."

"Welp, let's get you in bed."

He grabs me and tossing me onto the mattress like I weigh nothing, making me shriek.

"You ass," I say with a laugh as I roll toward him. "You just threw me on the bed."

"I'm ready to snuggle."

Nick scooches toward me and tosses the comforter over us as we get comfortable. The first time we were together and he said he was a snuggler, I didn't believe him. My experience with men is that none of them like this part. Now that Nick and I have been doing this for a few weeks, I have no reason to believe otherwise.

It's not just the hugs and light kisses. Our conversations in the afterglow of sex are becoming some of my favorite memories with him. Not just because it means we're resting up for the next round, but because he's so interesting. He loves art and poetry and music. He loves his sister deeply. He has interesting stories of places he's visited and intriguing tidbits about what being a professional athlete is like. We can talk for hours and we laugh constantly.

We're more than just no-strings lovers now. We've become friends.

As long as my heart stops at that label, everything is fine. I just have to keep reminding myself where the emotional boundaries are.

"What is life like on the road?" I ask once I'm settled against his chest, his hand lightly running up and down my back.

"Busy. Exhausting. A blur."

"A blur?"

He rests his arm behind his head, under his pillow, propping himself up just slightly. "It's non-stop. We play, eat, sleep, travel, play, eat, sleep, travel, the cycle repeating itself for however long we're gone."

"That sounds boring. There's no time to sightsee?"

"Not much. Sometimes our flights are four hours long. By the time we land, we head straight to the arena to get a short practice in and a feel for the ice."

I hum, feeling completely content against his warmth. So much so, my eyes close as I enjoy the feel of him. "That's unfortunate. I would have thought you'd at least go out on the town some nights."

He kisses the top of my head, eliciting a small smile from me. "My teammates do all the time. You know I'm more of an introvert than that."

"Yeah, I do."

"So I have a question."

"Hmm," I respond, on the verge of passing out.

"How come you don't tell your brother what a dick your boss is?"

My eyes pop open. We've talked about a lot as we've gotten to know each other. But the one topic that hasn't come up yet is Aaron. I don't think we've been avoiding it as much as he has no place in this happy little bubble Nick and I have built. Maybe that's why I'm surprised the topic has been brought up.

I lift my head, propping myself up on my elbow. "Women have a harder climb when it comes to the corporate ladder," I explain. I trace light circles around his chest. "That's kind of a common fact these days so I'm sure it's no shock to you."

He nods in agreement.

"But I think I wasn't expecting it to be as difficult as it is. Especially with family. When I first graduated, Gavin told me they wanted to put me under Aaron to train me. That was supposedly the plan from the beginning."

"And that didn't happen?"

I smirk. "What do you think?"

Nick leans his head back and closes his eyes. "I think I've met the guy twice and he's had little-dick energy each time."

A small laugh bursts out of me. "You and Bayleigh get the same vibe."

"And you don't?"

"I do. I just..." I pause to think through my words. "I've known Aaron since I was a kid. He was my brother Hoyt's best friend. I guess I'm sort of immune to his vibe."

Nick doesn't say anything. Just lets me sort through my thoughts as I try to explain why I continue to let Aaron walk all over me. To be honest, I need the time to figure it out myself. It feels like there are so many small reasons that added up over the years, until I finally remember the ultimate catalyst.

"When I started working under Aaron, I didn't really notice what was going on. I'd known him for so long, it was easy to justify like, 'It's just the way he is'. The more time that went by, the more I started noticing other people's reactions around me. That's when I started to realize how off-balance things in the office really were."

I lean down to rest my chin on his chest as I explain my side of things for the first time ever. "One day, I'd finally had it. He'd always pass his reports off to me, which felt like a compliment at first. That he trusted me so much. But I started to realize he just didn't want to do them himself."

"Shocker," Nick blurts out.

"I know. Anyway, we had almost finished building the newest wing of the conference center and were trying to fill all the shops before it was open to the public, so our deadline was really tight. We had several hundred applications to go through which meant we had to stay late. I'd come prepared. I knew it was going to be a long night to put our list together so I had a plan to order dinner and stay until it was done. But at five on the dot, Aaron just walks out. Says something about it being more my forté than his so he knew I had it covered.

"I was so angry. Not that I'd never been mad before. It was just the last straw. I stayed until almost eleven that night to finish up and when I was ten minutes late the next morning, Aaron reamed my ass in front of everyone for not taking the job seriously."

"What a dick," Nick interjects forcefully.

"That was definitely the consensus in the office that morning. One of my coworkers had brought me coffee, so they knew."

"What happened? Did you tell your dad finally?"

"I wanted to. We always have Sunday dinner as a family, or we did back then, so I was prepared to tell them exactly what was happening."

Nick's eyes pop open. "Tell me they blew you off."

"Worse. Aaron showed up."

Nick groans and shifts his legs, forcing one of mine between his.

"I sat through that whole dinner planning to somehow get them alone before the night was over, but then they started talking shop. We had just changed insurance companies and one of our employees was on maternity leave, but for some reason her short-term disability wasn't coming through. They kept laughing about how ridiculous the situation was and how her weekly phone calls were obnoxious. That she needed to calm down until it was all sorted out.

"Keep in mind, the whole situation was our fault. Totally and completely. She had turned in all the right paperwork, had planned in advance. There was nothing she could have done differently. There was some sort of glitch on our end and they made it into a joke, like a woman not getting the money she was owed wasn't a big deal when she's trying to pay for diapers and formula."

"Is it wrong to say I'm not really liking any part of your family right now?"

I laugh a little at Nick's honesty. "I didn't really like them that night either. I was about to say something, to put them in their place and tell them to stop being jerks when the words 'hysterical female' was thrown out by one of them. I don't even know who said it."

"Probably Aaron," Nick murmurs.

"Probably. But it didn't matter. Everyone else just nodded like they agreed, and I guess at that moment I knew it didn't matter what I said. If they didn't see the wrong doing for themselves, I was just going to be labeled as too emotional or a problem."

"Even with it being a family business?"

I nod sadly. "Even then. I'm the first woman in our family to ever work at this hotel. In its entire history. I'm already fighting an uphill battle. But the misogyny, whether they realize it or not, runs deep. I have to be super careful not to shoot myself in the foot because they'll believe Aaron over the 'hysterical baby sister'." I use air quotes, knowing full well I'm way less emotional than my idiot boss.

Nick wraps his arms around me and rolls us to the side so we're facing each other. "I'm sorry. That really sucks. I wish I could walk into their offices and force them to see reason."

I smile and scratch his jaw. "I appreciate the sentiment, but if you did, that would just confirm all of their biases."

My eyes flutter closed as he kisses my lids. "Is there anything I can do to help?" His lips drift to my cheek and over to the side of my mouth.

"Just this."

He gives me a peck on the lips and continues to the other side.

"The outlet, this outlet, has actually helped a lot. You make my body relax, which makes me sleep better, which makes my mood better."

"Does this help you relax?" Nick kisses down my jaw, around the front of my body and I know the direction he's going.

"So much yes."

"Good. I'm going to help you sleep really good tonight, baby."

Nick continues his way down my body, finally reaching his target where his tongue takes over and he does his best to work all the leftover energy out of me.

It works. I sleep like a baby.

CHAPTER EIGHTEEN

NICK

"Breathe in through your nose, and out through your mouth." Jackie models exactly how she wants us to breath into our stretches but even forcing the air in my lungs to come in and out slower doesn't keep the thoughts of last night's shit show at bay.

We lost. Again. At home. It wasn't a slaughter but it still wasn't a win. Even worse, Coach made it a point to remind me that in no uncertain terms, I was on the hook for a post-game interview.

It did not go well.

"Nick, what can you say about tonight's loss?"

"Uh, yeah. We lost. We don't like doing that."

"How does it feel to have let two zingers go right past you."

"It feels shitty, uh, I mean, not good. It doesn't feel good. I'll try harder next time."

What a fucking idiot. If anyone ever wondered why I'm adamantly against interviews, all they need to do is watch me stumble over my words. Even better, our head of PR contacted me this morning to see if she could offer me some interview training to help for the next time.

Of course I said yes. If I'm stuck doing this shit, I'd rather not sound like an incoherent moron every time a microphone is shoved in my face. Clearly breathing exercises from yoga aren't working.

"Bend your right arm behind your back and reach your left arm up and over, pushing into that lunge," Jackie stands behind me, adjusting my hips gently and nudges me deeper into my stretch. "Look up to the sky. Good. And hold."

As if on cue, she walks away and I hear a groan next to me.

"How long are we supposed to hold this position?" Tiger grunts through gritted teeth. "Aren't we on warrior twelve or something by now?"

"There aren't twelve warriors," I mumble and follow Jackie's instructions to swivel, put our hands on the ground, feet extended out behind us, *chaturanga* to downward dog.

"It seems like it," he continues to bitch. "Yoga is boring as fuck, man. I don't know why you come here."

I interrupt my moves to look over at him. "If you're so bored, why did you insist on coming?"

He lifts one hand off the ground—which he does easily, not because he has good core stabilization but because he's not even trying to do the poses correctly—and gestures to all the women in front of us. "This class does a lot of downward dogs."

I shake my head, not even caring enough to be irritated. Besides, all my annoyance is focused on the interview clips that made it on the news.

"Nick, how hard was it to come up against Vegas, particularly Maverick Hagen, tonight?"

"It was hard. I mean, I've blocked him before without a problem but he was hard tonight. I mean, he wasn't... hard. I wouldn't know about that. But, uh... yeah."

If I could crawl into a hole and die from embarrassment I would. I knew as soon as the words came out of my mouth what I had said, but I expected the sports reporter to cut out that clip. It didn't make sense anyway. Instead, they ran it and I reaped the benefits of about three dozen texts from my teammates giving me shit for it.

At least Coach understands now why it's never a good idea to put a recording device in front of my face in any official capacity. Not that he'll care. He's got bigger fish to fry these days. What with Patrick practically melting down over his pending divorce and Maks signing on to do whatever reality show he's doing. I haven't even asked. Apparently, Maks signed an NDA already and I don't enjoy my friends getting sued because I asked too many questions.

My mind never stops wandering through the entire class. Not through all the poses. Not through the breathing exercises. Not through Savasana, which usually clears my mind faster than anything else because we're laying so still, with nothing but the sound of our breathing and gentle music to distract us.

Not today, though. I end the class feeling just as tightly strung as I did in the beginning.

"Hey Nick," Jackie says, her after class bounce back in her voice.

"Hey, Jackie. That was a great class today." I'm lying. It was a shitty class, but that's on me, not her.

"Thanks. I do my best." She pauses and I look up from wiping down my mat. Jackie's biting her bottom lip and twisting a lock of hair with her finger.

Uh oh. I've seen those moves before.

"So listen. I was about to run and grab a chai lemonade from that little shop down the street. I need the fuel replenishment before my next class. I was hoping you'd like to join me."

Wow. She isn't subtle at all, is she?"

I briefly glance over her shoulder at Tiger who is making an obscene gesture with his tongue in his cheek.

Ignoring him, I try to turn her down gently. I have no interest in Jackie outside of this studio, but there are a lot of physical benefits to her class that I still need to take advantage of.

"I really appreciate that, Jackie, but your class is just the beginning of our workout. We're actually headed straight to practice now."

Jackie's face falls, but that doesn't mean she's given up. "Oh. Well maybe another time?"

Tiger throws up his hands in disgust at the fact that I turned her down. Then he uses his fingers to simulate sex. Apparently he thinks I don't know I'm being hit on and thinks I need some help getting laid.

I continue to ignore him, but it's getting more difficult when some of my classmates begin to stare.

The whole situation is a distraction that throws me off, so I say the first words that come to my mind. "I don't think my girlfriend would like that."

"Girlfriend?" Tiger blurts out.

Great. Now Jackie is going to know I'm lying. Sort of. Kind of? I'm not sure how else to explain having Prestyn in my life. Sure, we're secret fuck buddies, but we're also more than that. We're friends.

Yeah. Friends.

Friends with benefits.

She's a *girl* friend with benefits.

Which means, technically I'm not lying.

Jackie's eyes widen. "I didn't realize you had a girlfriend. I'm so sorry. I never would have asked if I had known."

Fortunately, she's distracted by another classmate wanting to chat about the health benefits of acai seeds, getting me off the hook of what could have been an even more awkward conversation.

Jackie's very obvious remorse reminds me of how Prestyn reacted when she found out Gary was married. It makes me respect Jackie a little more as a person, that she's drawn boundaries she's not willing to cross. Or maybe it makes me like her more because she reminds me of Prestyn.

Which is weird because I shouldn't be thinking of Prestyn when I'm in yoga. I shouldn't be thinking of Prestyn at all, but I do. All the time. I wonder what she's doing. I wonder if she's stood up to her boss yet. I wonder if she wants company.

There have been a few times I've texted to ask about getting together, not because I'm even thinking about sex, but because I'm thinking about her and can't quite find a way to say it without sounding like I'm slipping outside the boundaries of our well-defined relationship.

Maybe I'll invite her to a game next time we're together. Tell her I enjoy her as a person and like that we're friends. Yeah. That sounds like a plan. Maybe we can go to dinner after the fact just to hang out—

"Dude what the fuck?"

Tiger punches me in the shoulder as soon as we step foot out of the studio.

"Ow, you fucker." I rub the area that might actually bruise. "Why did you use your knuckle to hit me."

"So it would hurt more."

"Why did you hit me in the first place?"

"You have a girlfriend?"

Oh. That.

I hit the key fob so the trunk of my car opens. I toss my stuff inside. "No. But I wanted to let Jackie down easy."

"I don't believe you."

Right now, I regret having a trunk that closes on its own, because I'd really like to slam it for effect. "And I should care that you don't believe me, why?"

"Because I want to meet her."

I huff a laugh and walk around the car to the driver's seat. "That's not going to happen."

"So you *do* have a girlfriend."

We both climb in my vehicle and I hit the start button,

pulling my seatbelt across my body. "No. I have... I don't... Why the fuck are you in my car, anyway?"

"You're deflecting, which is fine. I have the mind of an elephant. I don't forget."

I roll my eyes and pull out of my parking space and into traffic.

"I left my car at the arena when I went out with the guys last night, remember?" Tiger explains. "You said you'd drive me to practice after yoga."

"Remind me not to do that again," I grumble as I look in the side mirror before changing lanes. "You're a pain in the ass in my class."

"No, yoga is a pain in the ass. A literal pain. Jackie always pushes me too hard when I'm doing Warrior Five-Hundred-and-Fourteen, or whatever. Besides, I think you like the company."

"I really, really don't."

"Plus, if I didn't go sometimes, how would I find out things like, *you have a girlfriend*."

"I don't. Have. A girlfriend."

"Okay." Tiger rests back in his seat, getting way too comfortable for this conversation. That scares me. He grins. "I get it. You have a fuck buddy."

Dammit. I really need to get with PR sooner rather than later so I can learn how to come up with better answers when I'm on the spot in any situation. If I had told Jackie I'm just not interested instead of exaggerating my relationship with Prestyn, I wouldn't be trying to throw Tiger off the trail right now. But there's no diverting his attention. Tiger loves paying attention to other people's messes, probably so he doesn't have to think about his own. I might as well be honest with him. To an extent, anyway.

"Tiger, drop it." I try to add some sternness to my tone, hoping to get across how serious I am. "I don't know what's happening, I just know it's not anyone's business except mine."

Even in my peripheral vision, I can see him narrow his eyes in assessment, trying to figure me out.

"So you're dating another dude?"

"Ohmygod," I shake my head in disbelief.

"I don't care, man." He holds his hands up defensively. "Love is love and all that. I just wanna know where you met. Did he come to a game or... Oh! Is it Phoenix? Our new center? He gives me a real metro vibe. And his hands are very soft for being on the cold ice all day."

"I'm not even having this conversation with you."

"I know, I know."

The car goes quiet, but I know better than to think it means the conversation is over.

"I'm just saying Phoenix is a good kid, is all."

"Would you stop?" I yell, half angry, half amused. "It's not Phoenix, alright?"

"Oh." He sounds disappointed. "You and Phoenix would have looked really good together."

I don't even respond, just shake my head. The last thing I need is rumors floating around the locker room about which team I bat for. Then again, maybe it'll get the jokes about my shitty interview to stop.

Just for the hell of it, I say, "He is a good looking dude, right?"

"I knew it!" Tiger yells in victory, like he's unmasked a huge secret about me.

He's going to be awfully disappointed if he ever finds out my sex life actually includes a woman.

CHAPTER NINETEEN

PRESTYN

"I did it."

Bayleigh singsongs before coming to a screeching halt in front of my desk, two iced coffees in hand. She gives one to me with a huge smile on her face.

"A coffee and not an Alani Nu?"

"I didn't have time to leave the property so you get what you get. You really need to convince one of the food and drink vendors to start carrying them."

"I'm working on it. And thank you. Also, you did what?"

She plops down in a spare chair and leans closer to me. "They've been doing some interviewing for the Director of Catering position but from what I hear, they haven't found anyone they really like."

This isn't news. I've heard it too.

"I finally called HR and asked if it was too late to submit my name for consideration," Bayleigh explains. "She sounded really pleased to hear from me and told me to send them an updated resumé as soon as possible. I sent it over ten minutes ago and already got the confirmation."

Bayleigh does a little happy dance in her chair, which makes me smile.

"I'm so excited for you, but, Bay, why didn't you apply before?"

Her smile drops minutely. "I don't know. I guess I kept thinking about how much experience the last director had and it freaked me out. I have the degree and all, but she was just light years ahead of me on experience."

"Yeah," I say with a tilt of my head. "Because she had been here for over ten years. You've only been here for what, five?"

"Four."

"Exactly. I don't know for a fact, but I'm pretty sure she'd been here four or five years when she took over the position. You probably have the same amount of experience she had when she was promoted."

Bayleigh's nose crinkles. "You think that's enough, though?"

"Well, let me see." I lean back in my chair, pretending to settle in. "You already know the ins and outs of the entire property. You live here which means no relocation expenses. You've taken on a leadership role with the rest of the staff in the department, regardless of Aaron's efforts." We both grimace at the mention of his name. "Yeah. I'd say you're a really solid candidate and your experience is definitely enough. Now it makes so much more sense why that position is still open. They can't find someone who brings as much to the table as you do. I honestly thought you'd applied a long time ago."

She takes a drink of her coffee before answering. "I really did consider it. I just psyched myself out. And then when Aaron had you running the events, I guess part of me assumed they were just going to combine departments forever."

I gasp. "Don't even put that into the universe. You know I love working with you, but if I never have to participate in running an event again, it'll be too soon."

"And if I never have to work with Aaron again, it'll be too soon."

Ugh. She just reminded me that she may be off the hook with him soon, but I'm never going to be free of his shit.

"Can you imagine," Bayleigh continues, a look of mischief crossing her face. "If I was his equal in title?" We both laugh at how fun it would be to see the look on his face when my best work friend became the same level of management as he is. "Oh man. I have to figure out how to take a picture of him when the announcement is made. *If* I get the job, of course. The only thing funnier will be when you become his equal. No! His boss!"

"You know that's not going to happen."

"But why?" she whines and then holds up her hand. "Don't tell me. I already know. Because you won't go to your brother and tell him the truth."

"You know I can't do that, Bayleigh."

"I know you say you can't. But I think it's a cop out."

I choke on the drink I just sipped, coffee dribbling down my chin. "A cop out?" Bayleigh hands me a napkin so I can wipe off my face and now my pants. "The men in my family have known Aaron basically my whole life. It doesn't matter what I say has been happening. He's part of their good-ole-boys club. They'll always believe him over me."

"Maybe. But you really think they'll believe him over all of us?"

"What do you mean?" The stain on my pants smudges as I scrub. Dammit. I wonder if I have some spare pants in the suite.

"If you told Gavin the truth, you really don't think he'd ask around, find out what other people have to say? We've all seen Aaron pass his work to you. Everyone knows he plays online games most of the day. And I'm sure there are a few owners of the businesses that no longer have shops here who have a thing or two to say about not being given timely information about rent increases."

"They all fill out a survey when they leave about that kind of thing," I grumble. "Doesn't mean anyone important looks at them."

"Yeah, because Aaron is the one who processes those surveys. You think he's sending complaints about himself higher up the chain?"

She has a point. Maybe I am just looking for excuses not to have that conversation with my brother. Maybe it's less about being a woman and more about me being afraid of rejection. Not that I want to admit it to Bayleigh. But it's probably something I need to think about a little deeper.

"Okay fine. You have a point. I just..." I shake my head, my thoughts all jumbled. "It's going to be a huge fight and I'm not sure how to even begin."

"Oh that's easy. You get yourself a full body massage before you talk to Gavin." She sips her drink and gives me a cryptic look that I think I'm supposed to understand, but I don't. When she realizes how confused I am, she rolls her eyes. "From your boy toy?"

I throw my hand over my mouth as I gasp. "How do you know about that?" I whisper-yell. "Does everyone know about that?"

There's no way I can talk to my brother now if he knows I'm having a secret rendezvous with Nick. I can't even imagine how the conversation would go. Would he take me seriously if he knows I'm having sex on hotel property? Granted, it's in the family suite, which is basically like a second home, but technically it's sort of at work, kind of. Things just got more complicated.

"Relax." Just because Bayleigh says the word doesn't mean it's going to happen. "No one knows except me. You told me about the night of the gala, remember? Besides, I don't have to be a genius to see that you sometimes come to work a lot more relaxed than you used to. And never when the Glaze is on a road trip."

"You've been paying attention to their away games so you know when I have sex?" I press my hand against my breastbone in horror.

If she notices my reaction, she ignores it. "I had a theory and I was curious if I was right."

"That's a little weird, Bayleigh."

"Oh I don't disagree. But you weren't telling me anything and I wanted to know. So spill—is this love or dating or just sex." She puts her elbow on my desk and rests her chin on top of her hand, batting her eyelashes at me. "I need to know all the things."

"You need to know none of the things."

I turn back to my computer, avoiding her gaze. Not just because I don't want to share any of the details, but because I don't even know the answer to her question. What are Nick and I doing?

Sure, it started as sex. Really good sex. But now, I feel like there's something more happening. Maybe it's just friendship. That could explain it. We're friends with benefits.

But is it just friendship? I think about Nick all the time. Seeing poetry books remind me of him. Every time I eat green chili enchiladas, I think of him. I even caught myself watching a Florida Glaze game on television the other day just so I could see him, and I don't watch sports. At least not on TV. In person is much more exciting, but it's still rare when I go.

When I'm with him, I just feel this connection. We can talk about deep topics, and very surface level stuff. We can be supportive of each other's struggles, and we can laugh about dumb memes on the internet. We just... click.

Honestly, I like him so much more than I should, so much more than I told myself I would when this all started, and it scares the crap out of me. This was supposed to be no-strings-attached. But somehow, I've added strings. Strings that I fear are attached to my heart.

Bayleigh sighs and I realize I've been silently staring at my monitor for way too long.

"Fine," she huffs. "You can keep your cards close to your chest. But the second this turns into something more than just getting laid, I wanna know, okay? The only thing I love more than a really hot sex story is a really romantic love story. And I have a good feeling you're going to have one."

I snort a laugh, reminding myself for the umpteenth time that that's not what this thing with Nick is about. It would serve me well to remember that. But Bayleigh is my best work friend, so I can give her that.

"Fine. If it turns into something—"

She squeals and I have to grab her forearm to keep her from jumping up in excitement.

"—which I'm not saying it will, but if it does, you'll be the first to know."

"That's all I ask."

"Prestyn!" Aaron's voice booms across the room, interrupting us and worsening my already irritated mood.

"Yes, Aaron," I say sweetly, mostly because it's the tone that makes him the angriest.

"You were supposed to get me that report ten minutes ago." He doesn't bother actually leaving his office, just stands in the doorway yelling at me for everyone in this office and the surrounding offices to hear.

"I emailed it to you earlier this morning."

Unsurprisingly, Aaron scoffs. "You know I don't like emails. I need hard copies, Prestyn. Every time."

Bayleigh rolls her eyes for both of us, since I'm trying to not be obvious about how annoying it is that the man can't print his own damn copies of whatever he needs, if he needs them. I'm almost positive most of the paper reports I give him end up in the shredder without ever being read.

"And what are you doing here?" Bayleigh's back stiffens, her eyes wide. "Don't you have a job to do in a different office?"

We both know he's speaking to Bayleigh, but the fact that he can't bother to even use her name further cements what a dick he is.

"I was just dropping off coffee." Bayleigh stands and grabs her almost empty plastic cup. "See you later," she whispers to me before scurrying out of the room.

I click on the email Aaron is asking about and open the report. Even with my concentration elsewhere, I can feel his eyes still boring into me. I glance around myself a few times before facing him head on.

"What?"

"Work time is for work. Not for gossiping with friends. Understand?"

I bite my tongue, wanting so badly to pop off about how work time is also not online gaming time. Instead, I shift my eyes back to my screen and press "print" without saying a word.

It takes longer than it should to print the entire report, because I have to refill the printer with paper when it runs out. It's a huge waste of my time when I could be checking in with all our businesses, but I finally have the whole thing in hand, ready to be delivered as demanded.

As I approach Aaron's office, his phone rings so I stop short of the doorway. Should I stand here and eavesdrop? No. But I also know if I walk in right now, he'll be pissed that I interrupted him. Might as well avoid one fight today. And it's a good thing I do, or I would have missed hearing just how far he'll go to keep his reputation as a douchebag.

"Bayleigh? Who's Bayleigh?" he asks, pausing for what I assume is the answer from whoever is on the other end of the line. "Is she the one that works in catering?" Another pause before he scoffs. "Are you kidding me? I just caught her in my office, not working, but sitting around gossiping during work hours."

My jaw drops open. While he's not wrong, Bayleigh is one of the hardest working and most responsible employees with have. She's damn good at her job.

"I don't know who you're talking to about her," Aaron continues. "But she's absolutely not a team player. If I were you, I'd toss that application in the trash right now and look elsewhere. She's barely competent at her current job. No way she can manage that whole department. Have you looked at my buddy, Kendrick yet? I told him to drop my name when he applied..."

Rage coursing through my veins, I don't wait around to hear the rest of the conversation. That asshole doesn't even know what Bayleigh does. He's never asked. And now he's trying to ruin her chances of getting a promotion to improve the chances for his friend? Because we need another person like him working at this hotel?

I storm out of the office, deciding I'd rather touch base with all our businesses today than wait one more second to give him a report he won't even look at.

Maybe Bayleigh's right. Maybe I need to get off my ass and talk to Gavin sooner rather than later. Even if I can't help my friend get a much deserved interview for the director position, maybe I can put a bug in my brother's ear about what's really going on.

If Aaron isn't dealt with soon, it isn't just mine and Bayleigh's reputations on the line. It's the respectability of the entire Caine Resort and Conference Center.

CHAPTER TWENTY

NICK

"Ow! Fuck!" Tiger calls out eliciting a "shhhhh" from Tucker.

"The kids are sleeping," Tucker chides. "Keep your voice down."

"I'd keep my voice down if you didn't run over my fucking toe," Tiger whispers, sounding way less threatening with his voice so quiet.

"Don't be a baby," Tucker banters back. "I didn't do it on purpose."

"If you would move the fucking poker table to the theater room before we got here, you wouldn't have done it at all."

"I'm not pulling the table out before we play on our home ice. It's bad luck."

Tiger doesn't respond to that. We can argue all day long about why it would be smarter to set up for poker night before we get here, but once superstitions are tossed around, the argument dies quickly with this bunch.

"Fine," Tiger finally says like a sullen child. "But you can at least start storing the table in the theater room so we don't have to sneak around like burglars. There's a closet in there, right?"

Tucker considers as we continue to roll the world's heaviest table down the hall. "I'll have to move some things around, but I'm not doing it until after the playoffs. I'm not messing with fate."

That seems to be an agreeable compromise for Tiger. He nods once and doesn't complain again. At least not until we're all in the theater room with the door closed. Then he points his toes into the floor and rolls his foot on the ground, checking to see how much damage is actually done.

"Shit man, that really hurt."

"As long as you can put on your skates tomorrow, you'll get over it." Tucker flips the legs of the table open and several of us heave it into the upright position, making sure everything is locked into place before dragging the chairs around to their spots.

"Where're the snacks?" Maks predictably asks. He brought his own bag of food, but that doesn't mean he won't eat Tucker's while we're here, too.

"Hurry up and get what you need, Ivanov," Patrick demands as he pulls out the cards and begins shuffling. "I've got a fucking divorce to pay for and now she's going after alimony, even though we have a prenup. I need to win some cold hard cash tonight."

Becker points at him. "And that right there is why I have no problem not dating."

Patrick gives him a pointed look as he bridges the cards. "Not dating or not getting laid? Because from what I hear, you're not doing either."

Becker tosses a chip at his head, which he easily dodges.

"You know who *is* getting laid," Tiger singsongs. I shake my head, knowing what's coming. What is their obsession with my sex life? First Becker and now Tiger. It's like they can't bother with finding a woman for themselves so they pay way too much attention to what I'm up to.

"Besides me?" Maks tosses a bag of chips on the table and puts down a large bottle of pomegranate juice.

Pomegranate juice.

Because of course I can't go for one night without thinking of Prestyn and all the things I wish I could be doing to her body right now. It's been a week since our schedules have lined up and I miss her.

Her. Not her body. Just her.

It's part of the reason why I agreed to poker night tonight. Not just because it's a superstitious tradition when we win, but I was hoping having some space would help me feel more detached from whatever is going on in my brain. I can feel myself getting emotionally attached to her and feelings were never supposed to be on the table.

Unlike more of Maks' snacks.

"We all know you have no boundaries, Maksim. Not with women and not with food. But do you ever stop eating?" Tucker asks him, as we wades through packages of cookies, mini donuts, more chips, that have shown up where our money pot is supposed to go. I think the answer is sitting right on top of this table.

No. Maksim Ivanov will likely die with a donut in his hand, a container of French fries sitting next to him, and probably a woman on his lap. It's inevitable.

Once we're settled, cards are dealt and the game begins. Fortunately, thoughts of my sex life are long forgotten.

For the most part, things are quiet, everyone concentrating on their hand. Tiger takes the first two rounds forcing a heated debate about whether or not he's allowed to sit in the spot he designated his "lucky seat" anymore.

After making him trade places with Patrick, we begin again, those superstitions assuaged for everyone except Tiger. Not that he has anything to worry about. The majority of us fold pretty quickly, leaving just him and the Captain standing.

Patrick rubs his bottom lip with his finger, his tell that he's got a decent hand. The question is, what does decent mean this round?

He glances up, looking around at all of us, a decision made. Picking up several blue chips, he tosses them in the pot. "Call."

Tucker sits back and blows out a breath, clasping his hands on top of his head. "That's a big pot, man."

Patrick locks eyes with Tiger who looks completely unruffled.

"Let's see what you've got, Captain," I say, my heart racing as I anticipate what's about to happen.

Slowly, Patrick lowers his cards to the table. "Full house. Aces over sixes."

Tiger's shoulder's drop amid the ruckus caused by the others.

"That's gonna be hard to beat," Becker says unnecessarily. "Whatchu got, Tiger?"

Tiger sighs deeply and tosses his cards on the table. "Just four of a kind."

The room erupts as Tiger tosses his head back and laughs maniacally at his win. I just shake my head, wondering why we still play with this guy.

"There is no way." Becker picks up Tiger's cards and inspects them. "He's got to be counting cards."

"Nah," Tucker begins pushing chips Tiger's direction. "His math skills aren't good enough to count cards."

Wrapping his arms around the pile, Tiger pulls his winnings towards him. "Before I decided to go pro, I considered trying my hand in Vegas."

"And why didn't you?" Tucker asks.

"I decided to do both. When I get done with hockey, I'm off to Vegas to be a card shark. It'll be my second career."

Patrick shakes his head in disgust. "Why do we let this guy play with us? We need fresh blood in here."

"You know who we should invite?" Tiger asks with a wink my direction. I roll my eyes, knowing exactly where this is going. "We should invited Phoooeeeeeeniiiiiiix," he sing songs.

Becker makes a face. "Why'd you say his name like that?"

"Because someone has a crush on the new guy." Tiger waggles his eyebrows while staring directly at me.

Very quickly, there are five sets of eyes looking my direction.

"What?" I ask, feigning innocence.

"You have a crush on Phoenix?" I watch Becker's face as he connects dots that don't actually go together. "Is he the person you're fucking? No wonder you didn't want to say anything in the locker room."

"What's wrong with me?" Maks throws his hands up in the air. "I'm a good looking man. Why don't you have a crush on me?"

"Y'all are a bunch of idiots." I push away from the table and head to the corner of the room to grab another beer and see if Tucker has any snacks left now that Maks has started eating.

Behind me I hear Maks arguing about his desirability. "I'm not saying I care who he fucks. I just wanna know why I wasn't his first choice. He knows I tan my butthole so I'm very attractive back there."

I try to ignore the conversation, but it's impossible. It's just too entertaining hearing all the wild theories when I haven't even said a word.

Sorting through the leftovers, I grab a small bag of chips and toss a chocolate chip cookie in my mouth.

"Did you really just come out of the closet?" Tucker approaches and reaches in the fridge for another beer. "I feel like I'm missing something."

"You're not missing anything." I gesture to the fridge for him to grab me a drink. "They keep coming up with these wild conclusions but never wait for me to confirm or deny, so I just wait to see what they come up with."

Tucker holds the fridge open and calls out my choices. "I've got Stella Artois, but there's also an ale. Looks like its pomegranate-flavored."

Of course it is. Just Tucker saying the word has Prestyn popping in my mind. My memories are thrown right back into what she tastes like, what she looks like when she comes, how the corners over her eyes crinkle when she laughs, the heat of her body when we fall asleep after an amazing orgasm.

"Nick?"

"Huh?" I realize I've been daydreaming.

"Beer or ale?"

"Ale, please."

He hands it to me and I pop the top off to take a drink.

"So you're fucking with them just because, huh?"

"Yeah. Seemed like a fun thing to do at the time."

"From the look on your face, they're not far off though, right? There's someone."

I glance up at Tucker and consider my next words. I don't want to share too much, but someone on this team should probably know at least part of the truth so if the rumors kick up a notch, they can help squash them.

"Yeah, there's someone," I admit. What, exactly, I'm admitting to, though, well, I haven't worked that out quite yet.

Tucker nods his head and takes another sip of his beer. "But it's not Phoenix?"

I snicker. "Hell no, it's not Phoenix."

"Good," Tucker says and blows out a breath. "We're too close to the playoffs to start having more issues with teammates."

"I agree. That's part of why I'm telling you the truth. I wouldn't want to make him uncomfortable, or whatever. He doesn't know these idiots that well yet."

Tucker shakes his head slightly. "Forget Phoenix. Maks is already losing his shit about not being your first choice. We're never going to hear the end of it."

A chuckle rolls out of me because he's right. "That man is probably going to swing his dick around even more than normal until someone finally tells him how pretty he is."

"Exactly. I need you to stick to women to calm his hairy ass down. Maybe you need to set them straight."

My phone buzzes in my pocket and I pull it out. It's the woman we're talking about without anyone actually knowing we're talking about her.

Prestyn: Are you home from your game yet? I'm bored out of my mind.

I fight the smile that wants to cross my face.

Me: At poker night and getting my ass kicked. Want some company?

Prestyn: Only if you don't mind coming to my place. I'm already in my jammies.

I start to type out a response but Tucker interrupts me.

"That's her, huh?"

I glance up, but don't say a word. Tucker holds his hands up in surrender.

"Alright, alright. I get it. You don't want to say anything until you've sorted out how you feel."

It's a little unsettling that he hit the nail on the head so quickly. "How did you come to that conclusion?"

He uses his finger to mimic circling my face. "Because I'm pretty sure I had that same expression when Lacy and I started hanging out. Not quite sure what was going on, not quite sure if she was feeling as deeply as I was, not really wanting to share with a bunch of guys who've been knocked in the head too many times until I knew for myself."

That... sounds pretty accurate.

"For a meathead, you're pretty astute."

He shrugs. "Feelings and trust. Those are the two basic dating problems we all have no matter what our relationships look like." He steps forward and claps me on the shoulder. "Don't worry about us. Go hang out with your girl. It's gotta be more fun than losing all your money to Tiger again."

"You sure you don't mind? It's tradition and all."

"If we weren't in my house right now, I'd be leaving, too. Sliding in bed with Lacy sounds way better than listening to

Patrick bitch about money and Maks list every reason we should all be in love with him and his body."

"Thanks, man."

He nods as he walks past me. "Okay motherfuckers," he calls out to the table. "Who's dealing? I'm ready to take back my money."

I toss the ale I just opened in the trash, feeling bad it's going to waste, but not bad enough to take it with me while I drive. Quickly, I text Prestyn.

Me: Shoot me the address. I'm on my way.

CHAPTER TWENTY-ONE

PRESTYN

Sinking down onto the length of him, my hands are on his naked chest helping me balance. We groan simultaneously at the contact, our bodies desperate for release.

It's been a week since the last time Nick and I were together and I missed him more than I should. It's not just the orgasms he can give me, although I'd be lying if I said that wasn't a perk, but its more than that. I missed *him*.

In a very short amount of time I've come not just to like Nick, but to crave him. Just being near him relaxes me. It's as if I've found a partner who likes being with me as much as I do him. Someone who wants me to unload my burdens on him. Someone who loves snuggling with me more than he loves just fucking me. Someone who is compatible with me in a way no one else has ever been.

I stop my thoughts right there. I know myself and if I don't squash the emotions before they bubble to the surface, I'm likely to cry from the overwhelming feelings and no man wants to see tears after hot sex. It's the fastest way to make someone run for the hills.

Focusing on the feel of him inside me, I begin to move.

"That's it, baby," Nick breathes. His big hands grab my hips and begin moving me up and down while I focus on going back and forth. The combination of directions has my eyes rolling in the back of my head, the feeling giving me so much pleasure and promising to end with an explosion like nothing I've felt before.

Nick leans forward, his teeth grasping one of my nipples as my breasts sway into his face. The unexpected prick of pain makes me gasp in delight.

"Turn around," Nick whispers.

My eyes flutter open, the words not making sense to my already mushy brain.

"What?"

"Turn around. Reverse cowgirl," he explains. "I wanna be able to see your pretty pussy."

Well when he says it like that...

I reluctantly push up further on my knees, hissing as he slides out of me. Quickly, I turn to straddle him again as he holds the condom down, wasting no time getting him situated back where I want him.

The change of direction feels different, but not in a bad way. I lean forward, rolling my hips and allowing my clit to rub gently against his balls.

"Fuck, that's a beautiful sight," he says behind me.

I can't help but smile. Then I toss my hair back and arch a little more, feeling sexy and powerful.

"Lean forward just a little more."

I do and we both gasp as his cock reaches the right spot inside me. It spurs me on, riding him faster and faster, Nick encouraging me with his words and pulling my hips hard against him.

Within seconds I explode around him, crying out with a loud, incoherent shout. When he pops upright and grabs my shoulders, slamming me down against him one more time, I know he's just as satisfied as me.

As I collapse forward, he falls back, causing his still erect cock to pull out of me with a "pop."

"Ah!" he yells and then groans. "Well crap. I was hoping to stay inside you for a while."

I chuckle into the blanket at his feet, my head still down around his calves. "Sorry. I couldn't hold myself up anymore. I wasn't expecting that position to do the trick so quickly."

"Me neither." He taps my leg so I can help get us disentangled. Like normal, he leaves me face down on the bed while he goes to clean up.

I stay put, letting my mind completely empty as I come down from my high.

"I like your place," he calls from my adjoining bathroom.

I know what he's admiring. The soaker tub was the selling point for me. It's big enough for two people, but I've never tried it with more than just me before. I feel my eyebrows raise as an idea hits me.

Climbing out of bed, my legs still a little wobbly, I make my way into the bathroom with him.

He chuckles at my inability to walk a straight line when he catches a glimpse of me coming in the mirror.

"Why'd you get up? I was just about to come back and wrap us in the blankets like a burrito."

I wrap my arms around his waist and kiss the back of his rock hard shoulders, loving his warmth on my chest.

"I was thinking maybe we could try out my tub. Take a bubble bath. Maybe give you a shoulder massage since you had a game tonight?"

He swivels and rests his arms on my shoulders as he kisses me. "Mmm," he mumbles against my lips. "That sounds really nice, actually."

"Good." I slap him on the ass and pull away. "Let me get the water going."

Nick leans against the counter, legs and arms crossed while I run the water and find the right kind of bubble bath for maximum coverage. As he watches me, he tells me about the hockey game tonight. About how many shots he blocked and how well the first line is doing in spite of the last couple of losses. I don't understand a lot of what he tells me, but I like that he's so comfortable. That he can just hang out naked in my bathroom and tell me about his day. It's like our relationship is progressing. But...

Is that what I want?

It is. I know it is. I like Nick so much. I could see myself falling for him. Hell, I probably already have. I just don't know how he feels. Is he just comfortable with me because no one knows we're together? Would it ruin things if other people found out?

I don't know the answer, but I do know we need to talk about it at some point. This tip-toeing around my feelings like a teenager isn't who I am. Or maybe it's just not who I want to be. Either way, we're heading for a hard conversation sometime in the near future. I just need the opportunity to address it.

Reaching my hand into the water, I swirl it around. Satisfied with the temperature, I climb in the tub. "You coming?"

Nick licks his lips but makes no effort to move. "You're really gorgeous, you know that?"

His compliment catches me off guard and I find myself biting my bottom lip as I peruse his body with my eyes. "You're not so bad yourself."

I hold out my hand, and he takes it, stepping into the tub in front of me so we can sit with his back to my front.

As we get situated, he leans his head back on my shoulder, eyes closed. From this angle, I can't reach his shoulders as promised, so I take the opportunity to scoop bubbles in my hand and slowly wash his arms, his pecs, his clavicles.

"Mmmm," he groans. "That feels really good."

"I figured your muscles could use some relaxing. You've

exerted a lot of energy today." I think for a second before changing my statement. "Maybe it was yesterday at this point."

He chuckles lightly and I feel the movement in my chest, our bodies so tight together it's almost impossible to find space between us.

"I'm sorry I'm keeping you up. I know you work early in the morning."

I shrug because I really don't mind. Sleep isn't nearly as relaxing as sitting in a hot bubble bath with the feel of his weight on me. "I'll take a nap after work tomorrow. Do you have to be at the stadium early?"

"Arena."

"What?"

He smiles and laces our fingers together, wrapping my arms around him. "Hockey fans would crucify you for that. You can either call it a rink or an arena but never, ever call it a stadium."

"Oh, well. Lesson learned," I say with amusement.

"Hey, would you ever want to come to a game?" he suddenly blurts out.

Nick shifts his body so he's trying to look up at me. The water is sloshing around enough that it comes close to spilling over the edge.

"We have a box for friends and family and I can get you a ticket or two. You could bring Bayleigh and have some fun. I hear they have great food, much better than the snacks at the vendors. Or so I've heard. I've never actually eaten there, but my sister swears by it."

He's rambling like he's nervous. I find it endearing and it makes me wonder if he's struggling with developing feelings like I am. No man babbles about food he's never eaten if he isn't feeling some sort of jitters, right?

"Anyway, if you'd like to go, just tell me when and I'll make sure you have tickets. No pressure or anything."

"I'd like that." I adjust my legs which are wrapped around his waist, his big hand rubbing up and down my calf. I'm sure he can feel the goose bumps from the combination of his touch and the heat of the water moving around my legs as he moves. "I'd like it a lot."

"Really?"

It's endearing how surprised he sounds that I would want to see what he does in action.

"When is your next home game?"

"Tomorrow ni—er, I guess tonight."

I laugh and pull my fingers from his hand, threading my arms under his so I can rub my hands down his chest.

"I don't think I can go tonight. I'm going to be too tired. But I can probably go to the next one."

"Yeah?"

He sounds so hopeful, it makes my heart warm, along with other parts of my body. I can't help but begin peppering kisses across his shoulder and around his back.

"Yeah. It's about time we met up at your job instead of mine," I whisper huskily against his skin. "Do you know how sexy it is knowing you're down there on the ice?"

He moans and I continue my ministrations, slowly lowering my hands as I nip at his skin.

"Knowing I've kissed every part of this big body."

He inhales sharply and I feel his cock bump up against my hand as I play with the hair leading to my favorite muscle.

"Knowing I've licked this treasure trail."

His legs widen in anticipation of where my hand is going.

"Knowing I've sucked this giant cock."

He gasps and exhales when I grab his girth with one hand, my other arm stretching as far as I can to roll his balls gently in the other. I begin stroking the length of him just the way he likes it, listening as his breath hitches, feeling as his body relaxes further into mine.

Nick reaches up and grabs my head, turning again, this time to kiss me. His tongue plunges in my mouth sloppily from the angle as I stroke and tug on him. He grabs my hand and helps guide me at that pace he wants. Suddenly, his kiss stops but his mouth doesn't move away as he cries out against my lips, his orgasm coming fast and deep.

As his body goes limp, I pepper more kisses along his shoulder.

"Oh no," he finally jokes, his breath coming in short gasps. "I dirtied up our bath water."

I giggle and squeeze him with my legs. "Whatever shall we do to get clean?"

He rests for a second before answering. "I guess we'll have to take a shower now."

So we do. And we dirty up that shower wall, too.

The trees are afraid to put forth buds,
    And there is timidity in the grass
    The plots lie gray where gouged by spuds,
    And whether next week will pass
    Free of sly sour winds is the fret of each bush
    Of barberry waiting to bloom...

My mind begins to wander, not even Thomas Hardy was capable of holding my attention. That's not a good sign before a game.

We all have our pre-game routines. Tucker listens to music. Patrick does a lot of hamstring stretches. Tiger wraps and rewraps his stick obsessively. Maks... well, he grooms the scruff on his face to perfection. Me? I read poetry.

Except tonight I can't stay focused. I can't keep my head in this book. That worries me for this game. I should be able to stay on task, to let the words soothe my mind. It's not working.

"Alright men, listen up."

Thankfully Coach interrupts us for his regular pep talk. Maybe I can focus on him since poetry isn't doing the trick.

"Chicago is a tough team. You know that," he starts, reminding us in his own way not to get complacent. "We've watched films. We've done the drills. We've studied for this test. Our only goal now is to win this game and increase our chances securing of a playoff spot."

A murmur of agreement rumbles through the locker room.

"Anything they can do, we can do better. But don't get lazy out there. Do not get complacent. Protect your goalie and obliterate theirs. You feel me?"

"We feel you," we respond, a little more lackluster than I'd hope, but I'm partly to blame for that.

"Oh hell no! Do you FEEL me?" Coach roars.

"WE FEEL YOU!"

The volume increases the next few times Coach prods us to respond and even my mind seems to be getting back to where it should be.

We strut out of the locker room and through the tunnel, amid flashes from cameras and cheers from the Glaze staff. The noise of the arena gets louder the closer we get to the ice. As the first of my teammates makes his way to the bench, the crowd begins to roar their approval as the music our PR team picked for our entrance pumps through the speakers.

I try to put all of that out of my mind as I take my skate guards off and toss them to the side, stepping out into the rink.

I do my normal three laps around the ice before taking my spot next to the net to stretch.

"*Don't look up, don't look up,*" I think to myself as I stretch and lunge, focusing on my yoga breathing and pushing deep into my muscles, making sure there are no areas of tightness in my body.

And then I look up.

I can't see into the friends and family box from here, but that doesn't change the fact that I know who is inside it.

Prestyn texted to confirm her ticket information earlier today and double check the parking situation. She may be a very low-key celebrity who isn't recognized often on the street, but I wasn't taking my chances with her tonight. She gets to park VIP. Once I felt comfortable that it was all taken care of, the nerves set in.

I don't know why I'm anxious. I've been a goalie since I was ten years old. Hell, I beat out thousands of other hopefuls to be drafted and beat out the last few candidates for the opportunity to protect the Florida Glaze net. I'm good at what I do. Excellent, if you're looking at statistics. So why am I nervous about playing in front of her?

I begin my backside pushes, making sure my IT bands are nice and loose as I try to ignore the reality of my tension. I know why I'm nervous. It's because I want to impress Prestyn. Like some Neanderthal caveman, I want her to see how good I am so I can beat on my chest and claim her as mine.

Just knowing I can't stop how I feel about her frustrates me to no end. I don't want to be in an official relationship. That means going public. Once it does, the door is open for other people to ask questions or comment about my relationship. To meddle and cause problems. Hell, it's probably the first thing the reporters will ask and I just stopped feeling nauseous before post-game interviews a few days ago. I'd rather not have that feeling back.

Besides, I like things how they are between Prestyn and I. Low-key, no drama, no interference from anyone outside our little bubble. If things could stay the way they are permanently, I'd be okay with that. I could fall in love with her in secret knowing we'd eventually tell everyone else. It would give us time to get used to the idea so there's no discomfort when the chiding begins, and there is *always* chiding.

"You planning on doing those pushes forever or you gonna move out in front of that net before warm ups are over?" Tucker skates a circle around me as he berates me.

"What are you talking about?" I pretend to not be scatter-brained as I transition into some side moves, getting the feel of my edge work.

"Your head isn't here," he says in response. "What's the matter with you tonight?"

As much as I will them to stay straight ahead, my eyes glance up to the box again.

Tucker doesn't miss it and whips his head around to see where I'm looking. When he turns back, his eyebrows are practically in his helmet. "She here?"

My lack of response is all the answer he needs.

Moving closer to me, he gets his helmet right up next to mine. "You can't impress her if you're playing like shit."

"I'm not trying to impress her," I lie unsuccessfully.

He doesn't fall for it. "So you're just losing your edge? We need to put in a back up?"

"No."

"Then focus on what is in front of you. Fuck who is in that box. She may not even be paying attention. Hell, she may not even be here yet. You don't know. Do your job and play your game."

I nod and he smacks me on the helmet. "Glad we got that straight. Now get your ass in front of the net so we can finish warming up."

I spend the next several minutes blocking pucks as they fly my direction. Some are faster than others but still aren't nearly as quick as they will be when it's the other team launching zingers at my head.

Most of the shots I stop but I'm impressed when I get deked by Becker. If he can do the same on the other side of the ice, we'll be in a good position to take on Chicago in spite of my wandering thoughts.

Feeling confident that my head is finally back in the game, I successfully keep my eyes where they should be for the rest of the warm up, not looking back when we head to the locker for last minute instructions before the game begins.

CHAPTER TWENTY-THREE

PRESTYN

I'm late. *So late.*

Maybe not so late. But late enough to know the game started a few minutes ago and I missed it. I'm so mad at myself, but I'm almost there. I'm power walking through the stadium... er, *arena* to get to the friends and family box.

Bayleigh wasn't able to come so I'm alone tonight, which might be a good thing. She doesn't need to see how nervous I am. She'd be on my ass about it all night if she knew the butterflies in my stomach refused to settle down.

It's not like I have anything to really be anxious about. I'm going to a local hockey game. Big whoop-de-do. I'm not even going to see Nick up close. No one will even know who invited me. Hell, I could tell them my dad asked for a favor because I was curious to see some of our clients in action.

That's how I know my nerves are shot—I'm making up answers to questions no one has asked before I even get to my destination. A destination I would have been to half an hour ago if I didn't get stuck obsessively putting beachy waves in my hair which caused me to get stuck in traffic after a fender bender between fans. I only know that part because the car windows were covered in Florida Glaze colors, just like the driver's face.

"Box One, Box One," I mumble as I follow the circular hallway into a more remote area. I know I must be getting close because the lingering crowd thins out. When I find a bouncer standing next to a door, I know I've made it.

I flash him the pass around my neck along with a smile of appreciation. He nods and opens the door for me so I can pass through.

"Whoa!

The concrete walls of the hallway gave me no indication of what to expect, but this is really nice.

The carpet is a pale grey with the Florida Glaze logo imbedded in the middle of the floor. The kitchen area has a huge buffet spread out and labeled with the name of the various foods and allergy warnings. Comfortable indoor seating and a large television dominate the room, for those who would rather stay in the warmth inside instead of braving the coolness in the arena. A dozen people or so mill about, drinks in their hands as they watch the game. Or in the case of one group clumped together, ignore it completely.

There are a couple of tall tables with matching stools facing the ice so you can eat without trying to balance food on your lap. And the chairs outside the box overlooking the arena aren't the hard plastic ones regular fans sit in. These have thick cushions and actually rock back. They seem to come in handy for a mom who is rocking the child I assume to be hers while they watch the game.

Wait... do I know that mom?

There are a couple empty seats next to her so I approach and sit down.

The woman looks up at me and smiles softly, then looks back at the game before doing a double take.

"Hi. Um, we've met, haven't we?"

I'm glad she takes the initiative. I still feel like an outsider even though I clearly have a pass saying I'm right where I'm supposed to be.

"We did. I'm Prestyn. I'm pretty sure we met at the Glaze gala a couple months ago at the Caine Resort."

She looks around and I can see she's searching her memories for details of that night, so I help her out.

"Tucker lost a trip to Tahoe when he was outbid by a dollar."

She laughs out loud, startling her sleeping daughter. Shushing her gently, the child settles in again.

"That's right, I do remember. I'm Lacy."

"Hi, Lacy. It's nice to see you again. Is Tucker doing okay? Still a sore loser?"

Lacy laughs, the sound deep and throaty, likely remembering Tucker's sad, puppy dog eyes when he realized he was outsmarted by the last person he expected.

"I wouldn't say he's over it. He's a big baby when he wants to be and that man has a long memory when it comes to Maksim's shenanigans, but he's fine."

"Well good. I have to say, that whole scenario was one of the highlights of that night for me."

The biggest highlight being the explosive orgasm I'd had at the hands and mouth of Tucker's teammate a few hours later, but I leave that part out.

Instead, I glance at the beautiful girl in her arms, her blond ringlets partially covering her face as she breathes deep. "Who is this little one?"

Lacy looks down at her daughter lovingly. "This is Sutton, our daughter. She's usually much more active at games, but the daycare took them on a swimming field trip today at the Y so she didn't make it long."

"Aw. Swimming takes a lot out of you."

"I know. I should have left her at home but she was so hyper when it was time to leave I thought I'd chance it. Wrong decision.

I guess she was trying to keep herself awake. Lucky me, she knocked out in the car and I got to carry her from the parking lot to this chair."

I don't envy her. It was quite a hike without carrying an extra thirty-five pounds in my arms. But then I remember something.

"Wait, don't you guys have a second kid?"

"Kody." Lacy shakes her head. "He's not really ours. He's my best friend's son so he's like a bonus child. He was going to come tonight because these two kiddos love hockey more than just about anything, but unlike this one," Lacy gestures down to Sutton, "when Kody is tired, he doesn't even bother trying to stay awake. He crashed before we got to the car, so he and his mom stayed home."

I'm so confused. Their situation sounds really complicated. "So they live with you and Tucker?"

"They live in the pool house out back. Ellie helped me get on my feet when I was in a really bad spot, so now we're returning the favor." Lacy shrugs. "Not everyone gets it, but it works for us. Family is who you make it, ya know?"

I actually don't know. I don't know that I've ever truly trusted anyone enough to get that close. Not even my own brothers.

"It's nice that you guys are so close," I say, meaning my words even if I don't understand how they do it.

Lacy just nods and quickly she gets distracted, her eyes straying back to the game below us.

"Go Tucker, go," she cheers quietly.

The crowd on the other hand, isn't as quiet. One of our players—I assume it's Tucker from the way Lacy sits up straighter, holding Sutton tight to her—quickly makes his way down the ice, deflecting anyone who gets in his way. The closer he gets to the goal, the louder the crowd becomes.

Suddenly he pulls his stick back and hits the puck. It sails in the air so fast, my eyes can't follow where it goes. It's only when a red light goes off above the net and Tucker raises his stick in victory that I realize he just scored.

"That's the way, baby!" Lacy yells as the crowd continues to cheer. Sutton stirs momentarily but as soon as Lacy leans back in the chair, she falls back into her snooze.

We watch the game in comfortable silence for a while, me just trying to figure out what's going on. Obviously I know what the teams are trying to do, but the smaller details are a little harder to determine. Eventually though, I seem to be able to follow a little easier. Even if I can't consciously figure out what is supposed to happen, my brain still seems to find a pattern to it all.

"Is this your first Glaze game?" Lacy finally asks, breaking the silence.

"It is. I really should have come sooner. I'm surprised by how interesting it is."

"I always find sports to be more fun in person than on television." She tears her eyes away from the game to look at me, one eyebrow cocked. "I assume you came as Nick's guest?"

I shift uncomfortably, wishing she hadn't asked me that question. I don't know exactly how to answer it, even though I practiced all the potential options on my way here.

I try for nonchalance. "Yeah. He found out I haven't been to one before and said this was the best way to experience it. Well, except for being on the bench, of course."

"Of course." There's an awkward pause which I assume means she's trying to come up with a tactful way of asking the question I know is coming. "Does this mean you and Nick have stayed in touch since the gala?"

"We've run into each other a couple of times since then." More like rammed into each other for mutual pleasure. "Just a couple weeks after the gala, I saw several of the guys again at a meet-and-greet. Seems like the Glaze organization likes using our hotel for their events."

Lacy nods as if she's buying what I'm selling, but the smirk on her face gives her away.

Desperate to be out of this conversation, I gesture over my shoulder. "Do you know if they have water here?"

"Water, beer, basically any kind of liquor, pretty much whatever you want. I've even requested milk for the kids a couple of times and they've always come through. See that guy against the wall?"

I swivel to look where she's gesturing. "Shortish, baby face, wearing a uniform?" I ask.

"Yep. That's Andy. He's great. If there's something in particular you need, just ask him."

"Awesome, thanks." I push out of my chair, thankful I'm getting a reprieve from our conversation but realizing she's sort of stuck where she is for the duration. "Do you need me to bring you back anything since I'm up?"

Lacy sighs in relief. "I'd love a bottle of water. Whatever Andy has. Thank you."

"I'll be right back," I tell her and take the few steps back into the box. I don't realize how chilly it is in the regular seats until the warm air in here hits me. Shivering from the temperature change, I head straight to Andy.

His face lights up as I approach. "Welcome," he says kindly, his deep voice at odds with his height. "Is there anything I can get you?"

"I really need two bottles of water, please."

"Of course." He turns to open the fridge behind him, pulling out two large bottles with squirt tops. That's a nice surprise. They're so much easier to use when you're trying to balance a plate of nachos in your lap, assuming nachos are on the menu. For some reason, being here makes me want to eat all the junk food you'd see at a sporting event.

Handing the bottles to me, Andy gestures to the buffet in front of him. "Are you hungry, Miss...?"

"You can call me Prestyn."

"Prestyn." He gives a short nod. "On tonight's menu, we have sliders, with or without cheese, hot dogs with all or none of the fixings, and beef fajita nachos."

My mouth starts to water just hearing about my options.

"If you're in the mood for something lighter, we have popcorn of course, as well as various forms of candy or ice cream. Or a traditional serving of cotton candy."

"That all sounds amazing," I say truthfully. "I'm really in the mood for some of those nachos."

"Of course. If you'd like, you can have a seat wherever you feel most comfortable and I'll bring it to you."

"That's really nice. Thank you, Andy."

"You're very welcome."

I make a mental note to tip him well tonight, not just for his effort, but the friendly and down-to-earth way he's making it.

"I'm going to give Lacy her water and then I think I'll just sit at one of the high top tables while I eat."

Andy pulls a glass plate from a stack on the side—because there's no plastic anything in this deluxe suite—preparing to fill it with nacho goodness. "I'll find you shortly."

Lacy is still sitting right where I left her, eyes still glued to the game. I'm not sure if she's the only significant other here, but she's still sitting alone which makes me wonder about the relationship status of the rest of the team. I would expect there to be a lot of wives and girlfriends here. At least, that's how all my trashy reality shows make it look.

I wind my way around a couple of people standing in the middle of the room as they chat. They're dressed in suits, so I assume these must be friends of the owner or something. They smile at me in acknowledgement as I pass, but don't stop their conversation.

I'm barely around them when someone else in a suit steps in

front of me. Only this suit is wrinkled and ill-fitting and belongs to the last person I was hoping to see tonight.

You've got to be kidding me.

"What are you doing here?" Aaron sneers, holding a glass of what smells like bourbon. At least that's the odor wafting off his breath.

"I was invited."

He scoffs. "By who?"

Like I'm going to tell him anything more than the bare minimum.

"A friend." I shrug nonchalantly hoping my indifference will be enough to pacify him. Instead, it seems to make him more angry.

"Daddy's little princess thinks she's so popular because she gets invitations to things, does she? You know who gets invited to things, too? Me. I get invited because I worked my way up in this business. I wasn't given things just because of my last name."

"How much of that have you had to drink?" I gesture to his glass as he gulps down a liquor that probably should be sipped. That's not a good sign.

"That's none of your business," he seethes and then moves closer, shoving a finger in my face. "I'm your boss. Don't you dare ruin my evening."

Clearly he's three sheets to the wind, which isn't good news for any of us. I've only seen Aaron drunk once before, at a Christmas party my dad threw when I was still in high school. He was a mean drunk then, and it appears he's a mean drunk now. I need to stay away from him tonight.

"Tell you what, I will hang out in the arena seats so I don't interfere with all your networking." I'm placating Aaron which I would normally never do, but I'm not sure how to handle Smashed Aaron without escalating him. He's giving off a really volatile vibe. I don't like it. "I know you're a super fan of the Glaze and I don't want you to miss anything, so I'll just stay out of your way tonight."

His eyes narrow as he sways on his feet, and I'm not sure if he's assessing me or if his brain is trying to catch up.

Finally he seems to remember what we were talking about when he sways my direction. "You just see that you do."

Then he stumbles past me, body checking me as he goes by. It doesn't hurt, but it doesn't feel good either.

I shake my head at my bad luck. My first time at a professional hockey game, and I have to be hyperaware of who is around me. That's going to put a damper on things. Thankfully Lacy seems nice and I don't think she'll have an issue with me sitting with her for the rest of the game.

I hand her a water bottle and she thanks me with a smile.

"Did I miss anything exciting?" I ask as I open my own bottle and take a drink.

"Nothing too exciting. Nick has blocked a couple of close shots but our defensive line is doing a better job of keeping the puck away from him than they have in a few weeks."

I don't understand most of what she just said, but I pretend and nod anyway.

"Excuse me, Prestyn."

I look up to see Andy next to me holding a plate full of steaming, delicious smelling nachos. Too bad my appetite has disappeared.

But I did order them and I'd hate for Andy to have gone through all that work for nothing.

"Thank you, Andy." I take the plate from him but he doesn't move, a look of hesitation on his face. "Is there something else?"

Andy leans over to speak directly in my ear. "If you need assistance with that man who was speaking to you a few minutes ago, please don't hesitate to signal me and I'll call security immediately."

I suddenly understand why Andy is the one charged with servicing this box. Not only is he serving food, he's keeping a close eye on all of the important patrons. I only hope he's compensated well for how far over and above he goes.

I turn my head slightly so I can tactfully ease his mind. "His name is Aaron and while he is technically my boss, he's not someone you need to worry about. You'll likely never see him again after tonight. He has no power or influence outside of his own mind."

Andy smiles gratefully and I see his shoulders visibly relax. I hate that he has to be on guard for not just the clients in this room, but also for his own job because of people like Aaron. Or more like the people Aaron wishes he could be.

"Thank you, Ms. Caine."

Ah. So he did recognize me. No wonder this situation put him on edge.

I give him a quick nod and we go our separate ways—he, back to his spot where he can see all the interaction in the room at once, and me, to my nachos.

"Everything okay?" Lacy's brows are furrowed and I know she didn't miss the interaction that just took place, she's just unsure what it means.

"It's fine." I try to play it off by shoving a chip in my mouth and moaning at how good it is, but I'm not sure she's convinced.

Neither am I. The only thing I can think about while I force myself to eat is how the chips are becoming a lump in my stomach, and how pissed I am that Aaron just ruined what was supposed to be a really fun night.

CHAPTER TWENTY-FOUR

NICK

Another game. Another loss. Another shitty interview about how we failed.

"Nick, you were looking really good up until the end of the third period. Can you tell us what the difference was when Scortiva got that shot past you?"

I don't want to, but I don't have a choice except to give yet another reporter yet another bullshit answer.

"I got deked," I say with a shrug. "Our defensive line was right where they needed to be, and I was ready for him. But Scortiva is a fantastic forward, always has been, and I misinterpreted the direction he was going. That's all there is to it."

"If you knew you had misinterpreted, why didn't you adjust for the save?"

This guy; I want to roll my eyes at him. A local sports reporter, he always has dumb questions. I know he asks them to try and get the best sound bites, but usually they make us look like idiots.

"It happens so fast on that ice, things are over before you even have time to move. As soon as I started moving to the left, I knew Scortiva was going right, but he's so quick, there wasn't anything I could do at that point."

More questions are called out, and it's exhausting me. I'm tired of interviewing. I'm tired of losing. And mentally I'm just exhausted from forcing myself to keep my brain on the game instead of pining over the woman who was waiting for me in the box. I don't think it affected my playing tonight, at least not, it seems, that anyone could tell. Trust me, these reporters would be all over me if they thought a woman was interfering with my game. But I'm just ready to be done.

With a quick look and eyebrow cock at the PR rep, I'm given a small nod giving me permission to go.

"Anyway, thanks so much for coming out tonight, guys."

More questions are called out as I walk away, but I don't stop to address them. I'm in a shit mood and I just want to get out of here. Being with Prestyn will hopefully get me out of my funk. If nothing else, at least I'll be able to relax a bit. She always does that to me—makes me relax. Just being near her feels calming. Maybe it's because she doesn't expect anything from me except what I have to give.

That's part of the reason I asked Prestyn to wait for me in the hall next to the locker room after the game. I was hoping we could go get a bite to eat and just hang out. Even if she watches a movie while I read, it'll be exactly what I need.

"How'd it go?" Tucker is adjusting the tie he's probably going to rip off his neck as soon as the door of his fancy Porsche SUV is closed.

I begin the tedious process of sliding all my necessary items into my pants pocket. "They're vultures, like always."

Tucker lets out a hollow laugh as he smooths down his lapels. "They're just on us because we're in the middle of this losing streak. What the fuck is the matter with us?"

I raise my eyebrows at him because we both know the answer to that question.

Tucker shakes his head. "I hope their divorce is finalized soon. We need our leader back. I really think he's losing his C next year."

"I don't see how he won't," I say honestly, although I hate that it needs to happen. "He's not doing his job. Hasn't been for a long time. She got in his head and fucked him all up. The only reason he's still good on the ice is the rage he's working out."

Tucker nods in silent agreement and we put that topic of conversation aside as we head toward the door. Regardless of what our feelings are about Patrick, there's no disrespecting one of our teammates. Team problems stay inside the locker room. Always.

"The good news about losing is you don't have to worry about us invading your house tonight for poker night. Maybe you'll get some sleep." I hold the door open for him as we step out into the hall.

"Doubtful. I'm too amped up. We'll see how tired Lacy is. If I'm lucky, I'll be able to work out some of the extra energy." He waggles his eyebrows suggestively, making me roll my eyes. Those two are almost as disgusting as Maks sometimes.

Wait. No. No one is ever as disgusting as Maks.

The hall has the normal crowd of people waiting on their loved ones who are still in interviews or getting dressed, and a few reporters straggling around. No one pays much attention to our arrival, except for the ones that are waiting on us to leave.

"Speaking of... hey baby." Tucker smiles at Lacy and gives her a quick kiss before taking the sleeping child out of her arms. "She didn't make it through the game?"

"She didn't even make it to face off."

Prestyn and I smile sheepishly at each other as we watch their sweet exchange. Tucker grabs Lacy's hand and with a quick nod of his head, the two of them head out, leaving Prestyn and I to our awkwardness.

"I'm starving." I lean my shoulder against the wall and look down at beautiful brown eyes staring up at me. "If you're interested, I was thinking we could go to grab a bite to eat."

"Just a bite?" she jokes.

"Okay, maybe a five-course meal. I haven't eaten anything of substance since lunch time."

Prestyn's bottom lip pops out from where she was just biting it. "Me neither. Unless you count a plateful of nachos in the box. But I only picked at them, so yeah. I could eat."

Something in her tone catches my attention. "Was something wrong?"

An expression I can't decipher flickers across her face. It was so fast, I would have missed it if I'd blinked.

"It's fine. I'll tell you about it later. I'm as hungry as you are so let's go."

I shrug off her comment, taking her at her word that whatever it is isn't a big deal. We've no more than turned for the exit, my hand on her lower back guiding her forward, when a man comes through the door and Prestyn stops dead in her tracks.

It takes me a second to recognize him, but then he sneers at Prestyn and I remember exactly where I've seen him before. It's her douchebag boss.

The brown suit he's wearing is disheveled and could use an iron, his tie is askew. And he's swaying on his feet just enough for me to gauge that he's probably had too much to drink. Something about this scene doesn't feel right. Already I'm on alert.

Aaron's eyes flick up to mine and his expression completely changes to one of awe.

"Nick Wiliams," he slurs. "Florida Glaze goalie. Wow. You had a great game tonight."

I really didn't, but he's not my favorite person when he's sober. I'm going to guess he'd be even lower on my list when he's three sheets to the wind. So I give him my standard answer.

"Thanks, man. Always appreciate meeting a fan." I put out my hand to shake his, hoping to keep his attention off Prestyn. It doesn't work.

"Oh I'm a fan alright. Been following the Glaze since the organization got here all those years ago. What's it been twelve? Thirteen years?"

"About that," I say making polite small talk as I look for an easy exit from this conversation. Prestyn's lips are pressed tightly together, her discomfort rolling off her like waves.

The last time we were in a situation with her boss, she didn't feel like this. Didn't give me a vibe like she was on her guard. Everything feels different this time, and I don't know if it's the alcohol or if I'm missing something.

Aaron shakes his head and then nods, like his head is trying to keep up with the thoughts rolling around in his brain. "Yeah. I've always been a fan. A super fan. I go to at least seventy-five percent of the games. That's why I have season passes. Because I'm the biggest fan."

We just let him ramble, my hand placed solidly on Prestyn's back. I don't know, or care, if Aaron has noticed it, but at least Prestyn knows I'm right here with her.

Suddenly Aaron's eyes leave mine and he's looking Prestyn up and down, a look of disgust on his face. "This one, though, she's not a fan. A spoiled heiress is what she is."

"Excuse me?" Prestyn's brows are furrowed in anger at his jab.

"Hey man," I say with a gentle tone I don't actually feel. "That's not necessary. You got back here to hang out with the players like she did, right? Are you hoping to get an autograph or something?"

Aaron's eyes roll lazily as he tries to focus back on me. Instead, his gaze gets caught on my other hand. The one on Prestyn's lower back. He lets out a slow, menacing chuckle. "Oh I get it." He scratches his jaw lazily, still swaying. "The princess couldn't figure out how to get box seats, so she used you to get them, right?"

"What the hell?" Prestyn glances up at me, clearly uncomfortable with his focus, eyes practically begging me to do something.

I'm trying. I'm trying to get us out of here without doing something stupid.

"Prestyn and I have been friends for a while, so I invited her. No big deal, man. I do it for all my friends." I try clapping him on the shoulder, hoping the gesture will make him feel like he's part of my circle.

It doesn't work.

Aaron snorts a laugh through his nose. "Friends? What kind of friends would that be?" Leaning in, he looks straight in Prestyn's eyes. "Like fuck buddies?"

Prestyn gasps and my stomach drops. I know he's plowed, but that doesn't change the fact that he's gotten too close to a truth we never wanted anyone to know about. Now I'm getting angry. And clearly this guy isn't going to go away nicely so I change my approach. I push him back gently to get him out of Prestyn's face, trying to maintain my sense of calm.

"You are crossing a lot of lines and I think you may have had too much to drink. Why don't we call an Uber or something so you can go home and sleep it off."

I signal one of the security guards to watch closely in case we need him. He immediately pushes off the wall and heads our direction, keeping an eye on things but not intervening yet.

"I haven't had too much to drink," Aaron slurs again, this time louder. People are beginning to notice something is going on and I don't like it. "I just think Daddy is going to find it very interesting that his daughter is getting on her knees for his beloved hockey team just to score box seats."

That's it. I've had enough.

Taking a step forward, I look down at Aaron and drop my voice low. "I know you are drunk, but do not ever say that shit to her again, do you understand?"

Aaron laughs. "So it's true. She had to blow you in order to get tickets, right? Seems like something she would do."

My nostrils flare and I'm seeing red. Security puts a hand on Aaron's shoulder and tries to pull him away. He just shrugs them off and turns back to Prestyn.

"Man, your life just isn't turning out like you expected, is it, Princess? Daddy didn't get you the job you wanted, so now you have to work for me. Had to blow the goalie to get box seats. You planning on spreading your legs for the captain so you can get some season tickets next?"

"Back off, man," I warn but he either doesn't notice or care.

Drunk eyes looking up at me, he snickers. "I can't believe you fell for this cunt's fake ass charm."

My brain doesn't think to stop me as my arm swings and I land a punch right to Aaron's jaw. He goes down like a sack of potatoes, unsurprising considering how much he had to drink. But it's Prestyn's scream as it happens that has me regretting my actions.

Suddenly the cameras that weren't paying attention to us a few minutes ago are swarming like flies, their flashbulbs lighting up the hall as they document this moment for all the world to see.

Fuck. I screwed up. I screwed up big time.

Fly under the radar, that's all I ever want to do. This isn't staying private. This is practically handing the press the keys to my life.

Frozen, I watch the scene around me as it unfolds. Security calling for a medic on the radio, microphones in my face asking questions, Becker suddenly pushing me backward, making sure I'm not going back for more.

My teammates voice sounds like it's under water as my brain finally catches up to what's going on. "...okay to drive? Nick. Nicholas."

Through my haze, I'm finally able to focus on Becker's face.

"What?" I shake my head and the last of the brain fog finally goes away.

"You good to drive? You need to go. Now. Before he wakes up."

Right. And I need to get Prestyn out of here before she's recognized.

A few reporters are already surrounding Prestyn and I realize it's too late. "*Ms. Caine, are you in a relationship with Nick Williams?*" They've figured us out.

Fuck!

Quickly, I straighten my suit and nod once to Becker. "I'm good. I gotta get her out of here. Just tell them I don't like when men try to bully women, even if they're fans or some shit like that."

"I got you," Becker says and moves out of my way. "I'll say he put his hands on her or something. Make you look like a real hero."

"Thanks."

Swiftly, I step around him and grab Prestyn's hand, pushing my way through the reporters, listening as security stops them from following us.

"Where are we going?" Prestyn asks quietly but I hear her like a roar in my head.

"Parking lot."

"But my car is in a different lot."

"We'll get it later. We've gotta go. They've figured you out."

Prestyn has to practically jog to keep up with my pace so I force myself to slow down a bit. I feel like looking over my shoulder, making sure no one is following us. Part of me knows I'm being a little too paranoid, but this is exactly what we didn't want. For people to figure out our relationship and put a spotlight on it. Yet here we are.

As soon as I open the passenger side door of my car, she climbs in.

"Your place or the hotel?" I ask before closing her in.

"What?" Prestyn looks just as scattered as I feel.

"Your place or the hotel?" I ask again. "Where do you want me to drop you?"

"Nick, my car is here. You need to take me to it."

"We'll get it tomorrow. Where are we going, Prestyn?"

She runs a hand through her hair before answering. "My place."

I nod once and shut the door, determined to get us out of this parking lot and to the safety of her place as quickly as possible.

CHAPTER TWENTY-FIVE

PRESTYN

The door *snicks* shut behind us, the loudest sound either of us has made since getting into Nick's car. The drive over was silent, not even music to distract us from our thoughts.

I was startled when Aaron showed up by the locker room. I was irritated when he started to go on about how I got the seats. I was enraged when he decided it was appropriate to talk about my sex life and alluded to me being a whore. But when Nick swung, I was shocked.

It's not like I haven't seen Nick get mad before. He was furious about my encounter with Gary and made no qualms about letting that anger show, but he's just so calm by nature, it was a little disconcerting to see him throw a punch.

In a weird way, it was also really hot.

From the beginning, Nick has always had my back. He's told me several times I don't deserve the treatment I've been getting from Aaron. He's encouraged me to stand up for myself, to make a case for myself with my brother. But for him to go all alpha male on Aaron for disrespecting me in such a vile way, I didn't hate it. Maybe because I can't remember the last time anyone stood up for me like that.

I toss my house key into the bowl on the table and slip my shoes off. "Want something to drink?"

Nick follows my lead and takes off his shoes as well, dropping his tie and suit jacket on the back of the couch. His phone ends up on the kitchen island as we head toward the fridge.

"It's probably a good idea for me to stick with water."

"No problem."

I grab a couple of bottles out of the fridge and hand him one before leaning back against the counter. I watch as he opens his and quickly downs the whole thing, leaving it empty and easier to fidget with.

Nick stays on the other side of the island, not even attempting to approach me, which feels too far away after what just happened. I don't like the distance. Then again, we probably need it if we're going to have this conversation. I have a feeling things are about to get serious.

"Are you okay?" I finally ask, breaking the ice.

"Yeah. No." Nick shakes his head slowly. "I don't know."

Understandable. But that still doesn't explain where his head is at. "What part is bothering you the most? That you hit Aaron?"

Nick scoffs. "I have no regrets over that part. He deserved it."

I smirk, because he's right. "Is it the fact that reporters were there to witness it?"

He shrugs and stares at the counter, eyes not able to meet mine. My heart sinks.

"Or is it because I was there for the reporters to see as well?"

Nick leans on his elbows, twisting the bottle cap off and on, over and over again. I stay quiet, letting him process his thoughts until he's ready to speak.

"I think I'm mostly mad at myself."

"For what?"

"A lot of things. I'm not mad I punched him, but I'm not happy that I lost my cool like that. It put us in a precarious situa-tion, and I know better. I should have called security over to help us sooner, but I waited, thinking I could defuse the situation myself."

"Nick, I've seen him that way before and even I didn't know how to talk him down. It's just easier to let him rant and let it go. He a mean drunk."

"All the more reason I should have gotten security involved from the beginning. And now there's probably video floating around of me punching the guy. Even worse, they know about you."

His comment stings more than it should, but I give him the benefit of the doubt. I don't think he's angry that people know I was there as much as we didn't have a chance to plan for the reaction to the news. We've been careful, just not careful enough this time.

"Nick, it happens sometimes. We're both public figures. We were at a public event. Someone was bound to recognize me eventually. It's something you have to get used to if this relationship is going to continue."

"But this isn't a relationship, right?" Nick, still leaning on the island, looks up at me with questions written all over his face.

What are we doing? What is this situation we've found ourselves in? Are we even on the same page?

I don't know the answers anymore. What started out as us being fuck buddies has turned into something deeper for me. It's not just attraction or scratching an itch. It's friendship, and caring, and love.

I *love* him. I didn't mean to, but how could I not? He's the first person I think of in the morning and the last person I think of at night. I want to be with him whether we're naked in the sheets, or sitting in sweats on the couch. I care about his ideas and opinions and whether or not he's getting enough sleep on the road.

I *love* him. I just don't know if he loves me back, but I'm about to find out. Because I don't want to hide this anymore. I don't want to just meet up for a torrid affair. I want dinners and hockey games and galas and vacations. I want video chats when he's on a trip and fireside chats when he's home. I want to introduce him to my family and get to know Delaney better. I want it all.

As his girlfriend.

As much as I hate Aaron for starting shit tonight, at least it got us here. Because now it's time to sort this out once and for all.

I take a deep breath, calming my nerves before I say the words I can't take back. "Maybe I want this to be a relationship."

Nick freezes, and for one solid second, I swear his eyes dance, and I'm sure he's going to smile and hug me and tell me he wants that, too.

But as quickly as that reaction comes, it's gone, replaced by dull eyes and a firmness in his lips that hint at resolve.

Then he shakes his head and I feel like all the breath leaves my body.

"I don't do relationships, you know that."

I try to put on a brave face as I argue his point. "What do you think this is, Nick?"

"A friends with benefits situation. Like we originally said."

"Friends with benefits don't text constantly during work hours. They don't hang out for hours, snuggling and watching television. They don't invite each other to hockey games and send each other bouquets of our favorite energy drinks."

Nick begins shaking his head vehemently but I continue.

"I know we started this whole thing as a way to scratch an itch and nothing more, but Nick, don't you think it's evolved into something more? Into something with feelings?"

That stops him. "Of course it has. I like you, Prestyn, so much. I'm not dense enough to not admit that."

For a split second, I think maybe, just maybe, we're going to move forward from here. But I'm wrong.

"But I can't do it. It's not even about you," he tries to clarify, as if that will stop my heart from breaking in half right here in my kitchen. "I just... I don't want to live my life in front of the cameras. I deal with it now because I love my job, but that's as much as I can do. It's torture to do interviews as it is. I can't add people poking into my life because of who you are to me and who you are in general."

And that says it all. He'll do it for something he loves, be in front of the cameras. But I'm not one of those things. I'm not something he is willing to sacrifice his discomfort for.

"I want to keep spending time with you, Prestyn," he says but the damage has already been done. "I do. I enjoy being with you. You're the only thing that relaxes me. The only person who makes me feel like I can just be me. I just can't do it on a stage for everyone else to see."

"You think I want to start traipsing around Tampa with you on my arm?" I finally find my voice, but just enough to fight back on what he's saying. "That I'll start calling tip lines to let them know where we're going to be so we can get some press? I don't like the spotlight anymore than you do, but sometimes that's my life. That's *both* our lives. You can't stop doing the things you want to do because someone *might* have a camera pointed at you sometimes. You'll miss out on too much."

"Can we just go back to the way things were?" he pleads. "Where we meet up at the hotel and spend time together and then go our separate ways? No one has to know we're together."

I huff and cross my arms. I'm so insulted that he only wants me if I'm willing to be his dirty little secret. That I'm good enough to be with in private, but nowhere else.

I can't do it. I can't give in, no matter how much my heart is breaking at what I have to do. I have too much dismissal in my life at the hands of the people who supposedly love me already. I won't do it with him, too.

"I think..." I pause to sort out my words. "I think our situation has run its course."

Nick's eyes widen and he steps around the island, stopping just in front of me. "Prestyn, that's not what I meant. I don't want to stop seeing you. I want to keep seeing you."

I shake my head. It's exactly what he meant. But this is not about me. It's about Nick and his own insecurities, and there's nothing I can do to make him get over this fear. It's something he has to do on his own. But I don't have to be there to watch him do it.

Grabbing his phone off the counter, I swipe to open it.

"What are you doing" he asks.

"Still doesn't have a fucking password," I grumble and click through until I find what I'm looking for.

Right there, on the second screen, is the hotel app giving him access to unlock the family suite. My finger hovers over it for less than a second before I make one of the hardest moves I've ever made in my life. I delete the app, and his access to my life.

I blink quickly, ensuring there is no wetness in my eyes before turning back to him and holding out his phone. "This is over. Please leave."

His face falls, and he takes a step toward me. "Prestyn—" he says gently.

I hold up my free hand to stop him. "I'm serious. We're obviously in two different places right now and I don't have the energy or desire to deal with another man in my life who behaves badly."

"Behaves badly? Because I punched Aaron?"

"No." I shake my head. My thoughts are a jumbled mess that I'm desparate to sort through. "I didn't mean it that way. You haven't done anything wrong." Except shatter me all over my kitchen floor. "I think we're just in two different places now. That's not going to work for me. I want to be with someone who *wants* to be seen with me. Or at minimum, doesn't want to hide me away like a dirty little secret."

He quickly takes a step backward, shock written all over his face. "That's not what I mean."

"I know. But it's how it feels. And I don't like feeling that way, so I'm asking again for you to leave." I push his phone out further, willing him to take it.

Nick stares at me, unblinking for a few seconds before he finally takes his phone out of my hands. He slowly slides it in his pants pocket as he looks around and licks his lips. He's stalling, but I don't know why and I don't bother asking.

I have to learn to stand up for myself, to fight for what is right, to ask for what I want and walk away when I don't get it. As painful as it may be, I know this is the right choice. This is the right path. Closing out this chapter may be painful, but it's the only way I'll find my happily ever after in the end, so it has to be done.

Finally, Nick steps forward and kisses me on the top of the head, murmuring, "I'm so sorry" against my hair.

As he pulls away, I swear I hear him sniff, but I refuse to look up. Refuse to see the expression on his face, knowing that his feelings aren't the problem, it's the resulting actions.

I stay frozen in place when he walks away, listening as the door closes behind him. It isn't until I count to one hundred, breathing through my pain, that I finally crumble to the floor and allow the tears to follow.

CHAPTER TWENTY-SIX

NICK

"It's about damn time we won a game." Tiger tosses a couple of blue chips into the pile on the table and sits back, the cards in his hand in a neat pile, held close to the table so no one can peek.

Becker follows his lead and throws his own chips into the pot. "Kind of hard to lose against Rochester. Their line-up is terrible this year. Where's their farm team again?"

"Lubbock," Patrick answers, his eyebrows furrowing as he looks at his cards.

"No wonder their team sucks." Becker places his cards face down on the table and stretches his arms overhead. "Isn't Lubbock in Texas? What the fuck is even there?"

"Tumbleweeds," Patrick answers, and ups the anty.

"You sure know an awful lot about West Texas." Tucker glances at his cards, then the table, then his cards again. "I thought you were from Minneapolis."

"Doesn't mean I don't know geography."

After a few moments of silence, Tucker makes his bet and turns to Maks, who doesn't bother looking at his cards while he munches on some Oreos. He just throws his own chips in the pot and leans back in his chair.

"You know who knows some good geography?"

Oh god. You never know where a statement like that is going when Maks is the one making it.

"Nick. At least the geography of that guy's face."

The table erupts in laugher and guffaws. I roll my eyes. I'm tired of talking about this.

The day after I punched Aaron, I was called into Coach's office and reprimanded. He didn't even really care that I'd taken a swing, it was just a standard ass-chewing. My teammates, on the other hand, won't let it go.

The worst part of it isn't that I hit the guy. I still say he deserved it. The worst part is it reminds me of why I snapped. Of who I was protecting. And of who I left behind when I walked out her front door.

I haven't heard from Prestyn since that night three days ago. It's the longest we've gone without talking and it's killing me. But I made my decision and I have to stick with it. It's what's best for us, even if my heart feels like it's breaking into a million pieces.

"Drop it, guys." I toss my chips in the pile and my cards on the table. "I call." I have no desire to relive any of that. I want to move on, to push the feeling of regret away, but they won't let it go.

"Who knew our little Nicky had it in him, eh?" Becker chides. If he was closer, he'd probably be ruffling my hair right about now. "I've never even seen him throw a punch on the ice, let alone on solid ground."

Tucker shakes his head and glances over at me. He must see something in my expression he doesn't like because the smirk on his face drops as soon as he looks at me.

"Oh I knew he could float like a butterfly if it ever came down to it, what with his grace in front of that net." Tiger shakes his head and stares at his cards while he keeps up with the conversation. "I always knew his form would be perfect."

"Did you guys see the slow-mo video?" Maks tosses into the

conversation and suddenly everyone is jumping up from the table, clamoring to see it again.

"Come on guys," I holler, throwing my hands in the air in frustration. "We're here to play poker, not hash out old shit."

They ignore me and crowd around Maks' chair to see his phone. "See? Look how gorgeous it is in slow motion."

I push away from the table to get a drink. I'm going to need one if they're going to continue "oohing" and "aahing" over a moment I don't exactly wish to take back, but I wish I could change the ending result of.

I'm pouring a generous glass of whiskey from the bottle Tucker brought in while the rest of us were moving that heavy ass table, when the man of the hour approaches.

"What's going on, Nick?"

"Nothing," I mumble, keeping my eyes on my drink.

Tucker harumphs and leans against the wall, arms crossed before saying the words I never expected.

"Prestyn break up with you?"

My gaze whips up to him before I can stop it. How did he know? And then I remember. Everyone knows. Because I'm the dumb ass that blew our cover with a single punch.

I know Tucker is my friend and I shouldn't deflect. He's been through worse, what with finding out about his daughter three and a half years into her life, and I was there for him. But it's almost automatic when I answer.

"We weren't together."

"You sure?" he challenges. "Because I've never seen you so relaxed until she came on the scene. So secure in your own skin. And in the last three days, you've been more tense than I've seen you in months. From where I'm standing, it sounds like she's more important than you're letting on."

I put the top back on the whiskey bottle and set it aside. "She's a great person. I'm sure everyone feels relaxed round her."

"Nah, man. It's more than that. She brings out the best in you and you're too afraid other people are going to see it."

I run my hands through my hair in frustration. "I don't know what anyone wants from me. She is Prestyn Caine. She's basically a hotel heiress."

"But that's not all she is, man."

"I know that." I don't need him to remind me she's so much more than what the public sees and it irritates me that he's trying. "But her life comes with responsibilities and one of them is to be the face of the Caine Resorts and Conference Centers which means anyone in her inner circle has to be that face with her."

One of his shoulders shrugs. "And you're the face of the Florida Glaze. How is that different?"

"My limelight is part of my job. Hers is part of her life," I argue.

"Weird. I don't remember seeing her in the news at all except for the night of the gala and a few days ago when *you* brought the spotlight on her."

I wince, because he's right. "And I shouldn't have done it. I don't like the limelight. You know that. It's not what I want for my life."

"And yet, you're in a job that requires it."

"I deal with it because I love my job," I say with frustration. How is he not understanding?

"Let me get this straight." Tucker takes a step closer. "You'll deal with it for the game, but you can't deal with it for her?"

"That's different," I say through gritted teeth.

"Is it? Because I've seen the look on your face over the last several weeks. I've lived the look on your face. You are sloppily, messily, head over heels in love with her and it scares the ever loving shit out of you."

I scoff. "I don't love her."

"You sure? Because you're awfully broken up about the loss of a fuck buddy."

My nostrils flair and I see red. "Don't call her that."

He grins at me. *Fucking grins.* "Why not? You don't love her."

I don't respond. I can't. He doesn't understand how this feels. Doesn't have any idea, even if he thinks he does.

"I get it. You're terrified. It happens when you start a new relationship and I'm guessing, if your life is anything like mine, there's some fear deep inside you that you'll be just like your dad."

My heart stops. How does he know about my dad's betrayal? Or does he?

"We're not bringing my father into this."

"We're not bringing mine into it either because he's not around for me to even know what he's like. Well, except when I signed on with the Slingers my rookie year. He showed up at a game." Tucker shakes his head and blows out a breath. "Talk about losing your temper. If my buddy Liam hadn't been there to hold me back, I might have dropped the dickhead's ass to the floor for the way he treated us."

I'm not sure how this conversation moved from my issues with Prestyn to our absentee fathers, and I'm not really sure which topic is easier for me to discuss. But suddenly my brain is spinning. Am I so wounded by my father's actions, by his secret life, that I'm cutting off the best thing that's ever happened to me so I don't turn into him? Am I hurting myself out of a desperate need to never hurt anyone else?

"Let me ask you a question." I missed whatever Tucker was just saying, so I'm not sure what he's going to ask me. "Did you even know who Prestyn was the first time you met her? Were there paparazzi following her around or did she take a bunch of duck-face selfies while you were together?"

"No."

"Right," Tucker says. "Because she's a normal person who happens to have a rich family. Sure, there's going to be some media involvement because of that, but she doesn't go looking for it any more than you do. I'm guessing that was part of the attraction in the first place, right?"

Crap. He's right. We'd discussed the benefits of being together and one of them was knowing the other hated the limelight. That what happened between us in private would stay private.

My mind continues to reel as panic begins to set in. *What have I done?*

"You're just going to throw it all away because of one incident that, let's face it, you're the one who triggered the media frenzy anyway?"

The more he talks, the more my breathing speeds up. He's right. I started all of this when I lost my cool. But that's not even the beginning. I could probably Google our names and mine would come up with a picture a thousand times more than Prestyn's does. My job keeps me in the spotlight, while Prestyn has perfected the art out of fading into the background and passing for "just another employee".

"If you hadn't thrown the punch, no one would have even blinked at you walking away with her. Way to go, man. You're cutting her off because of your own stupid issues and now she's paying the price for it. You're the most solid guy I know..."

I run my hand through my hair as my brain keeps spinning. My eyes scour the room, as if anyone sitting at the poker table can help me.

Briefly I notice Maks shoving a spoonful of cereal and milk in his mouth. *Where the hell did he find Capt'n Crunch?*

"...Not that it's hard with these bozos around." Tucker continues to drone on, but I'm not really listening anymore. "Listen, we all go to extremes to make sure we don't become our dad. I tend to take on responsibilities that aren't mine. I love Kody and Ellie, but damn, I invited a lot of people to live here." He blows out an exasperated breath. "And it looks like you refuse to be in any type of relationship so you don't accidentally hurt anyone. Except right now, you're the one being a dick. And in the end, yeah, you're hurting her, but you're hurting yourself more."

"I've gotta go," I blurt out.

"What?" Tucker looks a little startled that I interrupted his rant.

"I have to leave. I—" I put my glass down and pat my pockets, making sure I have my keys and wallet. "I can't be here."

"Okay." Tucker looks confused but claps me on the shoulder. "I get it. You have a lot to think about now."

"No... I mean, yeah... I..." My mind can't seem to wrap around my own thoughts. It's like a lightbulb has gone off, but it's so bright, I'm having a hard time adjusting. "I just need to leave."

"Okay. Do what you've gotta do. We'll see you at practice tomorrow."

I nod once, still feeling a bit shell-shocked from the realizations running through my brain. How could I have been so wrong? And how could I let fear control me like that without even realizing it?

Ignoring the heckling from my teammates as I rush from the room and out of Tucker's house, I race to my Range Rover. The ignition is no more than turned over when I connect my Bluetooth to make a call. It's late, really late, but I know she'll answer.

"What's wrong?" My sister's voice sounds groggy, but I know she's wide awake.

I only call at this time of night when there is an emergency. This may not be 9-1-1 worthy, but I'm still in full on panic mode.

"I'm afraid, Delaney. How did I not know it until now? And why is it so hard?"

"Wait. What are we talking about? What are you afraid of?"

"Did Dad really do that much damage to us? I thought we were doing fine, ya know? That we moved on and left him behind, but I'm not so sure anymore. I don't know what to think anymore."

She laughs, deep and throaty. "We've never been fine, Nicky. I married someone exactly like him and you don't let anyone get close."

"So, how do we fix it?" My voice is almost a whisper, the idea that I've screwed up beyond repair so strong it almost strangles me.

"Nicky?" she asks gently. "What did you do?"

"I pushed her away. I told Prestyn I didn't want a life in front of the cameras. That our lives were too different because of who she is and I pushed her away."

She sighs into the phone. "Oh, Nicky. I've been waiting for you to figure this out. You're in love with her."

My fingers tighten around the steering wheel, knuckles turning white in my panic and frustration. "How do you know that? Until a few seconds ago, you didn't even know I'd been seeing her."

"I know more than you think I know. The second I saw you punch some guy in front of her, I knew there was a reason my phone hasn't been ringing a lot lately. But you notice I haven't badgered you about it, either. Because I like her. A lot. Which is how I knew you'd fall for her."

Damn my sister and her matchmaking skills. If it wasn't for her, I never would have met Prestyn. Never would have enjoyed talking to her. Never would have spent the night with her. Never would have craved her body and her mind on a daily basis.

Never would have fallen in love with her.

As soon as I think the thoughts for myself, not hear them from someone else's assessment, but think it for myself, it all clicks. My feelings are so big, it's no wonder I'm afraid. It's not just about the possibility of me being hurt, it's about the possibility that I'll hurt her. That I'll destroy her and her family like my dad did me and mine. Because I love her.

It's everything Tucker already said, but when it finally clicks in my brain, my heart sinks.

"Nicky." My sister breaks into my thoughts. "Honey, you're

not him. You don't hide things from people. You're the same guy you were yesterday and last year and ten years ago. You're the same guy you were when Dad was arrested. With the exception of some emotional bruises, you've never changed."

"What do I do? I lost her. What do I do?" I plead, hoping she has an answer.

"You're the only one who knows that. So let's flip the question. What do you *want* to do?"

"I want to get her back."

"Good. Then the next step is to figure out how."

Oddly, I think I already know the answer to that. It's going to take me far out of my comfort zone, but for Prestyn, I'll do it. I just don't know if it's going to be as well received as I hope.

CHAPTER TWENTY-SEVEN

PRESTYN

"Knock, knock."

My knuckles rap on the door jamb and Gavin looks up from his computer. He waves me in silently and leans back. My older brother's elbows are resting on the arms of his office chair and his fingers are steepled together. He looks pissed.

Great. This isn't Gavin my brother. This is Gavin the general manager. Just what I need today. Well, just what I need the last few days.

I've been in a terrible mood since I kicked Nick out of my apartment. I'm sad and I know that. But it's mostly been presenting as anger. Not that I'm running around hitting people. I'm just snippy, so I've tried to give everyone a wide berth until I can pull myself together.

Unfortunately, now is not one of the times I can just avoid talking to someone. I have to suck it up.

I smooth down my dress pants and take a seat in the chair in front of Gavin's desk. "You wanted to see me? What's going on?"

He doesn't mince words, just goes for it. "A complaint has been filed against you for hostile and malicious work environment."

My jaw drops. I know I've been snippy the last few days but hostile?

"By who?" I ask, truly stumped as to who could be this easily offended.

When Gavin purses his lips, understanding dawns on me.

"Aaron. I should have known this was coming."

I shake my head. Of course the jackass would be a... jackass about all this.

"What? You don't have anything else to say?"

I look up at Gavin, eyes narrowed. I understand that he's angry about the situation, but really? He's going to treat me like he's my dad? I tamp down my anger because I know how this is going to end anyway. There's no use in even trying.

"I'm not going to try and defend myself against the golden boy," I finally say, shaking my head in disbelief that this is happening. The last of my remaining dreams seem to crumble away. I guess Aaron can congratulate himself. He officially drove me out of my own family's business. "It's just a waste of all our time anyway. So if I need to sign anything before I clear out my desk, just hand it over."

I reach my hand out and wave my fingers at him. Instead of giving me what I asked for, Gavin looks confused.

"Golden boy? Prestyn, what are you talking about?"

I drop my hand with a scoff. "Oh, come on Gavin. Aaron has been trying to worm his way into this family since I was a kid, using Hoyt to do it. He's got all of you convinced he's the best man for this job and he should be a Caine over me, and you all seem to agree so, why waste my breath? Apparently I've got a resumé to put together."

Gavin rubs his temple, his brows furrowed. "Prestyn, I'm not firing you."

"Oh, well that's good. So just a written warning or something? Suspension?"

"Prestyn, stop." He leans forward and puts his hand on his

desk. "I don't understand what you're talking about. You really think that about Aaron? About us? That we're letting him push you out?"

I roll my eyes and glance at the ceiling. "Oh, come on, Gavin. You guys have never seen me as anything more than your kid sister. Never given me a chance to prove myself. I have a Master's degree and you made me the assistant of the smallest department in the entire resort. Did Dad do that to you? No. You went straight to director."

"And we paid the price for that mistake. Pres, you've only been out of grad school for two years. You needed to get up to speed with how the business operates."

"I've been training my whole life. This is the only thing I've ever wanted to do. To be the first Caine woman to run this hotel. To be on equal footing with the men when it comes to daily operations. I spent summers here, shadowing everything Dad does. I spent holiday breaks helping behind the front desk, for free, I might add. Hell, by the time I was in high school, I was building relationships with the shop owners so I'd already know what they needed when I got here. But then you give Aaron a director job, put me under him, and let him railroad me daily."

Of all the expressions Gavin's face makes, confusion is not normally one of them. My rant stops short because of it.

"Pres, that is not what is supposed to be happening. Listen, when I started working here, yes, Dad made me the director of all business operations. And the first year I lost a lot of money for the company. A lot." This is news to me. He goes on. "I was in over my head. We didn't want to make the same mistake with you. Aaron offered to train you in that department and since its so small, once you were up to speed, then he'd have you work in the other departments. The whole point was to train you resort wide for a couple of years."

"Train me? Is this what you call training me? I literally do his job and he takes credit for it. All while he's making snide remarks to my face." I huff out a humorless laugh, not able to stop now that I've started spewing the truth. "Do you know how frustrating it is to be treated like dog shit by your brother's best friend every single day and there's nothing you can do, because he'll go running to Hoyt if he's unhappy? He used to do that when we were kids and you guys never even noticed. Would laugh at the things he would say."

For the first time, Gavin looks truly taken aback. "I... I didn't realize he treated you that way. That *we* treated you that way."

"I don't know how you can run this resort and still be that clueless."

"No, I mean I've heard him make off-hand comments, but I've always heard you put him in his place. I didn't realize you thought I didn't have your back. I just didn't want to fight your fight, especially if you didn't need me to."

I feel like my whole body deflates at his admission. "I don't need you to fight for me, Gavin. But I do need someone else in this family to see my value to the company and make it known I deserve the same respect as everyone else."

"I'm so sorry, Prestyn. I had no idea you felt this way. I don't think any of us did."

"It doesn't matter." His acknowledgement is great and all, but it doesn't change much. "As long as Aaron is my boss, I'm going to have to put up with it."

"Do you want me to move you to a different department? You're amazing with the event coordination."

I hold my hands up. "Oh no, no, no. I hate working events. I just know how to because I've been in attendance at them my entire life. After a while, you just know what needs to be done. Doesn't mean I like doing it. It hasn't been my dream."

"What is your dream?"

I look at my brother. Really look at him. For the first time, possibly ever, I feel like he's listening to me. Like he's really trying to hear me.

I take a deep breath and decide it's now or never. "I want to run this resort. General manager. Your job," I tack on with a cock of my eyebrow. "I'd like to be the director of our business sales—overseeing the retail operations and executive sales before tackling the whole company. And before I do that, I think we need to overhaul the retail operations department." I haul in a deep breath before running with my thoughts. "There are so many ways to diversify our shops so we give returning guests a new experience every time they come in. And I know we've discussed remodeling the conference center at some point. I have ideas on how to intertwine some of our premier businesses in those floorplans to increase their profitability. Or to have those as more like rotation shops depending on what conference we're having. Almost like kiosks or pop-up shops. Maybe a bookshop if we have some sort of author signing event, or a sports memorabilia shop when we have the meet-and-greets. Our shipping contractors can maybe take over the space during a business conference, or even a snack shop filled with travel brochures during a travel conference. We could tailor the space and offer it as a free temporary store for our current tenants..."

I look up, and stop talking, realizing I'm rambling. But Gavin's smiling.

"What?" I ask sheepishly.

"I need to apologize to you," he says without hesitation.

"Uh, you already did."

"No, I need to apologize again. I just blindly trusted Aaron to train you, to focus on making sure you were learning the ropes, I wasn't paying attention. I didn't realize you'd moved so far beyond that already. I love these ideas. And I'd love your input when we start talking to the contractors so we can see how to make it happen."

"Really?

"Really." He smiles but then blows out a breath and sits back, picking up a folder off his desk. "But we do need to get back to this complaint from Aaron. I've invited him to join us."

My shoulders tense and I bite my bottom lip, all my bravado and excitement vanishing instantaneously.

Gavin presses the intercom button on his office phone. "Georgia, is Aaron here?"

"Yes, Mr. Caine."

"Can you send him in?"

"Of course."

Seconds later, there is a soft knock on the door. I stifle a giggle. He knocks like the weak person he is.

Aaron struts into the office, looking at me briefly but quickly turning away, knowing he has the upper hand since he filed the complaint.

"Gavin, how's it going?" Aaron's oily grin makes me want to barf on his shoe. "Thank you for taking this matter seriously."

"I always take matters like these seriously," my brother answers, his fingers steepled in front of him.

"As you should. The Caine reputation is on the line and I'd hate to see it tarnished by Neanderthal brutality." Aaron nods once in my direction, like I'm the one who hit him.

I don't even stop my eye roll. This man is ridiculous.

"I'm in full agreement with you," Gavin says. "Which is why we do a complete investigation whenever something like this happens."

"Perfect." Aaron slaps his thighs. "And please know, Gavin, I have no interest in firing Prestyn. She just needs to learn her place and how to respect those in authority over her."

Something flashes in Gavin's eyes. Not sure what it is, but it has me paying closer attention.

"I'm glad you don't want her fired because there's no evidence to support your claim."

My eyebrows raise before I can stop them.

Aaron sputters. "What? It was all over the news."

"It was," Gavin agrees with a nod. "Which made it pretty easy to reach out to a few reporters, one of whom happened to have an open mic of the entire situation."

Gavin presses a key on his computer and Aaron's voice fills the room.

"Man, your life just isn't turning out like you expected, is it, Princess? Daddy didn't get you the job you wanted, so now you have to work for me. Had to blow the goalie to get box seats. You planning on spreading your legs for the captain so you can get some season tickets next?"

Gavin presses another key while Aaron sputters. "I...I don't even remember saying that."

"Really?" Gavin deadpans. "Because that's only one of the good parts. I can play it from the beginning if you'd like."

"No," Aaron practically yells before lowering his volume. "That's not necessary. I must have had more to drink that night than I realized. I had no idea."

"Hmm." Gavin pauses for a moment, assessing Aaron while he squirms. Finally he leans forward, elbows on the table and fingers interlaced together. "I think it goes without saying that I'm tossing your complaint. But I also believe you owe Prestyn an apology."

Briefly Aaron's eyes narrow. It happens quickly but I know Gavin saw it. Aaron just pretends he didn't take a split second to think about telling the big boss no. "You're right," he says instead. "I'll make sure to do that when we get back to the office."

"I was thinking you could just" —Gavin waves his hand around aimlessly—"get it out of the way now, since we're all here and it's in the forefront of our minds."

Aaron sneers, looking like he smelled something bad. It's probably the stench of his own ego. Swallowing hard, he turns to me, nostrils flaring. "I apologize."

"For?" Gavin prods.

"For making rude remarks."

"And belittling her, especially in public when reporters were around, right?"

Aaron swallows hard, his eyes closing briefly. "And for belittling you, especially in public when reporters were around."

I nod, just so he knows I heard him. But there will be no acceptance or forgiveness from me.

"Good." Gavin smacks his desk and looks around, as if he's lost something. Somehow I know he hasn't. "Now that that's settled, I want to bring a few other things to your attention."

I turn back, not sure where this is headed, but riveted nonetheless.

"Because our investigations are so thorough," Gavin begins, "I had to speak with quite a few people regarding this matter. That led down a rabbit hole of conversations with employees and even some of our business owners. Past and present."

My eyebrows shoot up. Aaron, on the other hand, shifts uncomfortably in his chair.

"As it turns out, your behavior at the game seems to be pretty typical of you." Gavin picks up the lone folder he flashed before me earlier and opens it, reading something inside.

"What do you mean?" Aaron looks truly stumped before loosening his collar as he plants his feet firmly on the floor. "Is this retaliation from Prestyn's friends? Because you know how it goes when you're the boss. They're always trying to one-up you. Trying to make the boss look bad so they can get away with bad behavior."

Gavin glances over at him, expression completely unchanged. "No, actually. I have seventeen signed statements from people in *your* department, in business events, and even in"—he flips through several pages before continuing—"catering, who all have very similar stories, some who could site examples from the day you first started this job."

Gavin tilts his head in question. Aaron's face turns beet red.

"That is preposterous. People are just jealous. You see my numbers and how well my department is doing."

"I do," Gavin says with a nod. "Which is why I went down yet another rabbit hole."

I press my lips together, trying not to smile. I may not have been getting the support I had hoped for, but I underestimated my brother. When he's tipped off to a problem, he's thorough.

"As it turns out, of the thirty-four businesses we have in our hotel, only three of them have spoken with you in the last two years. Yet every single one of them knew Prestyn and gushed about how easy she is to work with."

"Well, I have a full plate." Aaron sits back and crosses his legs, doing his best to give off an air of nonchalance. "That's why she's here. To be my right-hand man."

"That's actually *not* why she's here," Gavin corrects. "But that's not the point. According to everyone I spoke with, she's been the only *man* on the job for quite some time."

Once again, Aaron sits forward, anger radiating from him like a bad stench. "I resent that people have thrown me under the bus like this. It's clear Prestyn has coordinated a smear campaign against me."

Gavin doesn't flinch. "Aaron, what kind of shop is Tales of Time?"

He sputters. "I... what?"

Gavin turns the intensity of his gaze onto Aaron. "I asked what kind of shop is Tales of Time? And where is it located?"

Aaron's jaw snaps shut.

"How much rent do they pay every month and what is the owner's name?" Gavin snaps the folder shut and drops it on his desk.

Aaron says nothing, breathing deeply through his still-flared nostrils. It's clear, he's losing this battle in a very harsh way.

When he says nothing, my brother turns to look at me for the first time since this reprimand began. "Prestyn, what can you tell me about Tales of Time?"

I don't even need to think because I know these businesses by heart. "Ronny is the owner. They've been here since, I believe 2015. They sell things time related—watches, some specialty clocks, pocket watches and chains. They also do really well with the sale of small batteries since business men seem to like their watches working. Oh, and recently they stocked up on batteries for hearing aids and are selling them at cost because they've had a few guests who have come in looking for the kind of battery they need and decided it was a great customer service to offer our hearing-impaired guests.

Gavin smirks. "What about rent?"

This time I have to think for a second, but I'd rather do that then pretend to know something as fact. "I believe they're grand-fathered into our 2015 rates so they're due for an increase in the next year, but with them taking a hit on the hearing aid batteries, I'm hoping we can keep them where they're at. A guest posted a review about how pleasantly surprised they were to pay so little to get their hearing aid working again, and that kind of community service aspect makes them invaluable to our reputation. We got more traction on that post then we did on our last social media ad that we'd paid for."

Gavin cocks an eyebrow at Aaron. "That is the kind of thing the Director of Retail Operations should know. Or at least a good portion of it to help make good business decisions that don't just help your department's bottom line, but helps in the growth of the entire hotel chain. I'm frustrated and angry that my sister has been doing the job we pay you to do, while you use your position to lord power over anyone you deem insignificant."

My jaw drops open. When Gavin gets angry, he doesn't yell. It's so much worse than that. He gathers indisputable information and wields it as a weapon you can't dodge. That's exactly what he's doing now.

Aaron makes a last ditch effort to save his neck. "I will not sit here and take this kind of abuse from you, Gavin. You've known me too long to play these kinds of games with me."

"You're right. You won't sit here and take it. Because you're fired."

My jaw falls even further.

Aaron gasps next to me. "You can't do that."

"I can. But I will give you a choice. If you leave quietly, you can tell everyone you quit. If you make a ruckus, our official statement will be that you were fired for abusive behavior towards your employees. It'll be mighty difficult to find a job in this industry and certainly not at this pay scale with that kind of mark on your reputation."

Aaron raises his chin and straightens his spine. "And I'll go to Hoyt."

Ah, Hoyt. The oldest brother who never seems to see Aaron's flaws.

From the phone on Gavin's desk, comes the sound of a disgusted harumph. "I'll take care of Hoyt."

Two sets of eyes swivel to look at the phone that clearly has an illuminated red light, indicating someone on the other end. Except for the smirk on his face, my brother doesn't even flinch. Holy shit, Gavin is playing hardball.

"Mr. Caine. I... I didn't know you were with us." Aaron sounds like he's got something hard caught in his throat. I almost, *almost* feel sorry for him.

"Yes, I'm sure you didn't," my father and the CEO of the entire company says. "I always knew there was something shady about you, so don't think any of this comes as a huge surprise to me. But you aren't my concern right now. Prestyn, on behalf of Caine Resorts and Conference Centers, I owe you a huge apology."

My eyes glance over to my brother who barely nods, probably in agreement with my dad.

"I... thank you." It's the only thing I can think to say.

"And on behalf of myself, as your father, well, I think I'd rather have that conversation in private. Maybe over lunch tomorrow?"

I smile, a genuine smile for the first time in days. "I'd like that, Dad."

"I'm clearing off my whole schedule for the afternoon," he says. "Just in case you need to push it back. But I hope you're able to make time for me. We have a lot to discuss."

I blink back the tears I feel forming in my eyes. I'm so shocked about this whole thing. I came in here thinking I was going to be reprimanded and instead I'm being supported.

"I won't miss it, Dad."

"Great. Gavin," my dad says, shifting gears. "Thanks for including me in this little meeting. If you all will excuse me now, I need to make a phone call to your other brother."

Aaron's eyes widen, and I think for the very first time, he's understanding the gravity of the situation. All those years of schmoozing with my father, of trying to weasel his way into the family through almost any means possible, were for nothing. He's lost it all, decades of his life wasted because he couldn't find the one trait my father wants the most for this company—integrity.

Gavin disconnects the call and sits back. "Aaron, you can go clean out your office now. Make sure you let me know which story we're going with as you sever ties with the company."

Aaron pushes out of the chair with a huff and stomps to the door like the spoiled brat he is. "You'll regret this. I'll smear the entire Caine family name. I know all your secrets."

"Fortunately for us, there aren't many skeletons in the closet and anything about Hoyt you might know has probably already been found out by the media. I don't know if you know this, but Hoyt went through some pretty rough teenage years," Gavin says to me. "You may have been too little to remember. He was always in the papers for doing something stupid. Aaron was always in the background, too. Gonna be hard to dig up shit on Hoyt without Aaron's name being attached to the bad behavior, don't ya think?"

Gavin winks at me and Aaron storms out of the room, slamming the door behind him.

"Um," I look over my shoulder before turning back. "You have security following him, right? He seems a little volatile right now."

"Oh yeah. Georgia called them as soon as Aaron came in. She's had them waiting outside."

I can't help it, I start laughing. I feel so much relief to have Aaron gone and so much hope that my family truly sees my value now. The happiness is just bursting out of me.

Gavin tries to hold it together but he can't, and soon he's joining me with his own guffaws.

Eventually we pull ourselves back together, both of us wiping the moisture out of our eyes. "I have to say Prestyn, this is the most fun I've had at work in a very long time."

He has no idea.

"But let's get down to the nuts and bolts of it, shall we? We need to get all the paperwork processed so you can officially start your new job tomorrow."

"My new job?"

"Well, the job you've been doing, just with your new title and salary. All of those things that come with being a director."

I hold my hands up, stunned by this turn of events. "You're just giving me the job? Just like that?"

"Prestyn, that was always the plan. It just got knocked off course for a while. We should have seen it two years ago, but we just... well, I just kept waiting for you to tell me you were ready."

"Thanks, Gavin."

He swivels in his chair, placing his hand on the left side of his desk and cusses. "I can't believe I did that. I took the paperwork we need to the suite this morning and accidentally left it there. Can you go grab it for me while I call HR and get Aaron's dismissal started? We need a really strong paper trail for him."

"Sure," I say, not quite sure why my brother was in the family suite this morning. Maybe he was more nervous about firing Aaron than I realize and he needed some time away. I'm not thrilled about the idea of going back there, not sure I'm ready for the memories that are bound to assault me, but I'm hoping nothing can change my happy mood. Not even the reminder that the one person I want to share this news with doesn't want to hear it from me.

I agree to give Gavin about fifteen minutes to go over everything with HR. That'll be the amount of time it'll take me to grab the paperwork, make a pit stop in the restroom, and get back.

Unlike Aaron, I leave with my head held high.

Gavin wasn't kidding that this was the most fun day at work. And I suspect it's only going to get better from here.

CHAPTER TWENTY-EIGHT

NICK

I run my hands through my hair and breathe out slowly. It does nothing to calm my nerves. But I've come too far to back out now. Plus, I don't want to. No matter how much my yoga breathing isn't working to calm my heart rate, I have to try. I have to make this right with Prestyn.

After what feels like hours, but is probably only a matter of minutes since I got the text, I hear the door open and the familiar sound of Prestyn dropping her stuff on the foyer table.

She's not paying much attention to her surroundings, which is fine by me. It gives me the chance to catch my breath from how beautiful she is. Her dark hair is down today, in waves that cascade down the front of her chest, stopping level with her breasts. Breasts that look full from the form fitting white top she's wearing, that tucks into wide legged pants. She's so fucking gorgeous, my stomach flips.

But she also looks tired, with circles under her eyes that aren't normally there. A pang of regret hits me, knowing her exhaustion is likely from the same reason as mine. Because I'm a dumb ass who ran.

Just as she gets ready to turn for the kitchen, she looks up and sees me.

Her steps falter as she realizes I'm not supposed to be here.

I take it as a good sign when she stops completely, whatever task she was about to perform forgotten. She's not racing to get away from me. Maybe she'll give me a chance to beg for her forgiveness.

"I thought I deleted the app off your phone."

"Your brother reinstalled it."

My words hit their mark, her head tilts in confusion. "My... my brother? Gavin? Why?"

"It turns out, we haven't been as sneaky as we thought."

Prestyn's chin drops to her chest. "He's the general manager. Of course he figured it out," she mumbles to herself. Taking a breath, she looks back up at me, expression guarded. "What do you want, Nick?"

"To make things right between us."

She waves her hand in dismissal. "It's fine. I knew what I was getting into. I knew the rules."

Prestyn turns away from me, heading toward the kitchen again. My heart begins to race, knowing I'm running out of time. I don't have the luxury of drawing out this conversation. I need to get to the point immediately.

"The rules don't mean anything when feelings get involved."

She glances over her shoulder and shakes her head, grabbing a manilla envelope off the kitchen island and flipping up the tab. "That's my own fault. I've never had a fuck buddy situation before. I know now that I'm not built for it. I end up developing feelings, even if I don't want to. That's on me. That's not your responsibility."

"You're right," I step forward as she pulls a small stack of papers out of the envelope, glancing over them. "But it's my responsibility to make sure we're on the same page when I realized I'd developed feelings too."

She freezes, eyes staring unseeing at the papers in her hand. "What?" she whispers.

I take a few more steps forward, moving into her space. I don't ask her to turn around, I know she's still nursing wounds I caused, but I need to be close enough for her to hear me. "I didn't mean to, Prestyn, but I fell in love with you."

The papers slide to the floor, neither of us reaching to stop them.

"You...you did?"

I'm not sure if the disbelief in her voice is because she doesn't trust me or because she didn't see this turn of events coming. But she finally turns around and I don't miss the glossy sheen in her eyes. I take a chance and reach up to rub my thumb down her soft cheek.

The touch is like an electrical charge through my whole body, and the sense of rightness that fills me is overwhelming. How could I have been so stupid? How could I have let her go?

"How could I not love you?" I ask, continuing with my own train of thought. "You're smart and savvy. You have a tremendous business mind. You love your family deeply, even when they don't treat you fairly."

Her lips twist to the side with what looks like humor. "I've actually got a story to tell you about that."

Now she has me intrigued. "You do?"

"Later." She grabs my shirt in her fists and gently nudges me. "Keep telling me why you're in love with me."

I can't stop my wide smile. For the first time in days, it feels like I have a shot with her again. Like I'll get my second chance. So I continue with all the reasons she's the one for me.

"You see me as a person, not some jock. You respect my overwhelming desire for privacy and know how to handle yourself in a heated situation, even when I create it. You are witty, and funny, and the most gorgeous person I've ever known, inside and out."

She blinks and a lone tear falls from her eye. I feel my own eyes get glassy as the most private, tender moment of my life continues.

"I've fallen so hard for you, Pres, *so* hard it scares me."

"It scares me too."

"How come?"

"Because my life will always be at least a little bit in the spotlight, Nick. I can get by with shortening my name on my badge at work. That helps. But I will never have complete privacy. Not unless I move to a remote island and change my name. And I don't want to do either of those things." She shakes her head, as if we're at a stalemate. "It means sometimes dealing with reporters as long as you're attached to me, for the rest of your life. Do you really want that?"

I rest my forehead against hers, breathing her in. The truth is no; no I don't really want that. But there are a lot of things I don't want in my life. That doesn't mean I won't have to put up with them, and I need her to understand that.

Pulling away, I grab her hand and tug her into the living room. "I need to show you something."

She follows my lead without saying a word, until we sit on the couch and I press the remote to activate the television and my ugly mug pops up. I've already set up my phone to mirror on the screen.

Prestyn is visibly confused. "What is this?"

"An interview," I answer honestly.

"Wait." Prestyn holds her hand up. "You did an interview? Like after your last game?"

"No. I did one this morning."

She tips her head to the side as she takes me in. "Nick, what's going on?"

"Just watch, okay?"

She nods slowly, a small *V* between her brows as she tries to figure out what's going on. I press play.

The me on TV clears his throat and it's painfully obvious I'm uncomfortable with the situation.

"It's no secret I don't like doing interviews. I'm not good at speaking in front of a crowd, so I'm warning you guys now that you're going to have a lot of editing to do."

There are chuckles from around the room as the reporters settle in for whatever it is I have to say.

"I'm sure most of you are wondering about the fight that happened just outside the locker room a couple days ago and I'm here to address that."

Prestyn gasps next to me, her hands suddenly covering her mouth.

My least favorite reporter breaks in, but at least his question isn't stupid. *"Sources tell us that you hit a man named Aaron Ford, the Director of Retail Operations at the Caine Resorts and Conference Centers, Tampa Bay."*

"That's correct."

"Why did you hit him?"

On screen, I clear my throat again. Scratch my chin. Shift in my seat. Hell, just watching the discomfort I'd experienced in the interview makes me uncomfortable all over again.

Finally TV Nick answers. *"I walked out of the locker room as he was making some derogatory comments to my girlfriend. I tried to de-escalate him but he had too much to drink and continued with his very inappropriate comments, and it finally pissed me off enough that I took matters into my own hands. No man should ever call a woman the things he did, and I let him know it."*

Questions erupt around the room and it's hard to hear anyone. Finally one voice breaks through the rest.

"Was that Prestyn Caine, from the Caine hotels who dragged you away from the situation? Are you saying she is your girlfriend?"

TV me pulls at my collar. I really need to work with the PR department more so I don't look like such an idiot. *"We've been dating for quite some time,"* I finally say. *"We're both very private people so we've kept it on the down-low. But I guess that punch sort of gave us away, didn't it?"*

There's laughter around the room, but the only sound I hear is from the woman next to me. She sniffles quietly and I chance a glance at her. Her eyes are shining with tears, but she's smiling. I take it as a good sign.

"Are you concerned about legal repercussions?" someone calls out.

"I mean, that has entered my mind. But when it comes to defending someone you love, even from emotional harm, getting community service or anger management classes is worth it."

The questions continue as we watch in silence.

"How long have you and Prestyn Caine been an item?"

"I'd have to do the math on that and that was never my best subject, so you'd probably have to ask her."

"What did Aaron Ford say to her anyway?"

"I'll let him be the one to answer that question. When you do, make sure you ask him why he thought it was the right thing to do. I'd love to know his answer on that."

"Are there wedding bells in your future?"

TV me huffs out a laugh. *"I think it's a bit premature to answer that question. Besides, that's something I'd talk to her about first before I talked to you guys about it."*

More chuckles and commotion before the one question that gave me pause, although not for long.

"Do you regret punching Aaron?"

"Uh... No, actually, I don't. Maybe I should be a better man and take the high road more. And I hate that it means I have to do this. I don't like interviews. But I don't regret standing up for what is right, and I don't regret defending the person I love."

"Are you saying you love Prestyn Caine?"

TV me pauses temporarily before publicly admitting my feelings. *"I am. She's the best person I know."*

More questions ring out, but Prestyn puts her hand on my forearm.

"Turn it off," she says quietly.

I don't hesitate, more than happy to get my face off the screen. Watching myself do an interview is almost more painful than doing the interview itself.

"Why did you do that?" she asks.

"Do what? The interview?"

Prestyn nods, wiping away another stray tear.

"Because it's time I learn how to balance the parts I love about us with the parts that are required of us."

"And interviews like this are required?"

"Not required, exactly. But people are going to take pictures of us, or videos or whatever, probably forever. It's not something I can control, but it's also not something I should let dictate my life."

"How did you come to that conclusion?"

I chuckle at the irony of our situation. "I feel like I'm in another interview."

"You kind of are." Prestyn threads our fingers together and I revel in the feel of our hands holding tight. "I lost you for a handful of hours and it just about killed me, Nick. I need to know you're serious. That I'm not going to go through that again."

I turn my body fully to face her. I need her to see me, to be able to look into my eyes and see the whole truth. "I think I knew it all before, but it took losing you to force me to face it. I've done a lot of soul searching for the last few days and hashed out some hard stuff I think I was suppressing." Releasing her hands, I cup her cheeks, rubbing my thumb on her skin. "Losing you almost killed me too. I've spent so long trying to avoid cameras, running was like a natural reflex. But when I realized I'd left you behind, I felt so ashamed. And lonely. And... not whole. I..."

Pausing momentarily, I say the first words that come into my mind.

"I have no life but this,
To lead it here;

Nor any death, but lest
Dispelled from there;
Nor tie to earths to come,
Nor action new,
Except through this extent,
The realm of you."

Prestyn's lips quirk up. "Did you just make up those words on the fly?"

"No," I say sheepishly. "They're a poem by Emily Dickinson. It's called "I Have No Life but This"."

"I love that you quote poetry when you're emotional," Prestyn says with a sultry growl in her voice.

"I love that you love me for my nerdiness."

"It's not nerdy. It's sexy as hell."

I smile, feeling a weight lifting off my shoulders. Pulling back just slightly, I look deep into her eyes, trying to pour all of the emotion I feel into this moment. "I love you, Prestyn Caine. So much."

"I love you, too, Nicholas Williams."

I can't help the growl that comes from deep within me as I take her lips with mine, loving her with my mouth, my lips, my tongue.

Pomegranate.

We're so deep into the rekindling of our relationship, I barely register the door opening until a throat clears behind me.

"Oh good. You're still here."

We pull away from each other, not at all embarrassed to find Gavin standing in the doorway.

Prestyn wipes more tears off her cheeks. Only this time they're happy tears.

"Sorry," she says with a shaky voice as she stands. "I got a little sidetracked."

"I can see that." Gavin smirks and turns to the kitchen where papers are still laying all over the floor.

Prestyn bites her bottom lip and looks down at me. "I'm sorry, Nick, but I need to get back to work."

"It's probably better if you don't," Gavin says as he bends over to clean up our mess. "Aaron is apparently taking his sweet time cleaning out his office. Probably better to steer clear of that area. I'd hate to make HR have to do more paperwork if he accidentally swung at one of our security guards."

"I don't mind backing them up," I grumble but Gavin hears me.

"Now, now, Nick, no need to poke that bear," Gavin says with humor. "He's this close to revoking his lifetime Glaze fan membership card."

Prestyn laughs at that and picks up one final sheet of paper before taking a pen from her brother's outstretched hand, glancing through some paperwork and signing on the dotted line.

Retrieving his pen back, Gavin puts it in his suit pocket, and shoves the paperwork back in the manilla envelope, before shaking Prestyn's hand.

"I'd welcome you to the Caine family, but that seems a bit disrespectful under the circumstances."

I'm not sure what that means, but it makes Prestyn smile. When she throws her arms around him in a giant hug, I realize they've made some major strides this morning, strides I know nothing about. And that's okay. Some things should remain private.

CHAPTER TWENTY-NINE

PRESTYN

"Oh... don't stop.... I love yooooooooou..."

My words stutter as my body rides out one of the most intense orgasms I've ever had in my life. Nick is right behind me, figuratively and literally, shouting his own words of love and devotion. I want to hear them, I crave them, but I hang out in the stars for so long, I have to wait to come down before my brain fully processes anything he's said.

Nick's fingers gently rub my clit until we finally come back to ourselves.

We're laying on our sides, one of my legs thrown over his. It slides down onto the mattress as he pulls me into him, my whole body a puddle.

"I'm glad we were already spooning." His words rumble against my back. "Makes it easier to snuggle."

"Me, too." My hand gently pats his thigh. It's the only movement I can make besides breathing. "Now that we're going bareback, I need to go clean up, though."

He lightly pecks my neck, making me shiver. I've missed how affectionate he is. "Stay here. I'll get you a washcloth."

I could keep my eyes closed and rest. I'm exhausted after the last few days, but then I'd miss watching him walk naked into the bathroom. Plus, we have a lot to talk about and I don't want to miss that chance. We may be in an official relationship, but we still need to start it with all our cards on the table.

"How did you convince my brother to let you in, anyway?"

Nick glances around the corner at me before disappearing into the bathroom again. He emerges seconds later with that warm washcloth he promised. He lifts my leg and gently cleans me. "I just told him the truth. That I was in love with you but I'd screwed it up and wanted the chance to make it right."

"That's it? He just gave you access to the suite, no questions asked?"

"Oh he asked questions. He knew something was going on, I guess security wanted to make sure everything was on the up and up or something."

I roll my eyes. "What a crock of shit. They could have just asked me."

"I'm sure being the general manager had something to do with it."

"Mm-hmm." I don't even sound convincing to myself.

"Once I gave him a not-very-detailed rundown of our relationship and why we were hiding it, he went all big brother on me before giving me his blessing."

I pop up onto my elbow. "Wait, did he lecture you on my virtue?"

Nick chuckles and tosses the washcloth to the side before climbing back in bed. "Your virtue never even came up. It was more about not using you because of your last name."

Makes sense. "I guess he's had a rough day with people using the family name for their own personal gain."

"What does that mean?" He pulls me into a spoon again and covers us with a blanket.

"Aaron got fired today."

Nick stills behind me. "He what?"

I turn in his arms, throwing one leg over his as I snuggle in, just far enough away to see his face.

"I know that punch wasn't your finest moment." He grimaces, but I cup his cheek and smooth his eyebrow with my thumb absentmindedly. "But that wasn't the only thing caught on camera. Some of Aaron's choicest comments were also recorded."

"Are you serious?"

I nod. "There's more to it, but basically my brother caught wind of it all and did some investigating. He wasn't too happy to see how Aaron was representing the company."

"And disrespecting his sister, right?"

"Of course. But for HR purposes, that couldn't be the catalyst for him getting canned."

"I disagree." Nick closes his eyes, relaxing while we talk. "But continue."

"That's basically it. You already know I've been promoted to that position, you were here when I signed the contract. But that's what started it all."

Nick's hand runs lazily up and down my spine, creating goose bumps all over my body. "I'm glad my outburst was good for something at least."

"It was good for more than just that." Nick's eyes open and there's a question in them when he looks at me. "I think maybe we weren't being totally honest with each other and it was time to hash a few things out, don't you?"

His eyes shift back and forth between mine and he licks his lips before answering. "I'm so sorry I hurt you."

"It's okay."

"No. No automatic responses," he orders. "It's not okay. I ran away for no reason. Well, I guess there are reasons, just no good ones."

"What do you mean?"

With a sigh, he rolls on his back, throwing his arm over his head as he stares at the ceiling. "Tucker said something the other night that had me thinking about my dad."

Leaning up on my elbow so I can see his face, I rest my hand on his warm chest. "What did he say?"

"It wasn't anything major. Just how having a dad who ditched him sort of messed him up. He takes on too much responsibility to, I guess, be the exact opposite of his dad taking none. He mentioned that my fear of being in love could be related to that."

I think about how Tucker didn't just provide a home for his girlfriend and daughter, but how he made sure it had a pool house for the best friend who had saved them from the streets long ago, and I can see how he might care for the people he loves a little too much. But I'm not sure how that relates to Nick's situation.

"I'm sorry, I'm not seeing the connection."

"It's going to sound strange but my dad had three wives, right?"

"Uh huh."

"So in a sweeping generalization, he loved way too much. In the process, we got hurt. Maybe there's some deep part of me that's doing just like Tucker—the exact opposite to get as far away as I can from being him.

Finally it clicks. "By not allowing yourself to love anyone, you don't end up hurting them in the long run."

He turns his head to me, eyebrows furrowed. "Does that sound stupid?"

"No. In a weird way, it makes sense. Like you put up protective walls around your heart. When the walls started to come down and things got scary, you ran for cover."

"The cameras being there at one of my worst moments just happened to be a convenient excuse for me, since everyone knows how much I hate them. But maybe only you know how scared I really am."

I lean over and give him a slow, gentle kiss, threading my

fingers through his hair lovingly. "You are one very deep and astute man."

"It's all the poetry I read," he jokes making me laugh.

"Maybe. But just know, if you ever run like that again, I'll give you your space to work it out. But don't think for a second I won't call your sister to tell her what a shit you are."

The smile that crosses Nick's face melts the last hardened parts of my heart. Knowing we both understand how we ended up here has me doubting he'll ever spook that easily again.

He wraps his hands around my waist and pulls me closer, our lips just a breath away from each other.

"I love you, Pres."

"I love you, too."

He rolls me over and begins kissing my neck, down my clavicle, over the top of my breast, all the while murmuring soft words that I have no doubt come from one of his poetry books.

"Oh! might I kiss those eyes of fire,
A million scarce would quench desire;
Still would I steep my lips in bliss,
And dwell an age on every kiss;
Nor then my soul should sated be,
Still would I kiss and cling to thee:
Nought should my kiss from thine dissever,
Still would we kiss and kiss for ever..."

I relax as he takes control, showing me with his words and his actions how much I'm adored. When he pushes inside of me, leaving no space between us, I know with every fiber of my being that he is it for me. We have a passion others only dream about. And when it ignites, we both explode.

EPILOGUE

PRESTYN

Ten Months Later

Once again, tonight's event has been a total success. The ball-room is stunning, the people are generous, and it looks like we're going to beat last year's fundraising efforts.

Not that I'm surprised. Delaney and the event team from the Florida Glaze always put on an amazing gala.

It's hard to believe that only a year ago, Nick and I were meeting for the first time and our story was beginning. It seems like my life has never *not* included him. Maybe because while we're different people with our own thoughts and opinions, we fit together like the final puzzle pieces in a masterpiece made just for us.

Well look who's waxing poetic now. Nick must be rubbing off on me. Speaking of rubbing...

Nick's giant hand grabs my knee and squeezes as he leans over to whisper in my ear. "Are you almost ready to go? We've got plans and we can't be late."

I turn and smirk at him. "I'm as..." I bite my bottom lip and glance down at his, wishing we were alone and that mouth was kissing all over my body. Unfortunately, we're in public so we have to stay professional. I look back up at the man of my dreams. "Sorry. Got sidetracked. Like I was saying, I'm as antsy as you are but Delaney has to finish the silent auction first."

Nick closes his eyes and breaths out through his nostrils. "Fine. But as soon as Tucker loses, we're outta here."

"You think he's going to lose again?" I ask with a laugh.

"Undoubtedly."

I shrug nonchalantly and take a demure sip of my drink. "For Lacy's sake, I hope not."

Nick squeezes my knee again and his hand slides up my thigh. I push him away playfully, knowing we'll have plenty of time for that over the next few days and I can't wait.

The quiet chatter continues around us as the people I have come to know as friends all discuss the auction and prizes they've bid on and lost. It seems that everyone from their superstitious poker group tried to win something. Well, almost everyone. Notably absent is Patrick. Not that any of us are really surprised. Divorcing the owner's daughter has been rough on him.

Not only did he lose his C this season, which I've learned is a very big deal in the world of hockey, but his contract is set to expire at the end of the season. Considering his age—which I don't think is that old, but again, I'm learning hockey has its own set of rules—and the animosity from the owner, it's not looking good for him to be around much longer.

Nick has only talked about it with me a couple times and while he's not terribly surprised, I think it's reminded him that nothing in his chosen profession lasts forever. He could be traded without notice on any given day, which would suck. But even more so, he's got a limited number of years left before retirement. I'm looking at forty more years of gainful employment while he's looking at four. I can only imagine how jarring it must be.

"And our final item of the night..." Delaney's voice rings through the room. She looks lovely tonight, her blond hair pulled back in an intricate twist, her glittery blue dress hugging her curves dramatically. More than once tonight, I've caught a certain playboy by the name of Tiger losing his tongue when she's spoken to our table. I don't think Nick caught it, but I'm keeping my eyes peeled for that one. "...an all expenses paid, five day, six night trip to Cabo. Transportation generously provided by the Florida Glaze, and deluxe resort accommodations donated by Richard Caine of Caine Resorts and Conference Centers."

Tucker puts his clenched fist to his mouth. "Come on, baby. It's gotta be us this year."

Maks clears his throat loudly and gives Tucker a pointed look. Tucker just waggles his finger at his teammate.

"Nuh-uh. I was waiting for your little trick, so as soon as you outbid me at the end, I snuck up behind you and upped you by another dollar. You're not getting away with it this year."

"Our winner," Delaney says brightly. "With a bid of ten thousand, four hundred and three dollars..."

"Three?" Tucker says, his brows furrowed.

"... Becker Bell!"

Our group erupts with laughter as Becker stands up to take a bow. His date, a lovely woman named Sloan who he apparently met over the holidays, claps for her man, but obviously doesn't understand the gravity of what just happened.

"How the fuck?" Tucker's eyes are wild with confusion as Lacy puts her hand on his forearm, murmuring encouraging words to him.

Becker, in all his ornery glory, turns to his friend, and new rival. "I watched you watch Maks. After he outbid you, and you outbid him"—Becker slams his drink back— "I one-upped you again."

The entire table laughs, except for Tucker who is cursing up a storm. The scene is so reminiscent of last year's event, and yet, everything is totally different. In all the best ways.

"Can we leave now?" Nick whispers.

My hand automatically cups his cheek as I giggle at his

impatience.

"I'm dying to press you up against the glass and take you from behind while we watch the moon over the ocean."

Breathlessly, I turn my head just enough to be able to kiss him quickly. It's just a quick peck and he groans his displeasure.

"We have things to do first, lover boy. Besides, we need to wait for your sister."

Nick harumphs like a petulant child. "This is already not going as planned."

"No, it's going exactly as planned. With roadblocks popping up everywhere. Did you really think it would be easy?"

"I'm not going to entertain that with an answer. Can we at least start making the rounds to say our goodbyes? Delaney is just as antsy as I am to get out of here."

"How do you know that?"

He shrugs. "It's a twin thing."

I look up at his sister, a woman who started as the wife of a guy I thought I was going to date and turned into an amazing friend. She catches my eye and as discreetly as possible holds one finger to the sky, making a circling motion like we need to speed things up. I just shake my head at both of them.

"Patience doesn't run in your family, does it?"

"Not even a little." He pushes his chair away from the table and stands up, holding a hand out to me. "Ready?"

With the way his suit is hugging his body and all the goodness I know is under there, I'll go anywhere with him. But first, rounds.

It takes longer than either of us would like, but we're finally done giving hugs and shaking hands. I feel bad for not getting to know Sloan a little better—she seems really nice—but I don't feel bad enough to stay.

By the time we make it to the staff elevator bank to take us to the suite, Delaney is racing to catch up.

"Sorry, sorry." She's breathing heavy from power walking in her heels as she steps into the carriage. "I didn't think I was ever going to get away from Tucker. That man is serious about his auctions."

"What did he want?" Nick presses the button for our floor and we start moving.

Delaney's eyes roll and she gives a slight shake of her head. "He was asking about the validity of Becker's bid. Tucker just *knows* it was written down after the chime to end the auction."

I furrow my brow because that actually makes sense. "Wait. Was it?"

"Not according to the official judge," Delaney responds. "And even if it was, I'd still give it to Becker, just because the look on Tucker's face is so funny every year!"

The three of us chuckle as the lift climbs to the right floor. When the elevator dings indicating our arrival, my stomach flipflops with nerves. Somehow, Nick knows I'm anxious without me saying a word. He grabs my hand and brings it to his lips, dropping a kiss on my palm.

"You ready for this?"

I glance up at the man of my dreams, my private, poetry loving, sexy goalie of a man and smile. "I've never been more ready for anything."

"Aww, that's so sweet! Now move your tush," Delaney demands.

We quickly make our way down the hall and right on cue, my brother opens the door to the suite. Security must have alerted Gavin that we were coming because he looks like he's expecting us.

Gavin gives me a quick hug and I hear the emotion in his voice. "Welcome to your wedding, little sister."

Stepping into the room, my breath catches. The lights are dimmed and there are white candles of all shapes and sizes everywhere. In the places there aren't candles, there are white flowers —lilies and roses and gardenias. It's simple and gorgeous and... *us*.

"Oh wow. Bayleigh did an amazing job."

My favorite work friend, who is now the Director of Catering thanks to a fabulous interview and my brother who is smarter than he looks sometimes, takes that moment to get closer with her camera and snap a few pictures.

"Of course I did," she says as she clicks away. "This is why I'm in charge of event planning. Did you think I was going to slack off on the biggest wedding of the year?"

"I'd hardly call it the biggest," I say with a smile and squeeze my groom's hand. "There's what... six of us here?"

"Just the way we like it."

Nick leans down to kiss me, but Delaney puts her hand over his mouth. "No sir. I let it slide all night, but you are officially inside your wedding venue. You go take your place at the front. You can kiss your bride in about ten minutes."

He shakes his head with a smile, but does what his sister says, leaving me alone with her. Well, as alone as you can get in an open room with a few other people taking their places next to the floor to ceiling windows.

Gavin follows behind and they both shake hands with the minister who was paid handsomely to not only perform the ceremony on a very late Saturday night, but to also keep the fact that we're getting married on the down-low until we're ready to announce it to the world.

We're getting married.

I have to shake my head, hardly able to believe that this is happening. A year ago Nick and I met for the first time. Ten months ago, we worked through our issues and figured out that what we wanted was right in front of us and we weren't going to take it for granted. Then two weeks ago, Nick asked me to be with him forever and I said yes. On one condition—that we tell no one except my brother, his sister, and Bayleigh.

Not surprising, he agreed and we quickly decided tonight was the perfect night to elope.

Delaney pulls a small bouquet out of a vase and quickly wipes the excess water drips off before handing it to me. "It was sneaky of you to wear a white dress for the gala. You've been sitting in your wedding dress all night, and no one even knew."

"It wasn't sneaky, it was strategic," I reply. She reaches for my hair and sweeps some straggling locks back into place. "Saves time so I don't have to change and that way when the team gives Nick grief over not being invited, he can say they were practically there."

"It's no wonder you fit right in with that environment." Delaney nods and grabs a small tube of lip gloss from her clutch purse. "You're just as cunning as they are."

She dabs a few spots of color on my lips while Bayleigh buzzes around taking pictures. In a matter of seconds, Delaney deems me wedding worthy and grabs her own bouquet.

Bayleigh grabs her phone and quickly starts the music that will serenade me into my future.

Taking a deep breath, I steady my nerves, which is surprisingly easy to do considering I'm about to walk down the aisle. Well, I'm just walking across the room, but the furniture has been moved out of the way and more candles and flowers are strategically placed so I couldn't get lost on my way to my groom if I tried.

Gavin stands next to Nick, looking dapper in his tailored black suit, a huge smile on his face as he represents my side of the family in welcoming Nick.

Delaney moves to the other side to stand next to me, representing their family doing the same.

I hand Delaney my bouquet and grab the hands of the man who holds my future. The pastor Gavin hired looks back and forth between the two of us, a smile on his face.

"Friends, you wanted a very intimate affair with just the two of you and your witnesses. In line with that, we'll save all the pomp and circumstance for a different time. I'm told you wrote your own vows so Nicholas Williams, would you like to begin?"

Nick clears his throat and nods. I can see the nerves as he fidgets, but they're not nerves of anxiety. Only excitement. It reminds me of how he is on the ice before a game when adrenaline is coursing through him, when he just can't hold it in. It's flattering that he's that pumped up for us to be married.

"The golden gates of Sleep unbar

> Where Strength and Beauty, met together,
> Kindle their image like a star
> In a sea of glassy weather!
> Night, with all thy stars look down, -
> Darkness, weep thy holiest dew, -
> Never smiled the inconstant moon
> On a pair so true.
> Let eyes not see their own delight; -
> Haste, swift Hour, and thy flight
> Oft renew."

I smile, my heart filled by his romantic words. "Did you come up with those words on the fly?"

He chuckles lightly and squeezes my hands. "It's called "A Bridal Song" by Lord Byron. And I thought it was fitting for today."

Nick shifts closer to me as he continues with his words of love for me. "Prestyn, I never claimed to be the smartest man in the world."

I giggle and if I was paying closer attention to her, I could swear Delaney mutters, "No shit."

"I'm also nerdy, superstitious, and spook easily when there are cameras around." Bayleigh takes that exact moment to accidentally use the flash on her camera making Nick jump. His lips quirk to the side. "See?"

We all laugh and I'm grateful for the distraction from my own nerves. I feel more settled now that we've started and we're just being us.

"But for all my flaws, the only thing you seem to see in me is good. You encourage me when I'm down. You hold me account-able when I'm being an idiot. And you make all my fears disap-pear when we're together. You are the strongest woman I know with one of the biggest hearts. There's a reason everyone who works in this hotel loves you. But none of them love you like I do. I don't ever want to imagine a day in my life where you aren't in it. So I vow not just to be your husband, but to be your partner, your biggest cheerleader, and your safe place to land when things don't go as planned. I love you."

My heart swells at his words. This man I've loved like he's my other half committing himself to me alone for a lifetime. It is both the sweetest and sexiest thing I've ever heard.

"Prestyn Caine," the pastor says. "You have also written your vows."

"I don't have any beautiful poetic words for you," I say with a watery laugh. "But I'll do my best."

I take a deep, cleansing breath and focus on putting all my love into the most important words of my life.

"I didn't grow up seeing a solid marriage. I've been told my parents were deeply in love, but we lost my mom when I was so young I never really experienced being around it." Nick squeezes my hands gently in support. "Maybe that's why it's not something I ever thought I'd have, not something I was necessarily looking for. But then I got catfished by a man who had the most wonderful wife."

Nick drops his chin and shakes his head at the reminder.

"I think she's the first person who showed me how to look at people deeper than just face value because that's how she looked at me. It gave me the confidence to look at you that way, too, in spite of how rocky our relationship started. Nick, I love you. I love that you read poetry and do yoga and pummel people on the ice for a living. I love that you value your privacy as much as I do and believe some things are better when they stay between those who are the most important to you. I love that you encourage me to be strong and aren't afraid when I feel weak. There is no one I'd rather spend the rest of my life with. Not one person in this whole world. I can't wait for our forever to begin."

"Can I kiss her yet?" Nick asks quietly, eliciting chuckles around the room.

"Almost," the pastor assures. "Let's exchange rings first."

Nick slides the simple platinum band on my finger, immediately followed by my princess cut diamond engagement ring. I felt naked not having it on tonight and already feel better with it back on.

Nick's ring doesn't go on as easily. After much debate, we decided to get him a silicone ring so he doesn't have to take it off for practice or games. It also means our secret marriage probably won't stay secret for long, being that he has a home game tomorrow night and he won't be able to hide it in the locker room, but it's a price we're willing to pay.

Once the rings are secured, we get back to holding hands, anxiously awaiting the official announcement. Thankfully, the pastor doesn't wait long.

"By the power invested in me by God and the State of Florida, I now pronounce you husband and wife. *Now* you can kiss your bride."

Nick wastes no time, grabbing me around the waist and dipping me low to the floor, my hands cradling his face as we kiss for the first time as a married couple.

I hardly register our siblings clapping or the soft clicks of the camera, only focusing on the man holding me, trusting him not to let me fall, but I know he never will.

He sucks on my bottom lip, fully engaged in our kiss and I can't help but notice his taste. It's mint and wine and Nick...

And pomegranate.

The End.

BONUS EPILOGUE

BECKER BELL

One month earlier

It seems like hundreds of people are jostling around the tiny space, even though it's probably only a couple of dozen. I know airport restaurants don't have a lot of space, but when flights get cancelled, it doesn't make things easy.

Feeling something tap my foot, I look down. A small, wrapped package is next to my stool.

All the warnings about unattended packages race through my brain. I'm probably being dramatic, but I can't help it. I've flown so much, it's practically engrained in me to assume anything and everything is either a bomb or drugs.

I glance around the area, trying to figure out who it belongs to, but no one seems to be searching for anything. What do I do? Do I need to alert someone official that a random package has shown up at my feet?

Before I can make a decision, the package is snatched up off the floor.

"Sorry. My bag broke."

I glance up and almost rear back at the sight of the most beautiful woman I've ever seen. Her straight, auburn hair is pulled back in a haphazard ponytail that looks like it could fall out at any moment. What looks like a knit hat is hanging out of the pocket of her giant coat, dangerously close to falling onto the floor. And sure enough, she's holding a paper sack with a tear down the side.

Good thing I didn't overreact about her package or anything.

A random feeling of concern runs through me. She looks so disheveled and there's a hint of frustration hidden in the back of her blue eyes. I can't help but try to offer assistance. "Did you get them all? All the packages?"

"I think so," she says, barely making eye contact. "I'll have to count."

I watch as she navigates her way back to the table she's claimed, past a couple assholes who glare at her when she accidentally bumps their chair. A random surge of anger runs through me at the way they look at her like she's the problem. Yeah, because she can help the fact that they jammed too many tables into this tiny room.

Unable to tear my eyes away, I continue to watch as she puts the presents on her table. She looks so frazzled, and I can't help but wonder if her flight was cancelled, too. Her long fingers point up one at a time as she appears to go through a mental checklist, as if making sure all the gifts are accounted for. Her teeth gnaw on her bottom lip as she picks up the ripped bag and inspects it to see if it can be fixed.

That's when an idea hits me out of the blue.

"Hey, excuse me," I call out, flagging down the unlucky bartender that gets to deal with a packed house of stranded travelers.

She does her best to plaster a smile on her face. "Need another?"

"No. Well, yes. But what I really need though is to see if you have a to-go bag. A large one."

She looks a little surprised by my request probably since I

haven't ordered any food. "Let me see what we have in the back. I don't have any up here."

"Thanks."

I turn back to my fellow passenger and catch her expression the moment she realizes there is nothing that can be done about the bag she was carrying. With a frustrated puff of breath, she picks up a backpack, it looks almost like a computer bag, and starts inspecting the presents, clearly trying to see if any of them will fit without crushing the gift.

Fortunately, the bartender returns with a large plastic bag. "Will this do?" She holds it up for my inspection.

It's huge and white and reads "Airport Bar and Grill" on the side in blazing blue letters.

"It's perfect, thank you."

She hands me another beer, like originally requested and I hand her two twenties, tipping her as much for the bag as for the beer.

"Thanks for your help."

She nods and gives me a real smile this time as she rings up my order and shoves the change in her apron.

Grabbing my duffle and the bag in one hand, beer in the other, I leave my spot at the bar and maneuver around the same group of assholes I saw before.

When I bump into one of the chairs, one of the douchebags cusses.

"The fuck?"

I glare down at him, daring him to get in my face. As soon as he looks up and sees my size, he backs down.

That's what I thought. Asshole should learn some respect of other people and maybe I'd apologize. But I don't.

Instead, I approach the table where the beautiful woman is still struggling.

She doesn't even notice when I place my beer on the table, until I hold up the plastic bag in offering. "Will this work?"

She blinks up at me, the expression in her wide, blue eyes shifting from one of frustration to delight. And then she smiles and the breath is knocked right out of me.

Chestnuts will be roasting on an OPEN FIRE this holiday season! Don't miss Becker and Sloan's story. Scan the QR code to preorder it now!

ACKNOWLEDGMENTS

As always, it takes a village to raise a book baby, and this one was no different. I've never been a hockey player, nor have I worked in a hotel, so it takes a bunch of research and extra eyes to make sure I get it right.

To be fair, I may have still missed the mark on a few things. I'm only human, after all. But these people did their best to help me nor screw everything up.

Amber Higbie gave me the skinny on hotel jobs and how this story could incorporate all of Prestyn's dreams with the reality of the structure. **Renita McKinney** also hooked me up with some people who currently work in a giant conglomerate of a conference center and they were able to verify the many details that go into the job. Those people don't want to be named, but you know who they are, Renita! And they were wonderful.

Nikki Becker continues to be beta reader extraordinaire. And let's not forget the amount of time we spent on that poem!! Your honesty about the original is exactly what I needed!

Andrea Johnston fell into the role of... beta? But maybe it was Charlie reader this time? Whatever the exact roll was, you always find the wonky sentences. Always.

Kathryn Perez and I chatted for an hour about poetry and she pushed me in the direction I needed to find public domain poems. If y'all don't already know, you can't just publish snippets of other people's work. It has to be on the legal up and up, but figuring out whose work is public domain and whose isn't can be daunting! Kathryn worked through it with me to help find what I needed. And let's not forget my fellow author **Nicole French**! As soon as I said, "I need a poem like this," she not only knew where to look, she had the EXACT POEM in mind. It was brilliant!

I can't forget **Brenda Rothert** who always lets me "borrow" her teams and characters to give me some fictional locations and characters for my players to complete in/against. It makes writing that much more fun. (And as a side note, that reality show that Maksim Ivanov ended up on is Brenda's brain child. You can read about Maks' naked participation in Exiled! Trust me. You don't want to miss it.)

Gemma Brocato does amazing editing. **My mother** does amazing proofreading (go figure). **Jena Brignola** makes those beautiful teasers you see. And don't forget **Becca Manuel**. That trailer is... GAH!!

And of course, **Carter's Cheerleaders** and the **Nerdy Little Book Herd** for always cheering me on.

I couldn't do any of this without all of you, so with my humblest gratitude, I thank you.

ALSO BY M.E. CARTER

The Florida Glaze Series: Hockey Romance

Playing with Fire

Under Fire

Trial by Fire

Open Fire (Coming November 2022!)

The Hart Series: Football Romance

Change of Hart

Hart to Heart

Matters of the Hart

Matters to Me

Matters to You

Matter of Time

Matter of Fact

The Texas Mutiny Series: Soccer Romance

Juked

Groupie

Goalie

Megged

Deflected

#MyNewLife: Over 40 Romantic Comedy with a Sports Twist

Getting a Grip: Getting a Grip Duet Part 1

Balance Check: Getting a Grip Duet Part 2

Pride & Joie

Amazing Grayson

Little Miss Perfect (exclusively in the Getting a Grip Duet Complete Box Set)

Cipher Office Series: Romantic Comedy Set in the Weight Expectations Gym

(Part of the Smartypants Romance Imprint)

Weight Expectations

Cutie and the Beast

Weights of Wrath

The Charitable Endeavors Series: Romantic Comedy co-written with Andrea Johnston

Switch Stance

Ear Candy

Model Behavior

Better than the Book

Romantic Comedies co-written with Sara Ney

FriendTrip

WeddedBliss

Holiday Romantic Comedies co-written with Sara Ney

Kissmas Eve

New Year's Steve

Paranormal written as Anabeth Cartoon

Panther

ABOUT THE AUTHOR

My name is ME Carter and I have no idea how I ended writing books. I'm more of a story teller (the more exaggerated the better) and I happen to know people who helped me get those stories on paper.

I love reading (read over 100 books last year), hate working out (but I do it anyway because my trainer makes me), love food (but hate what it does to my butt) and love traveling to non-touristy places most people never see.

I live in Texas with my four kids, Mary, Elizabeth, Carter and Bug, who was just a twinkle in my eye when I came up with my pen name. Yeah, I'll probably have to pay for his therapy someday for being left out.

To keep up with all the happenings, sign up for my newsletter! www.authormecarter.com/newsletter

Instagram: @authormecarter

Facebook: Mary Elizabeth Carter (M.E. Carter)

www.ingramcontent.com/pod-product-compliance
Lightning Source LLC
Chambersburg PA
CBHW070444200726
48293CB00007B/2118